"You sure have a fixation with J.C."

Jared leaned over Kate as he spoke, dropping both hands to the ground to trap her within his embrace. "If J.C. was here with you instead of Jared, would you be using two sleeping bags or one?" Jared's face sharpened with need.

"Don't be silly," Kate croaked. "You're one and the same."

"Am I?" His voice deepened, husky with raw lust.

Her tongue appeared to dampen her dry lips. "Is this some kind of joke?"

Jared lowered his head farther. "You tell me."

The moment his mouth covered hers, Kate knew he was most serious.

ABOUT THE AUTHOR

Linda Randall Wisdom is well-known to readers of romance fiction. Long-term service in personnel, marketing and public relations gave her a wealth of experience on which to draw when creating characters. Linda knew she was destined to write romance novels when her first sale came on her wedding anniversary. She and her husband live in Southern California with a houseful of exotic birds.

Books by Linda Randall Wisdom

HARLEQUIN AMERICAN ROMANCE

Don't miss any of our special offers. Write to us at the following address for information on our newest releases.

Harlequin Reader Service
901 Fuhrmann Blvd., P.O. Box 1397, Buffalo, NY 14240
Canadian address: P.O. Box 603,
Fort Erie, Ont. L2A 5X3

LINDA
RANDALL
WISDOM

O'MALLEY'S
QUEST

Harlequin Books

TORONTO • NEW YORK • LONDON
AMSTERDAM • PARIS • SYDNEY • HAMBURG
STOCKHOLM • ATHENS • TOKYO • MILAN

To Mary Anne Wilson, who's shared the
adventures of stunt-driving shuttle-bus drivers,
delayed flights and waiting for the airline to find a
pilot, probably because they learned we were on
the flight! And to that late night we dragged our
suitcases through an airline terminal and you
asked me that all-important question: "Who
dared to say romance writing was glamorous?"

Published December 1990

ISBN 0-373-16372-X

Chapter One

"I don't think this is a good time for you to get married, Kate."

"Oh? And just when do you think is a good time for me to get married?" The feminine voice was heavily laced with amusement.

"When you're too old to care about looking for that next rainbow." While her grandfather's face was heavily lined, his voice and the sparkle in his dark green eyes were those of a much younger man.

Kate turned her head, eyeing him from her contorted position in the deep leather chair. "If that's the case I may as well wait until I'm as old and crotchety as you. Of course, I don't think my wedding night will be as exciting as I hoped it would be." A teasing smile lifted her lips. "Gramps, you're forgetting that our engagement isn't official. We haven't announced it in the newspaper or set a wedding date. We've basically discussed the idea of settling down together. Be grateful we haven't decided to just live together without the benefit of a marriage license," she couldn't resist goading.

"I'd prefer that over your making a mistake," he grumbled. "And Jared's too proper to just live with a woman. The way you two are talking about it, it sounds more like a business arrangement to me." He glared at his granddaughter. "And you're not a woman content to settle for that. You've too much of your grand-mother in you for that, unfortunately."

"Ah, but I also have your Irish stubborn nature, Shamus O'Malley." Her deep emerald eyes, so like her grandfather's, glittered with laughter as she faced the older man seated in a nearby chair. "So why don't you tell me the real reason why you feel I shouldn't marry Jared other than I'm too young at the tender age of twenty-nine."

"You know very well what I mean. He doesn't share your love for adventure and the outdoors, for the ex-otic," Shamus pointed out. "You'd be bored with him in no time."

"He plays a mean game of tennis, which is generally played outdoors, and he speaks Latin, which could be considered exotic."

Shamus's brows met in a thunderous frown. "He's stuffy."

Deep down Kate agreed that Jared seemed a bit too much on the conservative side. But she would never dream of admitting it to her grandfather. "There's nothing wrong with a man being reserved."

"He has no sense of adventure," Shamus argued.

"He eats in the faculty cafeteria; that's pretty adven-turous in my eyes." Kate heaved a sigh, silently wish-ing they weren't having this conversation. Why was Shamus acting this way? You'd think he'd be happy if she meant to stay here permanently instead of roaming the world most of the year.

He ran his hands through iron-gray hair and looked as frustrated as he felt. "I bet he doesn't even own a passport."

"So I'll give him an application for his birthday." Kate ran her hands through honey blond hair that hung in tangled waves to her shoulders. "You're digressing, Gramps. Here I am seriously thinking of settling down—something you should be happy about—and all you can talk about is how the man I've chosen is all wrong for me. Tell me something, if we're so wrong for each other how did we ever get together?" She was the picture of innocence.

Shamus shifted in his chair. "You're too young to get married," he mumbled, scowling fiercely.

Kate sighed. "Gramps, in four months I will be thirty, and my biological clock is beginning to speak up rather loudly. And for once, I'm beginning to listen to it. After all, wouldn't you like to see your great-grandchildren digging in the backyard looking for buried treasure and ancient bones?"

"Ha! More likely they'd be locked up in the library reading about the Civil War. I don't know why you're so worried about having a baby right now. Women in their forties have babies all the time," he pointed out. "That will give you another ten years to do what you want. Besides, nowadays a woman doesn't need a husband to raise a child."

She lifted her eyebrows in surprise. "Why, Gramps, I never knew you were so liberal."

"You know very well what I mean. Besides, if you want to marry someone that badly, look for a man better suited to your way of life."

"Maybe I don't want to marry someone like me! Maybe I want someone who's more suited to staying home and not running after every legend and treasure still not documented. Maybe I want what you and Dad never had!" She sighed, shaking her head as her cruel words sunk in. "I'm sorry, I shouldn't have said that."

"Yes, you should have. I always taught you to speak your mind. There's no reason for you to stop doing so now." Shamus looked weary. "You're right, your father and I never did have much luck with women. You were the first girl in the O'Malley family for six generations. I just don't want you to make a mistake," he said lamely.

"Gramps, something had to have happened to suddenly change your mind about Jared." Kate looked suspicious. "Do you think you could give me a hint?"

"Nothing sudden about it. I just think you should take your time before jumping into something as serious as marriage, that's all." He sat back, clearly finished saying his piece.

By now Kate was thoroughly convinced her grandfather was up to something and he intended that she be part of his scheme. But knowing him as well as she did she knew that she wouldn't learn a thing until he was good and ready to tell her. She bit her lip to keep a smile from blossoming. Oh, no, she'd just bide her time. Experience had taught her that Shamus O'Malley couldn't keep a secret to save his life. Kate knew all she had to do was appear disinterested long enough and the cagey Shamus would soon spill all. She glanced up at the clock on the mantel as it chimed five times.

"I've got to get ready. Jared will be picking me up at seven for Dr. Phillips's party." She pushed herself out of her chair. "Are you going?"

Shamus made a face. "That's a silly question, my girl. Phillips is a pompous ass and the less time I spend with the man the better. That's why I haven't attended one of his shindigs in the last eight years."

Kate grinned, well used to her grandfather's assessment of the college president. She walked over to his chair and draped her arms around his neck. "Yes, but that's what makes him such an excellent administrator. And if standing there in that moldy old greenhouse admiring his wife's roses keeps me in mind for that new teaching post next semester, well, so be it. Now, I'm going upstairs to get ready and if Jared arrives before I'm back down here, you be polite to him." She playfully twisted his ear. "Do you hear me?"

"Ow! Damn it, stop that!" He batted at her hand although it hadn't hurt at all.

"Then promise you won't say anything to Jared." She pretended to strangle him.

"All right, I promise!" he shouted. "I will not say a word to the man about how unsuitable he is for you."

"You better not or I'll take away all those smelly cigars that friend of yours smuggles in for you and I'll put every one of them down the garbage disposal."

"You were a lot more fun when you were six and thought your gramps was the most wonderful man in the world," he muttered, trying to look pathetic and failing miserably.

Kate kissed the top of his head. "Even when you're ornery you're still my favorite man," she murmured. "After all, how many men are willing to take a child to remote areas of the world to dig up old bones?"

"I sure wasn't going to let your father turn you into some damn flower child, was I?" he mumbled. "Now get going. You don't want to keep that stiff-necked Jared waiting too long if you're afraid I'll say the wrong thing to him."

Kate took the stairs to the third floor that housed her private living quarters. When she had turned eighteen

Shamus turned the third floor over to her and when she finished her decorating she had an area that resembled a loft apartment.

Kate spent little time in preparing for her evening out. She had lived in too many remote areas without a fraction of the luxuries she had at home. Therefore, it took her little time to shower and dress in a bright pink chemise-styled dress with a turquoise cummerbund. She slipped on turquoise high-heeled pumps and added several turquoise and silver bangle bracelets. With that finished she felt ready for the faculty get together she was attending with Jared Wyatt, the man she intended to marry whether Shamus liked it or not.

The first thing Kate heard when she reached the first floor was two men's voices speaking in low tones. She tiptoed toward the closed den door, fully prepared to unashamedly eavesdrop so she could learn if the conversation was harmless or, heaven forbid, not. She knew her grandfather wasn't above talking to Jared about the bad points of marriage to a woman who wore out a passport before it had a chance to expire.

"Are you sure you won't have a whiskey, Jared?" she could hear Shamus inviting his guest. "Knowing Kate she'll be a long time primping."

"Kate does not primp," she announced as she swept into the room. "And you know very well the doctor told you no alcohol." She smiled at the tall man standing across the room. "Hello, Jared." She reached his side in three steps and kissed him lightly on the lips.

"Kate, you look lovely." His slightly rough features softened as he gazed down at her.

"Isn't that dress too short for one of Dr. Phillips's parties?" Shamus asked. "He's the type to have a coronary if a woman's calves are revealed."

Kate looked down at the dress that ended about two inches above her knees. She didn't notice that Jared's gaze was directed to the same area. "It covers the essentials. And Kiki believes in wearing her dresses a great deal shorter at times and Dr. Phillips has survived her eccentric wardrobe over the years."

"Don't worry, Shamus, she's just fine," Jared assured the older man in the cool, controlled voice he was known for in the classroom. He glanced at his watch. "We should be leaving now if we don't want to be late."

Kate bent to kiss her grandfather's cheek. "Don't stay up too late."

"You're the one who needs to behave, not me. Just remember all those talks we had," he called after her.

"Our last talk was when I was fifteen and you didn't trust Christopher Bell," Kate retorted, her fingers outstretched to tweak his ear again.

Shamus covered his ears and scowled at her. "Go."

"Good night," she sang out.

After Kate grabbed a jacket to guard against the evening chill, she and Jared walked outside to his car.

"What do you think of our staying long enough to be polite then cutting out to somewhere with a bit more life to it?" she asked, looking up at him under artfully lowered lashes. "You have to admit that even the school's science lab has more excitement than one of Dr. Phillips's parties."

Jared shook his head. "Even Shamus would be the first to remind you that this particular party is one you remain at until the finish."

"Ah, academic politics," she sighed, settling in the front seat. "No wonder I never thought seriously about teaching here full time before. The required socializing would have driven me nuts in no time." She shuddered dramatically.

"Your lecture series on those Greek ruins ends in only a few weeks, doesn't it?" he asked, frowning at her words.

Kate nodded. "I have to admit I'll miss this group. They're very enthusiastic and ask some pretty insightful questions. I've had to do quite a bit of extra research just to keep up with them." She absently fiddled with her intricate braid accented by a turquoise ribbon woven through it. "I have several of your students in the group and considering they generally only consider the world interesting after the year 1720 they do pretty well with the early centuries."

Jared smiled. "Ted told a friend you've got great legs."

Kate chuckled. "I gathered that after my first lecture. He always sits in the front row and I doubt he listens to one word I say. After the first two sessions I began wearing slacks, but I think he has X-ray vision." She cast a quick glance in his direction, wondering if he was bothered by the idea of his students ogling her. After all, they were engaged to be engaged, weren't they? Nothing in Jared's manner gave away his feelings on the subject, which, at that moment, didn't endear him to her. She tamped down the feelings of irritation that had been surfacing more and more lately when she was in his company. While he was a very good-looking man with thick black hair and sapphire blue eyes that a woman could drown in, he was also just as her grandfather said—stuffy. More than once she wondered if he showed more animation in his teaching than he did with her. Still, considering her life-style, her chances of meeting an eligible man were next to nil and she figured if she could get Jared to loosen up he would be the perfect man for her to settle down with.

"You enjoy shocking people, don't you?" Jared commented, as he drove down the tree-lined road leading to the house that had been the university president's residence for more than thirty years.

"Not shock exactly, more like I let people know I'm an original," she quipped. "Gramps said I take after Dad in that respect."

As they parked near the entrance, Kate covertly studied her companion. Even though she had been dating Jared for almost eight months she doubted she knew any more about him than most people did. She knew that this was his second year teaching history at the college, that he was most definitely single, that he pretty much kept to himself, that he had dated a few of the women associated with the college and from what she had learned from friends she suspected that he was happiest keeping close to home. Just the kind of man she wanted. She had decided long ago if she wasn't going to have the kind of messy love lives her father and grandfather experienced she'd have to find someone completely opposite in personality. Which is exactly why she set her sights on Professor Jared Wyatt the first moment she met him.

And whatever Kate wanted, Kate got.

KATE WINCED as she listened to the ponderous music filtering through the door.

"Beethoven?" she guessed.

Jared shook his head. "Sounds more like Bach."

"Either way it sounds more like a funeral than a party," she mumbled, looping the strap to her pink leather purse over her arm. She reached up and straightened his tie. "There, now you're presentable."

He glanced at her impossibly long legs visible under the short skirt. "As you said, the essentials are covered."

Kate pasted a bright smile on her face as Jared rang the doorbell.

"You look as if you're here for a root canal," he commented, glancing at her.

"As far as I'm concerned attending one of these parties is the same as— Good evening, Mrs. Phillips, how lovely you look." Without missing a beat Kate's voice changed into a bright lilting tone.

The older woman returned her smile although hers was a bit cooler as she stared at Kate's long legs bared under the short skirt. "Thank you, Kathryn. I'm glad you could come. Professor Wyatt, it's nice to see you again." She nodded toward the tall man standing behind Kate. "Please, come in."

She led the way down a dark hallway filled with antique tables with ornate vases resting on top. Kate wiggled her eyebrows at Jared.

A museum, she mouthed.

"Kathryn, I must say you look more and more like your grandfather each time I see you," Mrs. Phillips commented. "To be frank, I can't see any of your father in you."

"I have Dad's nose," she offered helpfully.

The older woman looked at her suspiciously as if sensing Kate was teasing her. "Yes, well, we've seen so little of your father these past years. Does he still teach at Berkeley?" She said the word with obvious distaste.

Kate's smile was firmly pasted on her lips. "Yes, he does."

"Kathryn, my dear, how nice you could come." A bald-headed man advanced on them with hands outstretched. "Jared, it's good to see you."

"Good evening, Dr. Phillips," Kate greeted him.

Although he was a good two inches shorter than her five foot eight Dr. Phillips leaned forward as if imparting a secret. "When can we expect you to join our faculty on a full-time basis?" He eyed Jared archly then turned back to Kate. "I can't imagine you running off to one of those exotic countries so soon what with your new interests."

Kate found his heavy-handed teasing grated on her nerves, not to mention his clammy hand holding hers. "Let's just say that I'm considering your excellent offer." She carefully extricated herself from his grasp to accept the glass of white wine Jared now held out to her. She heaved a silent sigh of relief when Dr. Phillips was called away to greet more new arrivals. "I was ten years old the first time I attended one of these parties. Gramps decided I was old enough to mingle with the adults and brought me here kicking and screaming."

"And?" Jared knew there had to be a story to it. He had been seeing Kate long enough to be familiar with these anecdotes.

Her lips curved. "Mrs. Phillips was in the midst of showing an admiring group her infamous roses when they came upon Tommy Stone and myself playing doctor. Mrs. Stone fainted and when she came to she accused me of being the instigator. She insisted her darling little boy would never think of such a horrible thing even though it had been his idea."

"And all because of Kate little Tommy Stone is now an eminent psychiatrist dealing with sexual problems." A woman's throaty voice sounded from behind them.

They turned to find a woman who could only be described as sultry standing there. Her strapless deep burgundy cocktail dress complemented her voluptuous figure admirably.

"Kiki!" Kate squealed, hugging the woman. "When did you get back?"

"Obviously, not soon enough judging by the company you keep." She smiled at Jared. "Who's your friend, love?" Her husky voice rivaled Lauren Bacall's for that deep bedroom tone, and her porcelain features, haloed by dusky black hair, brought men to her feet bearing very expensive gifts.

"Kiki, this is Dr. Jared Wyatt, professor of American history. Jared, Cassandra Rogers Lassiter Fletcher, alias Kiki." She turned to the woman. "Did I miss anyone?"

Kiki lifted her shoulders in an elegant shrug. "André, but I wouldn't worry about it. I forgot all about him even before I filed for divorce."

"I can see André was a lasting memory," Kate drawled.

Jared touched Kate's shoulder. "Since I'm sure you two want to talk, I'll mingle."

She flashed him a bright smile. "Don't worry, I'll rescue you before it gets too bad."

Kiki dragged Kate off to a quiet corner. "Okay, sweetie, tell all," she pressed. "And don't leave out one delicious moment."

"Jared replaced Dr. Foster when he retired two years ago and we've been seeing each other for about eight months," she replied, sipping her wine. "I met him a couple of months after I returned from South America."

Kiki laughed softly. "And?"

Kate shrugged, pretending not to understand what her friend was getting at. "And he's a very nice man."

Kiki expelled a sigh of frustration. "Yes, but how is he in bed?" She leaned forward with an expectant expression on her lovely face. It was clear she wanted to hear a titillating confession.

Kate rolled her eyes and laughed. "You are incorrigible."

"Actually, darling, you're the incorrigible one. I'm the naughty one, remember?" Kiki's dark eyes scanned the group milling around the large room. Her expression was very much that of a spider looking for its next fly. "I don't believe the furniture has changed in this house in the last two hundred years." She pushed the toe of her burgundy peau de soie pumps against the design in the Persian carpet.

"You grew up here, you should know." Kate couldn't help but notice the direction of her friend's gaze. "Kiki, the man has no money. All he lives for is American history, and his idea of excitement is his weekly chess game with Gramps or a rousing tennis game, and you know me and sports. Remember Mrs. Reynolds, our gym teacher in the ninth grade? She never understood how I indulged in so much physical activity with Gramps's work and could still flunk gym. I'm sure I made school history."

"You always equated gym with bubonic plague." A tiny smile curved her burgundy-glossed lips as she surveyed Jared. "That might be what you think, but I see your Dr. Wyatt another way. I have an idea there's a great deal more to the man than meets the eye."

Kate shook her head. "Then you need your eyes checked. Trust me, he's your typical academian."

"Let's hear it for the academics."

Kate shook her head. "I'm shockproof, remember?"

"How's Shamus?" Kiki quickly changed the subject.

"His usual ornery self. Breaking his hip last summer hasn't slowed him down all that much."

"I'll have to stop by and see him." Kiki's gaze was boring into Jared's back. "Too bad you've already staked a claim on that one. I wouldn't mind learning about his views on American history."

"I already told you, he has no money and he doesn't have a crazy sense of adventure."

"He doesn't sound like your typical choice of man."

"I was ready for a change of pace. I was," she insisted at her friend's visible skepticism. "I've decided it's time to settle down."

Kiki shook her head. "You don't know how to settle down. Take a good look at yourself, kiddo. My idea of fun has never been digging around dusty old ruins and turning my nails into splinters, but I think that's when you're happiest."

"Now you sound like Gramps." Kate laughed, although an uneasy feeling crept through her stomach. To her, Jared was the kind of man one could be comfortable with. All she had to do was look at him now in his dark blue suit with the crisp white shirt and blue and gray striped tie to know he would easily fit into any situation. She narrowed her eyes, trying to picture him in rumpled khakis, sweating under a hot eastern sun. Well, almost any situation. His black hair was brushed into a neat style, he'd obviously shaved before picking her up this evening and she knew she'd find a clean handkerchief inside his coat pocket. No, he clearly looked as if he belonged here among the elite academic circles instead of laboring on an archaeological dig. She didn't feel half as comfortable in these surroundings as he was, although she'd known many of these people most of her life. She wanted more from her life than a sheaf of published articles and some rare archaeological finds.

"All right, people, come along. It's time to see my roses," Mrs. Phillips trilled, opening the French doors that led to the patio.

"A Venus's-flytrap would be nice," Kiki muttered as she wrinkled her nose. "You'd think that just for one year we could look at something other than her prize roses."

"I didn't think you were here last year," Kate commented.

"I wasn't and neither were you."

"I was in the Amazon dodging cannibals."

"And I was in Rome doing the same." She chuckled.

Kate looked up when Jared moved across the room to join them. She couldn't help but feel secretly pleased that he was nothing more than polite to Kiki whose beauty and wit usually had men swarming around her.

"On to the famous roses." His lips brushed Kate's ear as they entered Mrs. Phillips's prized greenhouse that dominated the rear of the yard.

"Where we ooh and ah and tell her we've never seen anything so lovely," Kate replied under her breath. Funny, she couldn't remember noticing before how enticing Jared's after-shave was. She wondered if it was new.

Kiki touched Kate's arm. "Who's that?" She nodded her head toward a tall blond man standing off to one side.

Kate frowned and shook her head. She looked to Jared for an answer.

"Craig Peters, philosophy and recently divorced." He filled in the blanks that Kiki would consider important.

Kiki's face lit up. "Sounds good to me." She turned to Kate. "Tell you what, I'll be by tomorrow for one of our breakfast gabfests," she told her before moving swiftly toward the blond man's side.

Jared chuckled. "She doesn't waste any time, does she?"

Kate looked up. "Kiki doesn't believe in wasting time where there's a man involved. If you'd arrived alone, she would have stuck to you like glue." *Ask him if he prefers her over you,* a tiny voice prompted. *Go ahead, ask him. You know you want to know.* "She's lovely, not to mention she has plenty of money thanks to all those divorce settlements," she said casually.

"Craig might not be rich, but from what I hear he'll give her a good time." Jared gently squeezed her hand.

She glanced sideways at his carved features and made a mental note to sit in on one of his classes. Maybe American history was where his passion lay.

Kate couldn't help but notice that Kiki and Craig slipped away barely ten minutes later.

"Are you sure you wouldn't like to sneak out early and find a place that doesn't consider Bach one of the top forty?" she asked Jared.

"If you don't mind, I'd like to speak to Dr. Carson first."

Of course, the department head. Always the political game, she thought. "No, of course not. You go on ahead. I'll wait here." Then she groaned silently when Dr. Phillips appeared at her elbow.

"Well, Kathryn, shall we talk more about your joining the faculty?" he asked jovially. "Since Shamus retired we haven't been able to find anyone with his expertise in the subject. We've always had an excellent archaeology department here, thanks to him, but with Shamus retired, the department doesn't have that old zip. Your lecture series is a godsend, but it still isn't the same as having you with us full time. An O'Malley on our faculty is an excellent drawing card for those future archaeologists, you know. Especially with the way you've followed in your grandfather's footsteps. What a shame your father didn't choose the field."

Kate thought of her father who had been happier in the sixties when free love and peace were praised. Patrick O'Malley, who preferred communes where pot was raised alongside whole wheat grains. No, he wouldn't have worked well in this conservative little college that dealt so strongly with academics instead of parties and where many of the male students still wore ties to class. No, Patrick wouldn't have been happy here at all.

"Dad always preferred cultural anthropology," she explained, pasting her polite smile on her lips. "He enjoys studying tribal habits over digging into ancient graves for evidence of their past lives. To be honest, I think Berkeley is more his style."

Dr. Phillips shifted uneasily, obviously remembering Patrick O'Malley's last visit and the young girl in tow whom he'd called Raincloud, his "woman." "Yes, well, at least you've always remained loyal to Sheffield, and we thank you for that."

"Gramps wouldn't have it any other way."

He turned serious. "I do mean it, Kathryn. We'd like to have you join our staff. I'm hoping your seeing Professor Wyatt means you might be thinking of remaining here permanently.''

"My finds have meant excellent publicity, not just for me, but also for the university,'' she reminded him. "But yes, I have been seriously considering the idea of settling down. Traveling without Gramps isn't as exciting as traveling with him. Since he's written books about his work and been successful with them, there's no reason why I can't do the same.'' She paused. "Of course, Dr. Phillips, the lecture series I've given over the years must show you that my teaching style is like my grandfather's.''

The good doctor looked pained. Shamus's teaching style had been ahead of its time, while Dr. Phillips always believed in the conservative approach. Still, he knew the young woman had learned much under her grandfather's tutelage and any college would be eager to have her on its staff. He knew he couldn't allow her to slip through his fingertips.

"I fully understand. I hope you'll be able to give me your answer well before the next semester begins. I'd like to see that department back to what it was under Shamus's direction.'' Seeing his wife gesturing to him, he smiled at Kate and walked off.

"Is he still trying to talk you into a full-time position?'' Jared asked, appearing at her side.

She nodded. "I feel as if I should put him out of his misery soon.''

"Ready to leave?''

The light flashed back in her eyes. "Ready and more than willing.''

"You don't enjoy these gatherings, do you?'' Jared asked once they were settled in his car.

"Not really. I feel as if we only attend these parties to pay homage to the good doctor. His wife's roses are only a front to make it look more social than business. Faculty attendance is mandatory because he likes his ego stroked and because he thinks everyone admires him instead of secretly considering him a pompous ass. Kiki once said he would have made a perfect Roman governor, although I can't imagine him wearing a toga."

"Where does Kiki fit in to all this?" he asked curiously.

"She's Mrs. Phillips's niece. Her parents died in a plane crash when she was nine. We met the first day of third grade when I blackened Toby Henderson's eye for calling her a snot nose and me a pickle face." She laughed softly. "Nine years later she and Toby eloped. They were married for seven months before Toby decided he was too young to be a husband."

"And now she only looks for wealthy men."

Kate nodded. "Oh, I know it sounds very mercenary on her part, but deep down she has a heart of gold."

"Probably because one of her ex-husbands had one made for her."

Kate looked surprised. "You didn't like her, did you?"

"I don't like any woman who looks at a man as if he were a slab of meat."

"But men can look at women that way and it's all right," she argued. "I hate that damn double standard!"

"I never said that either," he argued amiably. "No, I don't believe men should view women that way. I certainly don't look at you that way."

That's true, she thought. But why was she feeling more than a little put out by that fact? *But that's what you wanted, dolt,* she reminded herself. *You wanted a man who cared more for hearth and home and not following the sun. So why are you complaining now that you appear to have your hooks in what you decided you wanted?*

"I'd ask you in, but I'm afraid all that Bach gave me a headache." A weak excuse, at best. Kate's thoughts regarding Jared had left her more than a little irritated and now she only wanted to be alone to think things out.

"No problem. I have an early morning tennis appointment." His smile softened his refusal. "Tell Shamus I'll be by for our chess game at two."

She smiled and nodded. "I'll let him know."

Jared's good night kiss was light and altogether too gentle for Kate's taste. Yet she couldn't remember ever complaining about his kisses before. She silently damned Shamus and Kiki for prompting her to look at Jared in a different light. And silently damned herself for not wanting to ask him in for a drink since she felt uneasy with the conflicting feelings flowing through her.

When she entered the house, she was surprised to see the light burning under Shamus's study door.

She stuck her head inside. "Are you still up?"

He jumped, looking just a trifle guilty. "I wasn't sleepy so I thought I'd do some reading." He sounded grumpy.

Kate craned her neck but could see little of what Shamus was obviously hiding from her. What she could see appeared to be very old papers. She wondered what he was up to. "What are you doing, updating your memoirs?" she teased.

"Just some old papers I thought I'd look through before I went up to bed." Shamus's face took on a ruddy cast Kate had seen before. It meant he was up to no good.

She frowned. "What kind of old papers?"

"Just some diaries a friend sent to me for authentification." He went on sharply, "It's obscure erotica. Are you happy now?"

Kate shrugged, deliberately ignoring his defensive stance. "Only if I can read it when you're finished."

Chapter Two

"Tell me more about the man you've chosen to be the father of your children." Kiki picked through the box of doughnuts she had presented to Kate early that morning when she appeared on her doorstep demanding coffee.

Kate hated to hear it sound so cold-blooded. She wrapped her robe more closely around her as she slipped her bare feet under her. "I thought your interest was in philosophy."

Kiki looked miffed. "Craig is a very interesting man, but he prefers talking about the universe. He'd get along beautifully with your father."

"You mean he didn't talk on and on about your beautiful eyes and gorgeous cheekbones?" she teased. "That must have been very rough for you."

"We stopped by Ye Old Pizzaria." Kiki wrinkled her nose. "That place hasn't changed since you and I were students. Would you believe seven of Craig's students, all females, stopped by with questions? My God, were we ever that young and silly? The giggling alone would get on one's nerves. Either I'm getting older or they're looking younger."

Kate chuckled. "I know just what you mean. That's happened to Jared, too. Even though he's made a strict rule that if they have questions they have to see him during his office hours they always think of something and he's too polite to turn them away."

"Craig mentioned that Jared is rapidly becoming the fair-haired boy of the history department and that he'll have no trouble gaining tenure since my darling uncle is so pleased with him." Kiki eyed her closely. "Craig also said that while he's a crackerjack tennis player and good company for a morning run he's pretty closemouthed about himself, which we both know makes him perfect faculty material for this mausoleum. And you know what that means—he must be as stuffy as the other instructors around here."

"I wouldn't call Gramps stuffy and he taught here for more than thirty years," Kate argued.

"Shamus brought the college a great deal of publicity and recognition with his archaeological finds over the years," Kiki reminded her. "Uncle Raymond may not have liked his somewhat unorthodox teaching style, but he couldn't fault him for what he did for the school. And where Uncle Raymond's concerned the school always comes first." She adjusted the sleeves of her soft wool mauve sweater trimmed with a dyed-to-match V-shaped leather insert on the front.

"If that color didn't make me look so washed out, I'd steal it right off your back." Kate eyed her sweater enviously.

Kiki smiled. "That's probably why I bought you one in red." She tapped the large shopping bag by her side. "I brought Shamus some French cognac and a gorgeous sweater I found in Dublin. It's to make up for my not being here last Christmas."

"I hope you'll be around for a while this time. It seems we've never been home during the same time for the past few years," Kate commented, pouring herself another cup of coffee.

Kiki's mouth curved in a coquettish smile. "That's because you're off hunting relics and I'm hunting men. And here people thought we were so different."

"At least you can't marry and divorce relics."

"Of course, you can. Although they generally die off before you can consider divorce." Kiki licked sugar from her perfectly manicured fingers.

Kate's eyes narrowed. "When did you turn into such a cynic about men and life in general, Kiki?"

Kiki concentrated on stirring her coffee although she hadn't added anything to it. "After my third divorce I realized that love doesn't last forever and that I was more of a misfit than I thought I was." Her voice was so low Kate had to strain her ears to hear her. "Think about it, Kate, we were both raised without parents. You were lucky, though, you had Shamus, who is the dearest man I know. I was left with a couple who didn't want a child upsetting their well ordered lives. I was sent off to every extracurricular activity and summer camp known to man."

Kiki took a sip of her coffee, then continued. "Your mother preferred a commune over you and your father preferred Haight-Ashbury and Timothy Leary over everything else. But you had Shamus who loved you and took you everywhere with him. He redesigned his life for you. Not because he had to, but because he wanted to. They didn't even try to make any concessions for me. It was much easier to send me off to music and dance classes than to allow me into their lives."

For the first time, Kate didn't see the lighthearted Kiki she had grown up with, but a bitter young woman who was looking for something she obviously couldn't understand because she had never been shown it.

"Oh, Kiki, you never let on how you felt," she whispered, sensing her friend's inner pain. "Why didn't you ever tell me? I thought we could tell each other everything, but you never said a word about this before. You always made it seem like a game when you tried to outwit them. Except it wasn't a game to you, was it?"

Kiki managed a wobbly smile, but the expression in her eyes could only be described as bleak. "I guess deep down I'm jealous. Because I can see you settling down with Jared Wyatt and having those two-point-five children and living happily ever after while I'm still looking around for Mr. Right but always marrying Mr. Wrong."

Kate's coffee turned to bile in her stomach. What had happened to her friend to turn her into such a bitter, disillusioned woman? She wondered if Kiki would ever break down the self-erected barriers and tell her. She reached across the table and grasped her hand. "If Gramps has his way, there won't be a marriage for a while. He thinks I should hold off. Personally, I have a feeling he's up to no good and that usually involves a long plane trip and I end up with dirt and bugs in my hair for several months."

"What would you choose? Jared or Shamus? A house with a white picket fence or another stamp on your passport? Which would it be, Kate?" Kiki's voice turned low and intense. "If you had the chance to find something so unique the whole world would be astonished, would you honestly tell Shamus, 'No, thank you, I have a new life to prepare for and my traveling days are over'? If you had the chance to succeed where no one else had ever been able to, would you go for it or tell Shamus, 'No thanks, I've given it up to be a wife and mother'? Be honest, Kate, what would you do?'' She leaned toward her. "Be honest with yourself. Are you seeing Jared as a means to an end? A way to shut up your biological clock? Tell me," she ordered.

Kate froze. She felt sick all over again because she couldn't tell Kiki the truth.

"IT'S YOUR MOVE."

"I know that! You just remember that I'm an old man and my brain doesn't work as quickly as yours." Shamus studied the intricately carved medieval pieces decorating the chess board.

"If there's one thing that hasn't slowed down after all these years it's your brain." Kate spoke from the chair she was curled up in with a large book settled in her lap. Jared and Shamus had been playing for more than an hour and she sat with her book but hadn't read one word. Her talk with Kiki had left her feeling too unsettled.

"Smart-mouthed kid," Shamus mumbled. He studied the board, painfully aware the wrong move would cost him his knight. "I should have sold you to Hassan when I had the chance."

"When I saw him last year he said it was a shame that I've grown up to be such a beautiful woman, although, alas, I was now too old to be his youngest son's first concubine." There was a mischievous glint in her eye.

Shamus explained to Jared. "Hassan is the leader of a small but very oil-wealthy desert tribe. He's always had an affinity for blondes and he offered me fifty thousand dollars for Kate when she was eleven." He glared at his granddaughter. "Unfortunately, I turned him down. If I'd known she'd turn out to be such a handful I would have let him have her for half the price."

"If you'd known I'd be such a handful you would have doubled the price," Kate pointed out, giving up her pretense of reading.

She sat back, hugging her knees to her chest. She usually didn't stay around during Jared and Shamus's chess games. This time she wanted to. After her talk with Kiki even more questions crowded her mind and she still had no answers. What if Shamus had discovered something incredible and wanted her to go after it? Could that be why he was trying to talk her out of marrying Jared? She momentarily closed her eyes, feeling a headache coming on. Kate rested her chin on her knees, pretending to study a painting across the room while she was, in fact, covertly studying Jared.

Black hair was expertly cut to frame his rugged features. Her disgruntled mind said he came to life more when he spoke about his recent research into the French and Indian War than when he talked to her. Even the dark-rimmed glasses he wore added to his image. She clenched her teeth wondering why doubts were assailing her now. Hadn't she already decided it was time to stick closer to home, be around for her grandfather, who wasn't getting any younger. She could take that teaching job Dr. Phillips had been after her to take for the past five years. That was what she had planned to do. Wasn't it? She pushed herself out of her chair.

"Would you gentlemen like coffee?" she asked, sounding brighter than she felt inside.

"Sounds good to me," Shamus answered absently, watching Jared with an eagle eye while he made his move.

"Yes, thank you." Jared not only made his move but captured Shamus's knight.

"Damn," the older man mumbled, scowling even more. "I'm going to have to find someone I can beat." He glanced slyly at his granddaughter.

"Not me. I don't have any patience for the game." Kate leaned against the back of Jared's chair for a moment. She tried to tell herself she wasn't doing it so he could catch a whiff of her new perfume. She'd hoped to gain Jared's attention by looking sexy today. She'd hadn't missed how good he looked in a natural-colored crewneck sweater and navy chinos. But all he'd done was concentrate on his damn chess game! She had taken time to crimp her hair that morning so it flowed around her face in wild waves and she wore a teal fine cotton oversize shirt knotted at her hip and white jeans that faithfully outlined her slim hips. So why didn't he tell her she looked nice? Her eyes flashed fire as she looked down at the top of Jared's head. Damn it! What would it cost him to look up and just smile at her?

"I'll get the coffee." Her voice was tightly controlled as she pushed herself away from the chair.

"She's had a burr under her since she got up. Even her visit with Kiki this morning didn't seem to cheer her up," Shamus commented after Kate left the room. He eyed the younger man sharply. "Did you two have an argument last night?"

"No, last night was fine. Although she did appear a little unsettled at the party. I assumed it had something to do with seeing Kiki." Jared leaned back in the chair.

"I have to admit she's the kind of woman who could unsettle a stone."

Shamus grinned. "No, the only ones Kiki upsets are relatives and ex-husbands. I bet Raymond's and Lily's blood pressures shot up twenty points since she's been back." He grinned slyly. "I can imagine you were a surprise to her."

"I have an idea she prefers men with an impressive stock portfolio," he said wryly.

"While Kate likes men with excitement flowing through their veins." Shamus's eyes bored into Jared's. "It's in the O'Malley genes."

"And here she's dating a stuffy history professor who listens to her tales of traveling the world over while he has no desire to do such because he's perfectly happy to spend his time with his dusty old books." Jared smiled, but nothing else in his expression indicated what he might be thinking.

"Someone mentioned you studied an old Indian burial ground in Idaho a couple years ago," Shamus brought up. "Then there was something about you being up in the Black Hills for another long-term study. And some trouble that was quickly taken care of by the team leader. Rumor has it you were that team leader."

"Checking me out to make sure I'm suitable for your granddaughter?" He looked more amused than affronted that Shamus checked into his background.

"It wouldn't matter if you were or weren't suitable because she'll do what she wants no matter what anyone says." He leaned forward, crossing his arms on top of the table. "You know, in some ways you remind me of me years ago." He thought nothing of switching topics midstream.

"I hope that's a compliment."

Shamus's studied gaze didn't leave Jared's face. "I'm beginning to wonder if you're the kind of man the public sees. Age hasn't diminished any of my senses. I know very well if the man I was fifty years ago was looking to teach here today I'd be politely told there was no position available when what they really meant was I wasn't suitable faculty material. Phillips tends to forget the school is here to nurture minds, to show them more than just boring details written down in a book instead of firing them up to search for themselves."

"Maybe you should have gone after his job," Jared suggested.

Shamus grimaced. "And be bogged down with all that paperwork? No, thank you. I'm happier reading all the books I didn't have time for years ago and assisting Kate with her research. That's when she's the happiest." His words were deliberate. "When she's in the field."

"You'll have to give her up sometime, Shamus," Jared said gently. "She can't follow your dreams for the rest of her life or live your life for you. She has to start living for herself."

"And you don't think that's not what I want?" Shamus smiled, but there was no humor in it. "We'll just have to see who wins this particular battle, won't we?"

"COFFEE AND SOME OF ANNA'S rum cake," Kate announced, walking into the room carrying a large tray. She stopped just inside the door sensing the change in atmosphere between the two men. "Finish your game?" she asked unnecessarily. She could tell at a glance that they hadn't, but she felt the need to say something, anything to break the charged silence floating between the two men. She walked into the room and set the tray on a small serving table and pushed it toward the men. She picked up her own cup of coffee and wandered over to one of the floor-to-ceiling bookcases dominating the room.

"We're just taking a break." Jared was the first one to break the silence. He picked up the cup closest to him and sipped the hot brew. "Why don't you tell me more about Hassan, Shamus?" He sneaked a glance toward Kate. "He actually wanted to buy Kate, did he?"

The older man nodded. "That he did. Kate had accompanied me on one of my digs, which is where we met Hassan and two of his sons. He wanted Kate for his oldest son."

"Not as a wife but as his first concubine," Kate pointed out from her position by the bookcase. "I think Shamus was tempted, because I wasn't on my best behavior during the trip, but he knew Grandmother's spirit would have haunted him for the rest of his life if he had done it."

"That woman was a pain in the butt in life but in death she would have never left me alone just out of pure spite," he rumbled. Yet it was evident he had only affection for the wife who had died so long ago. He rose slowly from his chair and walked out of the room without looking back.

"I feel as if I've brought up a forbidden subject," Jared said after the door closed behind Shamus.

Kate shook her head. "No, nothing forbidden. Gramps likes to claim that Grandmother ran his life, but he still worshipped her. The fact that she died so suddenly early in their marriage was such a shock that I don't think he ever got over it." She gestured toward the leather couch situated under a window and took up one corner. She waited until Jared sat down before continuing her story. "The doctors said it was a brain tumor. No one had any idea she even had one. She was sitting there talking to Gramps one evening and she just looked at him, suddenly told him how much she loved him and died. Dad was seven then. What I know about her death I've mostly heard from others. When I was little Gramps would tell me how like her I was and he wasn't sure if it would be good or bad that I had her stubborn nature."

She smiled, looking down at her coffee. "He prefers to forget just how mule-headed he is. Marriages don't seem to work out very well for the O'Malley clan. My parents married long enough for me to be born before my mother took off with a guitar player. She said Dad's aura was too purple for her. The O'Malley family doesn't seem to have very good luck with the opposite sex."

"Kate." Jared grasped her chin and brought her face up. "It's not a matter of genetics whether people are lucky or unlucky in love. Look at your friend Kiki. How many husbands has she gone through? Then look at how long her aunt and uncle have been married."

"She's had five, I think, but it could be six for all I know." She focused on the natural-colored cable knit of his sweater. "But Kiki is a different matter. She tends to bore easily and she feels if she sleeps with a man she should marry him. I don't think she considers what 'till death do us part' really means."

Jared looked at her long and hard. "What are you really trying to say, Kate? One trait I've always admired about you is your outspoken nature. Don't prevaricate now."

Not caring for his close scrutiny, she jumped up. "I don't know what you mean."

"Yes, you do. Are you continuing what your grand-father began earlier?" Jared put his coffee cup to one side.

She eyed him suspiciously, relieved to have the chance to take the offensive. "What did Gramps say to you before I came in?"

"Man talk."

"Now who's evading the subject? I suggest you tell me or I'll get it out of him and my methods are not pretty. That man will not see one of his smuggled Cuban cigars for a very long time if I have anything to do with it." She leaned over him for a scant second before straightening up and moving away. "It had something to do with me, didn't it?"

He tipped his head to one side and watched her pace the room with jerky motions. "Kate, Shamus and I were not talking about you. Only about his work."

She sensed he was lying. "Stop sounding like a pompous fool!" She swallowed the embarrassed shriek that would have surely followed her words. "I'm sorry." Her apology was stiff and unnatural.

Jared stood up. "No, you aren't, Kate," he told her, looking as controlled as ever. "I guess I shouldn't be surprised that you see me that way. To be honest, I've always had a hunch that was why you went out with me—because you wanted to be with someone on the opposite plane from your family. Perhaps that's why we never set a wedding date, because deep down you knew you didn't want to settle down as much as you thought you did. I wonder if you only mouthed words you thought were appropriate for the discussion we had back then."

"On that point you are very wrong," she claimed, just before she threw her arms around him and kissed him so thoroughly she was positive he could feel it down to his toes. By the time she stepped back she was breathing heavily. "If that doesn't tell you something, nothing will."

The expression on Jared's face told her nothing. She silently damned him for not even showing a change in respiration. Wasn't the man the least bit human? He just sat there looking so damn calm she wanted to hit him! What didn't help was the tiny flicker of arousal in the pit of her stomach. She ruthlessly tamped the feeling down.

"If there's one thing I know it's a distraught woman," he said in his calm way that irked her no end. "This might be a good time for me to leave and allow you to collect your thoughts. Why don't we plan on having dinner tomorrow night when we can discuss this in a more rational manner." His kiss on her forehead was a bare touch of the lips. Before she could blink he was gone.

"This is all a nightmare," Kate chanted, throwing up her hands in anger. "I am still in bed and I'm dreaming this. When I wake up it'll be morning and everything will be just fine." She spun around, facing one of the bookcases, taking refuge in the orderly stacks of books Shamus had collected over the years. She frowned as her gaze ran along one shelf then backed up to run along the line of books again. Something was out of place; a rare occurrence for the fanatical Shamus who insisted every book had its place and should be kept in perfect order. She moved closer to the shelf that was at eye level and ran her finger along the spines. When she reached one particular book, she pulled it out, opened the cover and looked at the title page be-

fore closing it. She shut her eyes, trying to recall the last
time she'd seen this particular book.

"Last night," she murmured, stroking the cracked
leather binding. He had pushed some papers over it before she could see too much, but this was it. She ran her
fingers over the cover. "You've never dealt with this
time period, Gramps," she mused, her forehead creased
in a frown. "This is only a little over a hundred years
old." She slowly scanned the room to see if anything
else was out of place. "What has that schemer come up
with now?" Her features hardened with resolve.
"There's only one way to find out."

Kate knew exactly where she would find Shamus. She
headed for the enclosed sun porch attached to the back
of the house.

"Did Jared leave already?" He looked up when she
entered. "I thought I heard his car."

"Yes, he did. It appears he has the idea I'm not ready
for marriage yet. Now, I wonder where he got that
idea." She stood in front of him, her arms crossed over
her chest. "What did you say to him, Shamus O'Malley?"

He waved a hand feebly around. "Now why would I
say anything to him about you?"

"Because you're afraid I'll get married and not go
after some rare dagger or chalice or find some forgotten tomb of an equally forgotten prince for you, that's
why." If she hadn't been looking at him directly she
would have missed the flicker of guilt in his eyes.
"That's it, isn't it? That's why you were hiding that
book from me last night. That's why there's a book on
legendary gold mines hidden among your Egyptology
books when you *never* have a book out of place. You
almost had a coronary that time I put a book back on

the wrong shelf. You have something up your sleeve."
She leaned over, placing her hands on the arms of his
chair. "And that's why you oh so casually discouraged
me from accepting Dr. Phillips's offer. You found
something you consider important and you want me to
go after it. No. N-O. No. I don't care what it is, I am
going to go over to Jared's house and tell him I'm sorry
for the way I've acted, that I've regained my sanity and
I want to set a wedding date. Then I'm going to see Dr.
Phillips and accept his offer. And if you don't like it,
well, tough noogies, old boy, because that's the way it
is." She didn't give a thought that she was being rude to
her grandfather. He had always encouraged her to speak
her mind no matter how it sounded to others.

"Don't you want to hear about my latest find?"
Shamus asked with a calculating grin, unperturbed by
her temper tantrum.

"No."

His eyes gleamed. "This is more exciting than anything we've ever found, Katie girl."

"I wonder if I could borrow Lucretia Borgia's poi-
son ring for a few hours." Kate sighed.

"You won't need your passport or to update any of
your shots," he persisted.

"Of course, I won't. I won't be traveling more than
ten miles from here!" she shouted.

"The weather there is a hell of a lot warmer than it's
going to be around here," Shamus shouted back. "You
can't refuse this!"

She almost faltered under his confidence but quickly
found the courage to stiffen her backbone. "Not interested."

Shamus's smile made Kate feel uneasy. She sensed
whatever he had up his sleeve this time could prove to

be something that would change her life whether she wanted it to or not.

"I have positive information on the exact location of the Lost Dutchman Mine." He dropped his bomb.

Kate suddenly felt very light-headed. She slumped down onto a seat. "Some say that was nothing more than a legend."

Shamus's eyes were shining. "It's not."

If you had the chance to succeed where no one else had ever been able to, would you go for it or tell Shamus "No thanks, I've given it up...." Be honest with yourself, Kate, what would you do? Kiki's words came back to haunt her.

Kate never felt as sick as she did just then. "Oh, hell."

She closed her eyes for several moments. "What makes you think, and I do mean *think*, you have concrete evidence of the mine's location?" She silently groaned, wondering how she would dare ask such a question when, if nothing else, Shamus was a thorough researcher.

Shamus got slowly to his feet and walked into his study. He pulled out a large binder from one of the bookcases. He pushed aside the chess set and gestured to Kate to join him.

"What do you know of the Lost Dutchman Mine?" he asked, leafing through papers covered with his nearly illegible scrawl.

She shrugged. "Not very much. Just what I remember from that movie with Glenn Ford and Ida Lupino and bits and pieces from one of my history classes when we studied Arizona and the Superstition Mountains. In case you've forgotten my mind was usually wandering back more than a couple hundred years. If this is so important to you why haven't you discussed it with Jared? I should think this would be right up his alley."

He shook his head as he continued scanning pages until he found the one he wanted. "I prefer to keep this in the family." He looked up. "Not long before Jacob Waltz died in 1891 he became good friends with a widow in his town and even shared some of his gold with her. Since he wasn't able to physically take her to his mine the way he promised, he did give her directions. But they were very complicated and she went bankrupt looking for the mine. Her foster son took on the task. It's said he didn't find it, although he did concentrate in a particular area. Papers were later found proving that he did find it but kept it quiet to prevent the area from being overrun."

He handed her several of the handwritten sheets, which she quickly scanned. "But it was all in some kind of code and there were even varying stories told by other miners who claimed to be friends of Waltz. I've sifted through the many stories and worked on the code. I think I've finally cracked it." He showed her photocopies of writing that was decidedly old-fashioned, with misspellings and shaky lines depicting trails and inverted Vs for mountains. "One problem is there's no dates given on any of his papers and if this was drawn before May of 1887 the location would be distorted from a large earthquake they had then."

Kate picked up another sheet of paper wishing she could ignore the tingle traveling along the back of her neck. The tingle she only experienced when she knew she was to embark on something new. She could already feel the increase of adrenaline in her veins and the inner need to seek out what others have sought for so long and missed.

"The rangers don't like people in there for too long a period, because it's too easy to get lost. But with your knowledge of the wilderness I don't think you'd have too much trouble, although you would need a reliable guide who's familiar with the area. I contacted some friends to get some names of guides." Shamus's excitement grew with each word he uttered. "Of course, you'd have to plan to go within the next couple months before the really hot weather set in, but still, after the heat of the Mideast, this would be a picnic for you, girl."

A thin thread of sanity intruded on the excitement slowly building up inside her. "No!" Kate jumped up and backed away from the table as if afraid the papers would develop hands that would reach out and grab her. "I can't go." She could feel her breathing become more labored by the moment.

Shamus scowled at her. "And why not?"

"Because I told you when I found that Mayan ceremonial dagger that I was quitting my traveling. Not to mention I almost got killed getting that damned dagger," she reminded him. "And because I met Jared and we've decided to marry..."

"Ha! You told me you only got a tiny scratch! And as for the other, your plan to marry sounds more like a business contract to me." He snorted. "Where's the love involved? The passion? What about all those words you used to spout at me that you were going to marry someone just like me? What do you say to that?"

"I don't want to become a camp follower for the rest of my life!" she shouted. "I want to have a house with a garden and picket fence and a swing set in the backyard. I want to have a husband who will come home every night at a set time. I want to spend Sundays reading the paper and taking walks. I want a normal life!''

"A normal life?" Shamus bristled. "You've had the kind of life most children couldn't even dream of. You've met people all over the world, saw cultures people only read about in books or in *National Geographic*. How many people have done what you have? Seen what you've seen? Very few. You speak eight languages fluently and know enough of four others to get by. There's not that many women who grew up with the freedom I gave you. I allowed you to grow up to be an individual." He pounded his fist on the table for emphasis.

"That was because you figured I'd grow into someone like you," she argued. "I'm not saying it was wrong, because I love exploring the past and finding those treasures. But there has to be a time for that to stop. For me to go on to another level of my life. And this is the time." Her voice lowered. "Please understand."

But Shamus wasn't about to back down when he saw the realization of another dream so near. "Do you realize how long I've been poring over these papers, studying these maps against more recent ones?" he asked in a quiet voice that tore at her heart. "For two years, that's how long. I don't want to find this because of the gold, Katie. I just want to prove the legend is fact."

"Good thing, because you'd probably have to split it with the government. If they'd even allow you to take it out." She tried for a note of humor to steel herself from his manipulation.

He scowled at her. "That's not it and you know it. What's been written so far is the supposition that Jacob Waltz found a large vein of gold in those mountains. I want to tell people, yes, there was such a mine and here it is! Hell, I don't even care if the gold remains there, just as long as some kind of proof could be brought back." He paused, rubbing his hands over his face. "Kate, this may be my last piece of vicarious searching. I need it."

For the first time she looked at him closely. She saw the shadows under his eyes that were darker than usual, the deeper lines in his handsome, craggy face she didn't remember seeing before. She noted his hands, which used to be so strong when they worked on the digs, now trembled slightly, and his green eyes were somewhat dimmed with age. Shamus O'Malley looked every day of his eighty-two years.

Kate thought of the days they spent under the blistering sun in Egypt or the unending days of rain along the Amazon when Shamus insisted on his granddaughter working beside him to learn all the secrets of the past. During the school year he was there to help her with math and science, but the moment school let out they were off to find yet another rare artifact he had been researching during the winter. If they were away too long, no problem, Shamus was always able to tutor her in the necessary subjects and find someone qualified for the other ones.

"This is why you began to worry when it appeared Jared was serious about me," she said quietly, moving away from his aura of influence. She spun to face him, her hands clasped in front of her. "You hoped you could talk to me about this and I would immediately make preparations to hunt for the mine after we ironed out all the details." Shamus nodded silently. "Then why didn't you ever say anything about it to me before? Why now?" *Why now when my life seems to be suddenly spinning out of control?*

"Because I needed to compare one miner's journal against some other papers and I had to crack the code," he replied. "I wanted to make sure I was on the right track before I said anything to you."

"And now you feel confident you are?" She didn't need to hear his answer. If he wasn't on the right track he wouldn't be discussing this now.

He nodded again.

It's a sign, Kate. You've been wondering about Jared, whether he really is right for you and whether you truly were ready to settle down even with all your high and mighty talk about leading a "normal" life. Gramps says this is the last one, but you know better, because he'll always find another legend on the horizon and he'll hope you'll verify it.

She closed her eyes, feeling defeat in her bones. For once, she didn't feel the excitement of going after another rainbow. "I still have three more weeks of lectures."

"No problem. We have a lot of planning to do first."

She closed her eyes and breathed in and out several times. "You'll get the names of reliable guides for the area?" Her voice was barely above a whisper.

Shamus brightened now that he'd won the battle and, it appeared, the war. "I'll get them. You'll have to travel to Mexico to find them. Naturally, some are better than most, but you know your business, so I'm not worried about your having any trouble finding the right man.''

"You're that sure about this?" She took a last stab.

Shamus's lips curved in the rakish grin that years ago women all over the world fell for. "Trust me."

Chapter Three

As sleazy bars in tiny, sleazy Mexican border towns went, this one was no better and no worse than the others. And it didn't have to be a Friday night to bring out the regulars with the requisite number of typical barroom brawls to liven up the customers' evenings.

He sat at a back table in the tavern where he could see the entrance. A bottle of tequila and a cloudy glass were the only objects on the table in front of him. With the chair tipped back on its rear legs and his sweat-stained hat pulled down over his eyes, he looked relaxed, perhaps even asleep, which would be impossible considering the noise level. But those who had met him before knew differently. The *gringo* was not to be bothered. Those who had the alcohol-induced courage to challenge him usually ended up with more than a few bruises, and one sober challenger was treated for a broken collarbone. No, this man who appeared in the bar every so often seeking information or meeting people was not a man to be taken lightly. A few passed by the table murmuring a respectful "*Hola*, J.C.," but other than that terse greeting they left him to himself. Which was just fine with him. His less than clean chambray shirt was left unbuttoned to combat the heat in the small bar that intensified with every live body that entered the room. He poured tequila into the glass and sipped the fiery liquid while keeping his eyes on the doorway. It would appear he was waiting for someone.

It was late when the stranger entered the bar. For a moment, silence descended on the bar as the men stared at the woman standing near the entrance. Women coming in there were not unusual, but white women who were young and not looking shopworn were.

J.C. didn't move from his corner as he observed the visitor. He had to admit she was dressed appropriately for the occasion. Well-worn jeans, snug fitting but not too tight. A white cotton shirt that was buttoned high enough not to reveal any cleavage. No jewelry, not even a watch. Her boots looked scuffed and broken in. Her honey-blond hair was pinned back in a conservative style that emphasized her delicate features. Good, nothing to grab on to in case of a fight. The lady obviously knew what she was doing. When entering a strange situation, don't try to draw attention to yourself.

She walked confidently, looking neither right nor left until she reached the bar. If she was aware of the men watching her with hungry eyes she gave no evidence of it.

Pedro, the bartender, looked at her with little surprise in his eyes. He'd been working there too long to think it unusual to see a lovely *señorita* who was obviously not a prostitute walk into his bar.

From J.C.'s vantage point he could hear every word she spoke. He gave her points for fluent Spanish in the region's dialect. He hid a smile when she asked for a glass of tequila.

"*Señorita*, are you sure?" Pedro asked, looking a little worried.

She smiled. "Very sure."

J.C. smiled. Good girl. If you want information, you have to be ready to drink with the natives.

She didn't flinch when Pedro deposited the bottle on the bar, displaying a pale worm curled up in the bottom. She downed her drink quickly without one flicker of emotion on her face.

"I'm looking for Joaquin," she told Pedro. "I'm told he can usually be found here."

The bartender looked worried. "Oh, *Señorita*, a lovely lady like you would not want Joaquin. He is a very nasty man." Something occurred to him. "Unless you happen to work for him." He looked her up and down. "If you do, you must leave and return to his house. I do not want any trouble here from his women."

"I don't work for Joaquin, but I am looking for him to work for me. I understand he sometimes guides people into certain mountain regions," she explained, being deliberately vague. "I was also given Luis Ventara's name." She tapped the rim of the glass with her fingernail, indicating she would take a refill, and laid money on the bar.

"If you want a guide, you should speak to J.C. first," Pedro advised, gesturing toward the rear corner table. "He does not guide, but he can give you names of men who are very reliable. Men you can trust."

She barely spared him a glance. He didn't mind because he knew exactly what she saw. A man with several days' growth of beard, face pretty much hidden by the hat, a shirt that hadn't seen a laundry in weeks. He probably looked like a drunk who recently passed out and no one bothered to throw him out just yet. He hid a smile. She didn't look very impressed with what she saw, although nothing in her expression gave her away. He just sensed it. He couldn't wait to see what she thought of Joaquin or Luis.

"What about either of the other two names I mentioned?" she asked coolly, returning her gaze to the bartender.

"You want Joaquin, *Señorita*, you have him." A stocky man with a few strands of oily hair plastered across the top of his head and a belly straining against his sweat-stained shirt front moved to the bar, blocking the woman from J.C.'s sight. "What can I do for such a beautiful lady?" He smiled, revealing a mouth missing several front teeth.

"I was told you were a reliable guide into the mountain regions of New Mexico and Arizona," she explained.

"But, *Señorita*—" Pedro tried to interrupt but a searing glance from Joaquin stopped him.

"I am at your service. Where do you wish me to take you?" He looked her up and down in an open leer that undressed her within a matter of seconds.

"I have a few questions first." She reached for the tequila bottle. "Perhaps if we sit down?"

Joaquin immediately headed for a nearby table and promptly pushed the occupants away. With a bow he offered her one of the recently vacated chairs.

"I know many mountain regions," he bragged. "Which one do you wish to travel to?"

"The Superstitions. I'm an archaeologist and I'm looking for an Apache camp that was abandoned years ago," she told him. "It's deep in the mountains and I know the trail can be treacherous, but I'm willing to pay for your time. Half now, the other half when we return."

Joaquin peered at her closely. "Who else will go on this trip?"

"That's not your worry. What I need is an answer now because I intend to leave soon. If you can't do it, just say so now so I can look elsewhere." Her tone was crisp and businesslike, her gaze cool and collected.

He reached for her hand, sliding his beefy fingers across the back. "Now why would you want to go into the mountains? You are much too beautiful to want to do such a thing. You should be where you can be admired for your beauty."

She looked down at his hand then up at him. "I wouldn't advise you to touch me."

Undaunted, he continued stroking her hand. "But you are so very soft and sweet smelling."

Her other hand lashed out, the fingers grabbing his wrist at certain points. He yowled and jumped to his feet, cradling his throbbing hand.

She gazed at him levelly. "I told you not to touch me."

"No one treats me that way!" He reached out and grabbed her shoulders, jerking her to her feet. "Especially not a woman."

"*Señorita*, he is not the right Joaquin!" Pedro shouted. "This Joaquin is very mean to women! You do not want to do business with this man!"

As if they were mentally connected, J.C. knew what the woman was thinking. There wouldn't be any help from the others, who were content to sit back and watch the show. And if she wasn't careful she could very easily be raped and no one would give a damn about it. Correction, he thought, one person would.

She countered with another move, using both hands to break Joaquin's bruising grip on her. When he reared back to slap her across the face, she kneed him. His roar of pain set off the charged atmosphere; it was the only excuse the others needed to begin their own battles.

"Damn!" J.C. jumped to his feet. He reached her in seconds and promptly tossed her over his shoulder.

"No!" Joaquin shouted, angry at losing his prize so easily. "She is mine to deal with."

J.C.'s reply was explicit as to what he would do to Joaquin if the lady was touched. Amid a few cheers, some swearing and a lot of grunting from various small fights going on around him, J.C. stalked out of the bar.

"Put me down!" she screamed, punching him furiously in the back.

"Shut up," he growled.

She frowned, wondering why the husky tones sounded somewhat familiar. "Who the hell do you think you are?" she demanded. She couldn't help but look down and notice how the worn denim fitted his muscular buttocks. Very nice, she thought. If the face looked as good as the back, she would plan on patronizing this dump more often. She catalogued what little she could see and feel: a broad shoulder, arms well muscled enough to handle her tall frame, the enticing scent of warm male skin with overtones of cheap cigarettes and equally cheap whiskey. Too bad she hadn't gotten a better look at his face.

"I'm the man trying to keep you out of trouble, that's who." He spied an unfamiliar Jeep parked near the town's idea of a hotel and guessed it belonged to her. "That was one mean S.O.B. you were tangling with, lady. By now Joaquin is probably irate over losing the chance to add you to his stable and no one in their right mind wants to be around him for a while."

"That's what he thinks." Resigned to her upside down position she remained as still as she could. "He would have been missing a few pieces of his anatomy first."

He grinned. "I would have liked to have seen that."

"Tell me something, who exactly are you?"

"They call me J.C. What do they call you?"

She put on her haughtiest tone, considering she didn't feel in control of the situation. "Dr. O'Malley."

He chuckled. "Well, O'Malley, you sure put yourself in a hell of a position back there."

"I'm in a hell of a position right now!"

J.C. walked into the sorry excuse for a hotel lobby and leaned over the counter toward the rack holding keys. "What's your room number?"

"Four."

He was glad she didn't question him for his reason for taking her directly to her room or demand he put her down immediately. He had an idea she'd turn violent once he put her down and she got a good look at him.

The narrow, unpainted hallway was dimly lit and smelled strongly of stale sweat, beer and unidentifiable odors.

"Here you go, O'Malley, direct-to-door service." He leaned down, tipping her onto her feet and gripping her shoulders more to keep her from hitting him than to help her balance. "Most bellmen would expect a tip. I'll just settle for a heartfelt thank you. Although I'm not above receiving a good lusty kiss."

Kate regained her balance and looked at her unwanted savior under the dim light bulb. Her eyes widened as she got a full view of the man's face in the pale yellow light. Jared Wyatt!

"You . . ." She swung out and her hand connected with the side of his face before he had a chance to defend himself. "You . . ." Her fury left her at a loss for words.

"Cretin? S.O.B.? Jerk?" J.C. offered.

"The description I'm thinking of is a great deal more disgusting." She clenched her hands at her sides. "What do you think you were doing in there?"

"You were in the middle of what promised to be one hell of a battle, so I got you out of there before you ended up with a few broken bones." Settling his hands on his lean hips, he bent down close to her face. "Lady, I just saved your butt in there. It wouldn't hurt you one bit to thank me."

"Why should I thank you when I didn't need any help?" she snapped. "Do us both a favor and mount your white horse and ride off into the sunset."

"Whoo-ee." J.C. grinned, unperturbed by her fury. "And here I thought only redheads had nasty tempers. O'Malley, you've got one to equal a hundred redheads. I bet you're hell on wheels in bed." His voice lowered to a husky purr.

Kate's rage faltered. This was not the man she was familiar with.

He held out a hand. "J.C. Wyatt, at your service."

"J.C." She uttered a short laugh as she ignored his outstretched hand. "Buddy, I've got a better name for you. How about liar and fake? I can't believe this! You just stood there, smiling at me so serenely while I stumbled over my explanation about why I needed to do this for Gramps. And said perhaps it was for the best, that we needed time apart from each other to make sure we

were doing the right thing. You were so nice about it I felt as if I was whipping a puppy! I've felt like the worst kind of idiot these last three weeks,'' she screeched.

He winced at the strident tone. ''Tone it down, O'Malley, or you'll be breaking what few windows they have around here. As for how you felt, that wasn't my fault.''

''Damn you, Jared Wyatt, I was feeling guilty for what I did to you!'' Her face was bright red from anger.

He shrugged. ''They say guilt's good for the soul.''

''You—'' She punched him in the abdomen.

''Ow! Damn it, Kate, knock it off! If you want to prove you're as macho as the next guy you can find another way to do it.'' He grabbed both her wrists and held them out of striking range. ''Maybe I should have left you with Joaquin. He could have used his special method of pounding sense into that hard head of yours.''

''I was handling him just fine until you barged in.'' Her eyes spat fire at him.

''Right. Using that Oriental mumbo jumbo that paralyzes the nerves may have looked good at first, but it doesn't work against a gun or a knife.'' He released her wrists. ''If I hadn't been there he would have had *you* working for him before the night was out, baby. Not the other way around.''

''I have been taking care of myself for the past twenty-nine years and doing just fine without the likes of you,'' she declared loftily.

''Oh, yeah?'' Without giving a hint of his intention Jared rushed her.

Kate immediately countered his move with one she learned overseas that left him gasping for air. Undaunted, he hooked his boot around her ankle and dropped her to the floor before she had a chance to retaliate. Within a breath he was straddling her hips, holding a knife against her throat.

Considering his position he appeared the amiable wolf. "You must have missed one of your lessons, sweetheart." He grinned, enjoying his victory.

Kate's smile was chilling. "I don't think so."

It was the pressure against his belly that caught his attention. He looked down to find the muzzle of a tiny but very lethal-looking handgun in her hand.

"Strapped to your ankle?" he guessed.

She nodded. "And I have a very sharp knife in my other boot. The ammunition I use for this gun is very unusual and quite probably illegal. But I've always believed in the best." Her eyes were icy emeralds. "And I used to believe in you. Now get off me before I decide to use the gun. Considering the mood I'm in right now it wouldn't take much for me to pull the trigger."

He cocked his head. "Aren't you afraid someone will hear the shot? Mexican jails aren't a pretty sight."

"Around here no one will notice or even care. I'd hazard a guess that gunshots and fights are a fact of life in this town. Ten to one they see you as just another drifter. I wonder what they'd think if they knew you were really a professor." Her words dropped like ice cubes. Her eyes flicked over his clothing. "Interesting disguise. Is this to enable you to fit in among the natives? And even a name change, no less. Tell me something, *J.C.*, what other surprises do you have up your sleeve?"

He grinned, enjoying her portrayal of the cool lady of the manor. He had her on her back—a most interesting position if he said so himself—with a knife at her throat, and she hadn't turned a hair. He attributed it to the fact she still had her gun nestled against his belly. "We've got some things to talk about, O'Malley. Think we could try it without all the hardware?"

She arched up, unbalancing him. She jumped to her feet and quickly extracted the key from his hand. Within seconds her door was unlocked and she was inside. "Jared, J.C., whatever you call yourself, go to hell." She slammed the door, just barely missing his nose.

"By the way, O'Malley, I'd put a chair under the doorknob if I were you. That lock looks pretty flimsy and I don't think you'd want Joaquin to visit you later tonight. I'm a heavy sleeper and might not hear your cries for help." He ambled down the hallway to room six and unlocked the door.

Due to the equally flimsy walls he could hear every word Kate shrieked.

"If I'd known in the beginning that you had this kind of bad temper, O'Malley," he said to the wall he shared with Kate, "I wouldn't have considered marrying you."

"That son of a—" Kate eyed the cracked pitcher atop the scarred dresser. Her fingers itched to throw something, anything. With great effort she restrained herself.

Instead, she paced the narrow length of the room trying to come to terms with this turn of events.

"It doesn't make sense," she muttered, picking up her duffel bag and digging through the contents. "Jared doesn't wear tight jeans. And he always shaves. He doesn't pitch women over his shoulder and he most certainly doesn't patronize border cantinas." Her brow creased in a frown as she dug through the bag until she found a bottle of purified water, toothbrush and toothpaste. "What's he doing here?" Her words were garbled as she energetically brushed her teeth. "And how did he turn out so—so—" Her hand halted in mid-motion. "Oh, my God, the man is a living, breathing sex symbol." She quickly spat into the pitcher.

A mental picture of Jared as she'd seen him less than five minutes ago flashed before her eyes. The pit of her stomach dropped just as if she was racing down a roller-coaster track.

"Which is the real man?" she whispered. "Jared or J.C.? And if it's J.C. he's not going to let me put him off." A low moan was torn from her throat. "And I don't think I want to."

WHEN JARED ENTERED the restaurant at eight o'clock on the dot he found Kate sitting at a corner table sipping a cup of coffee and not looking at all pleased.

"You're late." She glared at him as he sat in a chair across from her. "Jared Wyatt is never late."

"And good morning to you, too." He smiled. "Yes, I slept well, thank you. And while Jared might be punctual, J.C. doesn't believe in looking at his watch every five minutes."

Kate kept glaring at him even as he smiled at a young giggling waitress and gave her his order. She mentally compared the man sitting with her to the man she met last night and the man she knew back home.

Jared was always clean-shaven, soft spoken and extremely polite, and he wore conservative clothing; in essence, the perfect college professor. J.C. wore jeans that were bleached white from long-time wear and an equally worn chambray shirt. His scarred leather belt boasted a silver and turquoise buckle that looked handmade. The hat he tossed on the third chair was far from new, as were his boots. And most importantly, the beginnings of a dark beard covered his face. She tried to ignore the tiny ripples of desire in the pit of her stomach as she studied him through downcast lashes. There was something about the man seated across from her that aroused her primal instincts. She wasn't sure this was a wise idea, but whoever said hormones were wise?

"My, my, if only Dr. Phillips could see you now," she drawled, settling in her chair, one arm draped across the back. "I do wish I had brought my camera with me. I'm sure he would have been fascinated to see you in front of the tavern with your old buddy Joaquin."

"That sounds like blackmail." He didn't sound the least bit worried.

She smiled sweetly. "Blackmail is such a dirty word. No, I'd call it more an unveiling," she replied. "After all, Dr. Phillips hired a man who was as conventional as he was. At least he *thought* so. How you must have been laughing at all of us."

"I never laughed at any of you, Kate," he said quietly. "There was never any intent to defraud anyone. That position offered me exactly what I was looking for and I'd done enough research to know that Dr. Phillips preferred a certain kind of instructor. All I did was become what he wanted on the outside; on the inside I'm still the same. In essence, I made him happy. So far he's had nothing to complain about where my teaching is concerned, so what's the harm?" He looked up and smiled at the waitress when she deposited his plate in front of him. "*Gracias*, Juana."

"*De nada*. Do you wish anything else, *Señor* J.C.?"

"No, thanks."

"How long do I have to wait before you explain exactly why the Jekyll and Hyde routine?" Kate demanded.

"Personally, I'd prefer the image of Bruce Wayne and Batman," he countered, drinking his coffee.

Kate smiled sweetly. "Let's go for broke and talk about Bugs Bunny and Elmer Fudd."

Jared winced. He scooped up some eggs with a warm corn tortilla and ate hungrily. "It's very easy. J.C. Wyatt isn't the kind of history professor Dr. Phillips would hire; Jared Wyatt is. It's just as easy to answer to Jared as to J.C. I've done it lots of times."

Kate found herself intrigued. "What about credentials? How did you get away with them?"

He grinned. "My full name is Jared Carson Wyatt, hence the J.C. Anything I've published in the past has my full name as author. It was only my research team in the past who called me J.C."

"So basically, you lied to all of us. You let us think you were one person when actually you were someone else." Her tone was accusatory.

"I'm one and the same. It's just that these clothes are more familiar to me than the suits I wear to class." He wiped his mouth and folded his arms on the table. "Now you. Why did you come down here to hire a guide?"

"Private business."

He shook his head. "Your grandfather must have been crazy to allow you travel down here by yourself. The Joaquin you almost hired would have gladly taken you into the mountains, but you wouldn't have come out alive. Of course, he would have had some fun with you first."

"You're not scaring me," she argued. "I've already proven to you I can take care of myself. In the past six years since Gramps had to retire from his travels I've gone into countries some men would hesitate traveling through. Gramps taught me to control my fear of the unknown and I've met enough people that I haven't had to truly worry about my safety. That doesn't mean that I'm careless, only that I know whom I can trust and whom I can't."

"I gather you've included me in the latter," he stated, his dark blue gaze boring into hers.

"I'd say you've given me more than enough reason."

Jared stood and pushed back his chair. He dropped some money on the table. "I assume the Jeep by the hotel is yours?" Kate nodded. "Good. I hitched a ride here with a friend of mine who flies medical and food supplies in. I can just ride back with you."

"You could at least wait for an invitation," she pointed out, stung that he could so cavalierly assume she would want his company. She was equally stung that she did want his company because she was growing more and more curious about this new side of Jared Wyatt.

"If I did that I'd still be here when my friend comes back in a month." He walked her outside.

Kate would have walked away except a surly Joaquin lingered near the bar doorway sending her looks meant to kill.

"Good girl," Jared murmured, when he caught the direction of her gaze.

"Just cautious. He already looks drunk and I'd bet he's a mean drunk who loves to get into fights just for the hell of it." As they walked along she appeared as cool and collected as if the temperature was moderate instead of well over one hundred. "If you want that ride be out front in five minutes. I won't wait."

Kate would have loved nothing more than to leave Jared behind but she had no reason to. When she walked outside with her duffel bag over her shoulder several minutes later, he was already seated in the Jeep. But Kate had another plan up her sleeve. Without saying a word she started up the engine and drove out of town.

"When are you going to tell me why you were down there looking for a guide?" Jared shouted over the engine's roar an hour later.

Kate didn't indicate she heard.

"Excuse me, ma'am, is the passenger allowed to talk to the driver?" he persisted.

"I don't like to talk when I'm driving," she said crisply, without turning her head.

Jared settled back in the seat, crossing his arms in front of his chest, his hat tipped over his eyes. "No problem," he mumbled, "we'll be on the road for almost a week. I'm sure there'll be time when we can talk."

Kate's smile grew broader. "That's what you think," she said under her breath.

She pushed the Jeep to its limit once she crossed the Texas border.

"I would think you'd bypass the city," Jared commented, when Kate raced onto the freeway.

"I just need to make a stop first," she said cryptically, studying the road signs until she found the off ramp she wanted.

Jared sat up a little straighter when Kate pulled up in front of an airport terminal.

"I thought the Jeep was yours," he commented.

She smiled, twisting her body to reach into the back of the Jeep. "It is, but I have several stops to make on the way home. I figured you'd prefer a nonstop return." She tossed him his knapsack. "I'm sure you won't have any trouble finding a flight home."

Jared studied her set features, taking in the emerald eyes glittering with barely repressed fury. He slowly climbed out of the Jeep with his knapsack in one hand.

"Am I to gather you're angry with me for some reason?" He was pretty sure he knew the reason, but if he could keep her there long enough he might be able to persuade her to take him the rest of the way. He knew they needed that time to talk.

"Angry, no. Furious, most definitely. If I had my way I would stake you out on an anthill at high noon with honey poured all over your body. And that would only be the beginning," she informed him with acid dropping from each word. She ignored the strident car horn honking behind her. "I suggest you stay out of my way once you're back at the school or you'll be very sorry. Trust me." She gunned the engine and raced off with a squeal of tires.

Jared chuckled, not the least intimidated by her threats. As she gunned the engine and the tires spat rocks at him, he shouted, "Does this mean our engagement is off?"

Chapter Four

"I want the man hurt." Kate paced the width of Shamus's study with furious strides. "I want him hurt bad. I want our name carved on his chest with a dirty knife. I want—"

"Wait a minute." Shamus held up his hand. "That kind of statement sounds more Italian than Irish, darlin'."

She advanced on him with murder in her eyes. "Don't you dare stand up for that snake!" She threw her hands up. "He's a liar and a fake! He lied to you, he lied to me, not to mention lying to Dr. Phillips! Who the hell does he think he is to do this to us?" She picked up a crystal vase and drew it back in a pitching motion.

Shamus winced at Kate's strident voice. The last thing he wanted to hear in the morning was one of the ranting lectures she was well known for. He leaned over, carefully prying her fingers from the neck of the vase. "The way I see it you're angrier over the fact that he's more like you and me than the man you wanted him to be."

The dark flush staining Kate's cheeks indicated his guess was accurate. "I don't appreciate being made a fool of, that's all," she said stiffly, turning away. "And you shouldn't, either."

"Even if he had a good reason to do what he did?"

She spun around. "What kind of reason?" She narrowed her eyes. "Have you talked to him recently?"

Shamus shrugged. "Never said I did."

"Don't evade me, Shamus O'Malley." She shook her finger at him. "Have you talked to him?"

"Stop shaking that finger at me like you were some old-maid schoolteacher," he ordered testily. "I can talk to whomever I please."

"When did you talk to him? Shamus, tell me or else I'll scream the house down. And you know I can do it." She inhaled deeply, fully prepared to carry out her threat.

He held up his hand. "All right, don't turn blue. He called me from Texas after you rudely dumped him without bothering to find out if he had the funds to get himself home." His eyes, as sharp as his granddaughter's, silently criticized her.

She felt a slight guilty twinge that she hadn't thought to ask if he had the money to fly home and swiftly tamped it down. She told herself that wasn't her problem. "Last I heard airlines accept credit cards."

"Do you carry credit cards on trips like that?" Shamus pointed out. "He didn't even have enough cash on him for bus fare."

She refused to bow under his silent intimidation. "Then he should look into carrying travelers' checks. There wasn't any way I would share the Jeep with him for two thousand miles. It couldn't have upset him all that much. I've been back for three days and I haven't seen even a trace of him," she added, furious at herself for sounding sulky.

"Last I heard you threatened him with bodily harm if he dared come within a mile of you."

Kate pushed her hands through her hair, resisting the urge to scream at the top of her lungs. During the five days it took her to drive home and the three days following she had done nothing but compare Jared and J.C. And she hated herself for it even as she kept reminding herself that the man had obviously lied to her. At the very least, he hadn't told her everything about himself as she once thought he had. She thought about their past talks. No, he really hadn't talked as much about his past as she thought he had. Or she hadn't truly listened to him.

"You're on his side," she said to Shamus. Her voice was dangerously soft. "For some crazy reason you've suddenly decided he's not so bad after all."

"I'm not on his side, Katie. All I'm saying is that you should hear the entire story before you convict the only man I can trust to guide you into the Superstition Mountains."

But Kate was past listening to reason. "What? The man who wasn't good enough to marry me is suddenly good enough to ride into the mountains with me?" She laughed harshly, her eyes glittering with fury. "I'd rather have Joaquin guide me than that hypocrite. As far as I'm concerned Jared Wyatt is no longer a part of my life and if you dare to interfere in this I will make your life miserable, Shamus Patrick O'Malley. Not only will your cigars end up in the garbage disposal, but I will also pour all your hidden bottles of whiskey down the sink and I will insist that Anna follow that diet the doctor gave you. And that will only be the beginning." She shoved her hands into the deep pockets of her sweater.

"You're overreacting, Kate," he said softly. "You're allowing your emotions to rule your head instead of using your common sense as I've taught you to do. You've always been a levelheaded woman, a scientist who looks at all sides of an issue. Besides, I felt your idea of marrying Jared Wyatt was more for the sake of having a home and family than for the sake of love."

Kate stiffened at his accurate shot. She knew he was right, even if she refused to admit it. "I don't like people lying to me," was all she could reply as she turned away.

She picked up a large file folder filled with Shamus's notes from his desk and cradled it against her chest. "I'm taking this upstairs to look over when I get home tonight from my lecture." She walked toward the door.

"Just because you felt a man did you wrong once before doesn't mean Jared will do the same," Shamus called after her.

Kate may have closed the door softly after her, but the action was as effective as a slam.

When she reached her apartment, she set the folder on her desk and headed for the kitchen to make coffee. She had just sat at her desk to review her lecture notes when she heard a knock at her outside door. Few people knew about her outside entrance, only a handful of friends. And Jared, a little voice told her. Either way she didn't care to be disturbed and ignored it.

"I know you're in there, Kate." Kiki's shout could be heard clearly through the door. "Stop pouting and let me in."

Sighing heavily, Kate crossed the room and threw open the door. "I am not pouting."

Kiki studied her closely as she walked inside. "Yes, you are," she pronounced. She spied the coffee cup on

Kate's desk and immediately headed for the kitchen to get herself a cup without waiting for an invitation. "Has Jared called?"

Kate was irritated by the not-so-innocent question. "I suggested if he wanted to remain alive he not try to contact me. If I could have, I would have gone a step further." The dark expression in her eyes told her friend that next step would have been most unpleasant.

Kiki sipped her coffee, eyeing Kate over the rim of the cup. "Rumors about the good Dr. Wyatt are flying around the campus," she commented. "Such as that he's not just an excellent history instructor, but also a well-known historian who spends his free time in the field delving in some dangerous areas of Indian culture. That he might be more like Shamus than the uptight individual everyone thinks him to be." A sly smile curved her lips. "I can't wait to see the *real* man."

Kate seriously thought of murdering her best friend. She didn't even want to think of Jared Wyatt, or J.C. "I don't care to discuss him, Kiki." Her voice held a hidden warning.

"I don't understand you, Kate," Kiki blurted. "You've got this gorgeous man who's ended up perfect for you; the adventuresome spirit, the need to explore and live life to its fullest. What's so wrong with that? You sure didn't seem very happy when you thought he was an old stick-in-the-mud. Now he's just what you need."

"Perfect," she said flatly. "Did you know my grandmother hated all the traveling? She hated the dust, the constant change in time zones, different customs, foods and primitive conditions. Yet she never said a word to Gramps. When he wanted to find that rare artifact or research a legend, she quietly packed their bags and went with him. But all she wanted was a full-time husband and a real home. Gramps never knew how she felt because she didn't want to worry him. He didn't know about it until after her death and he found her private journal. Dad once overheard his drunken ramblings of how he failed her and he told me about it when I told him I was getting my degree in archaeology. He said the time would come when I might decide I didn't want the traveling any longer and I'd want a home of my own. I was convinced he was wrong. After all, he's still chasing after all those odd tribes. Do you realize both men never remarried after the first time? That should say something.''

"Or deep down they knew they couldn't replace those women in their hearts. And you've decided you want more and since Jared isn't who you first thought he was, naturally, he couldn't give you the kind of life you've decided you need now. How much easier it must be for you to just cut him out like a nasty infection," Kiki stated flatly.

Kate was tired of everyone trying to tell her how wrong she was. "Is this why you stopped by? To tell me how wrong I am?"

She shook her head. "No, it's just that I'm one of the few people who know the real you." She turned at the sound of someone knocking at the door. "More visitors."

"Probably Kirk Chambers. He attends my lectures and is looking for extra money. So I'm having him wash and wax my car." Kate headed for the door and opened it. The welcoming smile on her face faded when she saw her visitor. "What do you want?"

Jared looked past her toward Kiki and flashed a wicked grin. "If I told you the truth you'd probably push me down these stairs," he drawled. "Mind if I come in?"

"Yes, I do."

Smiling as if he hadn't heard her, he ambled inside, his hands settled deep in the pockets of his black leather bomber jacket.

"How about some coffee?" Kiki greeted him, holding up her cup.

He smiled at her, recognizing an ally. "Love some, thanks."

"How do you take it?"

"Black."

Kate glared at Kiki. "He won't be staying long enough to drink it."

Ignoring her friend's rudeness, Kiki went to get Jared a cup of coffee. "Look at the time! I really must be going," she announced with false cheer. "Just remember her bark is worse than her bite," she confided in Jared in a mock whisper.

He glanced toward Kate who looked as if she could cheerfully strangle the two of them. "I don't know, her bites might be real interesting." His voice was low and intimate.

"That's my cue to leave," Kiki said hastily, hurrying to the door. "I see Kirk out there. Is your car unlocked?"

Kate's gaze was riveted on Jared's face. "Yes."

"I'll tell him to go ahead and start. Bye."

Kate felt the jarring need to call her friend back, to keep her there as a buffer against the new emotions she felt where Jared was concerned. She remained in the middle of the room, watching Jared wander around the large expanse sipping his coffee, occasionally halting to study the few paintings and sketches hanging on the walls and some pottery vases and figurines on a wall unit. He picked up one statue, cradling it carefully in his hands.

"Pre-Colombian?" He turned his head.

"Yes." Her reply was clipped. "A copy, of course."

He nodded as he returned the statue to its shelf. "Of course." He turned and rested his hip against the side of the unit. "Funny that in all this time we've dated I've never been up here." His bright sapphire eyes bored into her. "You've always preferred I pick you up downstairs."

"Yes, I did." Kate found it difficult to keep her eyes on his face when the rest of him looked so intriguing. She wasn't used to the new Jared. But then the man standing before her wasn't Jared, she reminded herself; he was J.C.

He wore jeans that were old and faded and she thought tight enough to cut off a man's circulation and a faded gray sweatshirt under a leather jacket that looked as if it had been manufactured during World War Two. His hair looked as if he hadn't had it cut recently and she couldn't miss the dark stubble along his cheeks and chin.

J.C. looked like a man who would control every situation. Kate had always felt in control with Jared. Now she felt that control dangerously slipping, and she didn't like it.

"Shamus said you were up here and suggested I come up to discuss our trip into the Superstitions," Jared explained.

"People generally come up here by invitation." She silently patted herself on the back for her cool tone.

Jared continued his wandering, stopping at the partition that hid the sleeping area. He glanced around it, studying the wide platform bed with drawers built in underneath. A slate-blue, rose and cream striped quilt covered the bed while accents were a slate blue vase on a small round table under the window and a rose-colored ginger-jar lamp. "Very nice. You've done a great job of using your space." He turned to her. "Kate, whether you like it or not, we'll be making this trip together because your grandfather recognizes the fact that you need a reliable guide into the mountains. And like it or not, I'm your best bet."

"Gramps has been wrong before."

Jared fixed her with a stony gaze equal to hers. "Not this time. He hasn't told me the whole story, but it doesn't take much to figure out the Superstition Mountains means the Lost Dutchman Mine."

"I'm going to investigate a rumor of a camp once occupied by the Folsom Man," she replied smoothly, mentioning one of the many primitive tribes known to have once roamed the same mountains.

He grinned and shook his head. "No way, sweetheart. I spent some of my formative years in that area and any proof of that tribe has long since been gone. Besides, your grandfather loves legends and the Lost Dutchman Mine is about the most colorful story for that area." He set his cup down. "As I said, I'm your best bet. In fact, I'm your *only* bet."

Kate couldn't help but notice the gleam in his eyes. It was a look she had seen many times in the past when Shamus prepared for another quest. Not to mention seeing it in her own eyes when she found a new map or journal about a legendary object.

"Think of it, the two of us under the desert stars and moon. Alone," he continued, his eyes gleaming with a more predatory purpose. "Talk about a perfect spot for an engaged couple to really get to know each other."

"Our engagement is off. Thank goodness it was never official," she pointed out, fervently wishing he wouldn't cross his booted feet at the ankles, drawing her attention to those tight jeans of his that pulled even tighter over interesting areas of his anatomy. She could have sworn the temperature in the room rose at least twenty degrees. "It was just something we discussed the same way we discussed the weather."

"I don't know. The weather wasn't as interesting to talk about as the idea of our sharing a—life—together." His smile was pure J.C.

Kate's stomach dropped a mile. She was certain he meant to use another word, especially since he was looking over his shoulder at her bed at the time. Her glance drifted toward a tall vase.

"You've got to learn to keep that violent streak of yours under control," he advised, straightening up. He glanced at his watch. "I should be going. I've got a class to teach in a half hour. I only wanted to stop by to let you know you've got your guide."

She breathed a silent sigh of relief at his mention of leaving. "Are you sure you have enough time to change into one of your suits?"

Jared looked down at himself. "I'm properly dressed. I guess it's time Dr. Phillips realizes that a dress code is not more important than teaching skills. How about I pick you up around six? We'll grab a bite to eat and talk about this trip we'll be taking together."

"There is no *we*," she insisted. She felt the beginnings of panic—an unknown phenomenon for the woman who had faced fierce desert tribes in the past without flinching. "And I'm busy tonight. I have a lecture to give."

"No problem, I'll pick you up there," he told her as he opened the door. He halted for a moment. "And, Kate, don't think about running away. Because I'll track you down." With that parting soft-voiced threat he left.

"This is all a miserable nightmare!" Kate gasped, spinning around. She ran to the window, fingering the sheer drape just enough so she could peek outside without being seen. She found Jared by the garage talking to the student who was busy washing her car. Confident that she couldn't be seen, she concentrated on the tall dark-haired man who looked too sexy for his own good. She wished she had the good sense to turn away, but curiosity was too strong. Then, as if he sensed her regard, Jared looked up at the window. The wolfish grin on his face told her he knew she was looking at him. She resisted her inclination to move away, but she was not so certain he couldn't see her.

See you later, he mouthed, still smiling. He turned to Kirk, said something to him and walked away.

"Damn him," she muttered, turning from the window. "Even his walk is more J.C. than Jared."

"UNFORTUNATELY, THOSE who weren't immediately killed from the first lava flow were soon suffocated from the smoke and falling ashes. When the town was first discovered, archaeologists thought the townspeople had escaped when the volcano erupted." Kate's voice was well modulated and clear enough to carry even without the use of the small microphone she wore clipped to the draped neckline of her mint-green sweater. "It wasn't until much later that most of them were found in caves along the sea's edge, all of them obviously dead from suffocation. The ashes and smoke were so thick in the air that the people couldn't breathe. This was the first chance scientists had to study the Romans because the bodies were left intact and they were able to study their life-style in great detail." She nodded at one student who raised his hand. "Yes?"

"I thought it was only Greeks who were killed by Vesuvius," he commented. "Such as in Pompeii."

Kate shook her head. "No, there were Romans also living in neighboring towns, although many of them did escape the eruption by putting out to sea, but there were only so many boats and most of the people perished." She walked across the front of the room then turned to write something on the blackboard. As she wrote, she missed the small stir among the students as a latecomer entered the room through the front door, instead of the rear as so many do when coming in after a class or lecture begins. "As I've tried to point out here—" She halted as she turned to find the newcomer seated in the front row with a very wicked smile on his face. "The, ah, the ones left behind gave us an idea of jewelry, clothing." She coughed softly to regain her voice. "The women carried handbags not all that dissimilar to the ones carried now." She appeared to take a deep breath and carried on.

Jared knew he was the reason for frantic whispers going on in the rear rows. His concession for his evening with Kate was a clean shirt; the jeans and leather jacket were the same as this morning.

He settled back in the chair and enjoyed watching Kate work. She was dressed in a slim-fitting gray tweed skirt that ended just above shapely knees and a mint-green sweater that draped her breasts in a way he wouldn't mind draping them. Dark gray stockings and high heels accentuated her long legs. He scowled when he caught one of his male students openly appreciating them. The young man reddened under his instructor's dark glare and swiftly lowered his eyes, pretending to write in his notebook. Jared really couldn't blame him. Any red-blooded man would enjoy looking at legs like Kate's. He sure did.

Jared's reason for walking in on Kate's lecture was deliberate. He had a hunch she wouldn't have thought twice about not being around if he arrived to pick her up when she was finished. This way she couldn't escape him. And when they were up in those mountains, he was going to make sure she never had a chance to escape him.

When Kate finished her lecture, Jared hung back as several students approached her with questions. He hid his smile at her wary expression.

"Ready?" He walked up when she was left alone and took her briefcase from her hand.

She lifted her chin. "Do I have a choice?"

He shrugged, appearing more nonchalant than he felt. "Yes, but I hope you'll make the choice of going with me."

If Kate hadn't seen that brief flicker of uncertainty in Jared's eyes she would have turned him down without a qualm. This wasn't the arrogant J.C. standing in front of her, but a good part of Jared expecting her to refuse. She knew now she couldn't. Uncertainty or not, she wasn't about to give in easily. "All right, but only because I'm starving and I expect an extra-large pizza with everything on it."

Jared smiled. "Your wish is my command."

"I would think J.C. would prefer tooling around town on a motorcycle," she commented, when Jared assisted her into the passenger seat of his car.

He looked surprised by her remark. "You sound as if J.C. and Jared are two separate people."

She was pleased at unsettling him, even a little. "Aren't they? I admit I don't know J.C. very well, but I think I know enough of him that he doesn't believe in doing things the conventional way Jared does." Her gaze bored into his eyes, made even darker by the dim lights winking at them from the dashboard. "At one time I thought I knew Jared quite well. Apparently, I didn't."

The only sound was a sharp indrawn breath. "If you think you're going to get me angry, you're wrong, sweetheart. Because, where you're concerned, I intend to keep my temper." His teeth flashed white, looking too predatory for Kate's peace of mind.

Her smile equaled his. "My, my, talk about a challenge. There's nothing more intriguing than seeing a man's face turn red, then purple, and his blood pressure rise to the danger point. I can see I'm going to have a lot of fun."

Jared firmly gripped her chin between his fingers. "I should have known you wouldn't make this easy for us. All I'm asking is for some understanding." He held up his hand, asking for silence. "Now, if you don't mind, I haven't had time to eat since this morning and I'm starving. Let's shelve any discussion until after we eat, okay?"

She gave a slight nod.

During the short drive, Kate kept a suspicious eye on Jared. She chose to initiate the conversation rather than let the silence hang heavily between them.

"How did your classes go today?"

He grimaced. "Let's just say I've had better days."

Kate relaxed in the seat, turning to look out the window so Jared didn't see her grin. "Your female students must have been pleasantly surprised to see the new you. I bet they gave you an A plus."

"Surprised is a good description," he said. "All of a sudden everyone needs student conferences because they can't understand their next assignment or the paper I've asked them to write or they're not even sure what to write and could I give them some advice."

She choked back her laughter. "Why, J.C., you've become a very popular man, haven't you?"

He slanted her a look that wasn't pleasant. "Not funny."

"I think so."

"You would. You've got Kirk Chambers salivating all over the idea of being privileged enough to wash that hot little Fiat of yours, and Steve Hinshaw is determined to follow you on your next dig. Then there's—"

"You've made your point," she hastily interrupted. "But I learned how to deal with those problems a long time ago. Obviously, you never bothered to."

"Yeah? Why do you think I turned into a bookworm professor? Not just for the administration; them I can handle. But there's too many kids who lead with their hormones instead of their brains. I'm here to teach them history, not sex education," he spat out. "When you become a full-fledged professor instead of an occasional guest lecturer and when you're bored with your field work and you decide it's time to return to civilization, you'll understand what I'm talking about."

"*Bored* with field work? *Occasional guest lecturer?* You're doing an excellent job of insulting me," she said.

"I am as serious about my work as you are about yours."

He pulled into the parking lot of a pizza place popular with the students. "You're right, only a serious scientist would decide it's time to hang up her passport and settle down with a dependable staid professor type and raise a family."

"They've wanted me to teach full time here for the past five years," she said stiffly.

Jared smirked. "Yeah, I can picture you in those bulky tweeds like Miss Hammond. We'll have to get you some thick-rimmed glasses, too. But I'd hide those great-looking legs of yours. They're a dead giveaway that you're not the typical old-maid schoolmarm."

Kate counted to ten, first in Arabic, then in Latin. Once the car was stopped, she opened the door and jumped out, without waiting for Jared to come around to assist her.

"I hope we can find a table," she said for the lack of anything witty to say.

"Doesn't matter." He pushed open the door, sending a blast of rock music and hot air at them. "We'll get it to go, because what I want to talk to you about shouldn't be discussed in public."

Kate had an excellent idea what he wanted to talk about. "No anchovies." She walked in front of him, standing off to the side of the crowded room as Jared headed for the order counter.

He nodded.

As she waited for him, she couldn't help but notice the speculative looks directed their way. Judging from the whispered conversations and appreciative expressions, word of Dr. Wyatt's new image had reached a majority of the students. While she still wasn't happy with him, she had to admit she didn't like the way he smiled at some of his female students and spoke to them in what appeared to her to be a very friendly manner. She refused to admit the dark feeling coursing through her was jealousy.

"Dr. O'Malley?" A girl's tentative voice sounded at her right shoulder.

Kate turned and greeted the dark-haired young woman with a warm smile. "Yes? It's Susan, right? You sat in on my series on Egyptology last year."

She nodded. "Rumor has it you're going on a dig soon and I'd like to know if there's any way I could go along. I'm a junior so there wouldn't be any problem of my going and I can pay my own way. I work part-time at the inn as a waitress," she explained. "And I'd work really hard and do anything you wanted me to. I just want this chance."

Kate smiled, pleased with the young woman's sincere enthusiasm. "So you've got the archeology bug, do you?"

"Yes, ma'am."

Her smile froze. Not thirty yet and she was already hearing that oh-so-polite ma'am. "To be honest, I've been thinking of retiring from field work and teaching here full time, although I would probably think up something for next summer if the administration goes along with the idea. I'm just glad to hear that someone is eager to get into the nitty-gritty work. Believe me, manicures are pretty quickly destroyed on a dig, along with professional hairstyles and clean skin. We won't even talk about plumbing or lack thereof. It's no picnic, but it does offer you the chance to view the past in a beautiful way." She flushed, realizing she was getting a bit too enthusiastic. "Sorry, I tend to get a little crazy when I find someone sharing my passion for past cultures.''

Susan looked a bit uneasy. "I never realized that kind of work is so dirty."

"I'm afraid so. Tell me, was it my lectures that got you interested?" she asked.

The younger woman shook her head. "No, I've been in love with the idea for quite a few years now. That's why I came here to study since the archaeology department is so well known." For a split second her gaze was caught by the sight of Jared approaching them.

"Then what did get you interested in archaeology?" Kate pressed, by now curious.

Susan's eyes lit up with another kind of passion. "Indiana Jones." She turned when she heard her name called. "I better go. Thanks, Dr. O'Malley."

Kate's smile felt frozen on her face.

"Think she'll show up wearing a fedora and carrying a whip?" Jared appeared with a large cardboard box. "No wonder there's so many female students flunking out of archaeology."

She turned her head. "That was quick."

"I called the order in earlier," he explained.

Kate lifted the lid just enough to peer inside. "Good boy. If I had seen anchovies on it, I would have run screaming from here." She looked toward Susan who was now sitting at a table with several friends. "I worked very hard to put together that series of lectures," she muttered, as they walked outside. "I never did so much studying in my life as I did to prepare for those. It wasn't even *King Solomon's Mines* that got her interested. Just an incredibly sexy guy." She paused. "Come to think of it, I could have easily developed a fascination with the subject if Indy had been my professor. Gramps was a great teacher, but it wasn't the same. You just can't develop a crush on your grandfather."

"Dr. Wyatt!" A buxom redhead waylaid them in the parking lot, but her hundred-watt smile was all for Jared. Her eyes lit on the cardboard box and her smile dimmed. "Oh, you're not staying."

"No, we're not, Eva." He smiled back.

"That's too bad. I thought we could talk about that assignment you gave us on Lewis and Clark. I have a lot of questions."

"I bet you do," Kate muttered under her breath.

"There will be a discussion in class on Thursday," he told the student while he steered Kate toward his car.

"See you then." The young woman made it sound as if there would be just the two of them in class instead of thirty. With a twitch of her hips she sauntered toward the door.

Kate rolled her eyes. "Oh, please, you're making me lose my appetite. You came here for a reason, didn't you? Is it so everyone can see that Dr. Wyatt has a great body for tight jeans or because you wish to sit here and be admired by the female portion of the student body? J.C., you devil, you," she drawled, ruthlessly ignoring the burning feeling in her stomach.

Jared sighed, looking more than a little irritated by now. "I wanted pizza, all right? Nothing more."

"Did you happen to run into Dr. Phillips today?" she asked.

His features tightened. "Yes."

"Did he happen to comment on your choice of attire?"

"Yes."

"He didn't like it." She made it a statement, not a question.

"He suggested that the next time I do yard work I time myself better so I'm able to change my clothing for my class," he bit out.

"You worked so hard to maintain that nerdy exterior and you've blown it to bits in less than ten hours. Don't despair, tell him you were going through a mid-life crisis. I'm sure he'll understand," she offered helpfully as she settled in the car seat with the cardboard box nestled in her lap.

"You're not helping, O'Malley."

"Sorry." Her tone indicated otherwise.

"Do you realize I've never seen your apartment?" Kate later asked as she waited for Jared to unlock the front door. "You were such a gentleman." She walked into the lighted entryway. A quick glance showed her where the kitchen was and she carried in the pizza. "Very nice." She looked around. "No dirty dishes in the sink." She opened the refrigerator door and peered inside. "It's even filled with moderately healthy food. Mine is usually lucky to have more than a bottle of wine and a few cans of diet soda."

"Why don't you get out some beer?" Jared suggested, as he transferred several slices of pizza to two plates and carried them over to a breakfast nook.

Kate grabbed two bottles. "Your bookcases look as crammed as mine."

"The bedroom is even worse because two windows take up space I could use for bookcases," he replied, reaching around to grab a steno pad and pen. "I guess you realize that this is one of the best times to travel into the mountains since the temperature is sometimes below a hundred degrees. I'll have to take a leave of absence, but if I hint around that it has to do with something of great historical significance, which it does, I'm sure Dr. Phillips won't mind."

"Ah, yes, he does buy into the old 'publish or perish.'" Kate inhaled the rich fragrance of tomato, cheese, sausage and various spices. "I'm starved. You better get your share quickly or I'll eat it all. Then we can talk about how you figured out what I was going to look for."

"Shamus told me."

Her face turned to stone. "Gramps told you?"

Jared nodded. His tongue curled around a string of mozzarella cheese hanging from his pizza and brought it into his mouth. "He told me when he asked if I knew of any reliable guides who knew that region."

"He got Joaquin's name from *you*?" She was positive steam was pouring out of her ears. "You were the one who set me up with that moron?"

"It wasn't my fault you chose the wrong Joaquin." He flipped the open notebook around to face her. "Look, we'll argue about that later. Let's just get this settled, shall we? Shamus is all for me guiding you into the Superstitions. All I ask is my share of the credit for the find. *If* we find it. No one has been able to yet and due to rain and the shifting of the land over the years, it won't be easy."

"What you're saying is if I'm going, you're going," she said finally, glancing at his pad and its detailed lists of supplies, possible routes and departure dates. She had to hand it to him, he was very thorough—a trait she appreciated in anyone she dealt with.

"That's the way it is."

She looked again at the list. "On one condition. Our unofficial engagement is officially off and this trip is strictly business and I'm in charge."

Her statement didn't faze him one bit. "If you want our engagement off, it's off. This trip is business because it deals with our careers. As for you being in charge, *I'm* the one who knows the area and *I'm* the one who will have to haul your butt out of trouble if we run into anything unplanned."

"I think I've already shown you that I can easily take care of myself."

He sighed, beginning to lose his patience. "Fine, then if there's trouble you can haul my butt out." He flipped the pages in the notebook. "I've already checked with the airlines and there's no reason we can't take a flight out to Phoenix a week from Monday. That will give me time to show a substitute teacher my lesson plans and for you to prepare whatever you need to. I also want a closer look at Shamus's papers before we leave."

But Kate heard only one word. "Fly?" she asked weakly.

He looked up, surprised by her question. "Yes, fly."

"We could take the Jeep."

Jared looked skeptical. "No, thanks, I wouldn't appreciate being dumped in some small town while you continue on, convinced you can do this by yourself. We'll fly."

Kate set her slice of pizza carefully on the plate. Her appetite suddenly disappeared. Should she break the news to him now or wait until later?

Chapter Five

"What do you mean you hate to fly?" Jared stared incredulously at Kate.

She shifted her feet, uncomfortable enough with her confession without him making an issue of it. "I didn't say I hated flying. Merely that I don't like it."

He looked around the crowded airline terminal then at the ceiling. "I can't believe I'm hearing this."

Her head shot up. "You refused to consider my suggestion that we drive to Phoenix!"

His jaw tightened. "Flying saves time we sorely need. For someone who's traveled the world as much as you I can't believe you hate to fly," he bit out, adding sarcastically, "I don't imagine trains or boats are always available for your convenience."

"It's not that she hates it." Shamus spoke from his position as observer, amused by their confrontation. "She's scared to death of flying."

Kate shot her grandfather a glare filled with murderous promises. "Let's not discuss it, shall we?"

"*Not discuss it?*" Jared's voice rose. "Our flight leaves in twenty minutes and you're telling me now that you hate, correction, fear flying. Would it have been so difficult for you to mention it to me earlier? Even just a hint?'' Heavy sarcasm dripped from his words. ''Such as when I first brought up our flying to Phoenix?''

''I told you I couldn't work with this cretin,'' Kate shot at Shamus, placing the blame squarely on his shoulders.

''Calm down, you two, before you draw a crowd,'' Shamus advised in a no-nonsense tone. He laid his hands on Jared's arm. ''Kate can fly one of two ways— tanked or tranqued. Take your choice.'' He held up a small brown bottle with a prescription label pasted on the front. ''If you choose the latter I suggest you slip one of these in her food.'' He held it out to Jared.

Jared rolled his eyes, clearly disgusted with the situation. Then he stared at the bottle. ''I can't believe this is happening.''

Kate snatched the bottle out of his hand and dropped it in her oversize tote bag. ''You're off the hook,'' she told him in a sickeningly sweet voice. ''Now if you'll excuse me, I have a flight to catch.''

Shamus laid his hand on her shoulder in a grip meant to detain her. ''Listen to me, my girl, you are not in charge this time. Jared is,'' he told her. ''He knows more about that area than you or I do. If you were going to Egypt or even the Orient, I'd step back and allow the two of you to battle it out, but not this time. You can't do this alone, Kate. Just be a good girl and go along with whatever Jared says.''

Her face stiffened at his words. ''I've always gotten results before and I never needed a partner then.''

Shamus's eyes bored into hers. ''Trust me this time. The two of you can work together just fine if you forget how alike you are and start compromising.'' He looked up at the sound of the disembodied voice announcing that the flight to Phoenix was now boarding.

He reached out and gathered Kate into his arms. "Find the mine, darlin'." There was an intensity in his voice she had never heard before.

Tears pricked her eyes. She wished he had the strength to go with them. "We'll find it and we'll tell the world that you were the one to track down the maps. We're only doing the legwork."

He smiled and kissed her forehead then her cheek. "Just come back in one piece," he murmured. He stood back, his heavily creased face wrinkled in a smile. "And no fighting between the two of you." He turned to Jared and offered his hand. "I don't trust her with just anyone, you know."

Jared smiled. "I know." He grasped Kate's arm and steered her toward the tunnel leading to the waiting jet.

"I feel as if I shouldn't be leaving him," she muttered, pulling away from his touch and walking swiftly down the tunnel ahead of him. She smiled briefly at the attendant and walked toward her window seat, settling down after stowing her bag under the seat in front of her.

"If you'd like I can put that in the overhead compartment for you," Jared offered, after stowing his own bag overhead.

She shook her head. "I have some reading material in there." She sat rigidly in the seat, eyes staring straight ahead. She didn't have to turn her head to know that Jared sat next to her. He shifted in his seat to fasten his seat belt and finally settled back. She was too busy concentrating on drowning out the sounds of the engines warming up. She didn't bother listening to the flight attendant's speech on the emergency exits. She had memorized the location of emergency exits on all planes long ago.

Jared eyed her. "What's so wrong with flying that you need to take something in order to handle it?"

"It's unnatural. We don't have wings and something heavier than air shouldn't be able to stay up without falling immediately to earth. You don't see rocks flying, do you? Or a horse?" She stared straight ahead, still intent on tuning out the jet engines.

"Pegasus was a great flier."

"Now I'm sorry I had to put my knife in my luggage."

He leaned over and almost crushed her hand with his grip. "You brought that knife with you?" he muttered while his eyes spat out their fury.

"Of course. I always take it with me. I never know what I might run into."

Jared closed his eyes, his lips moving; whether in prayer or profanity was anyone's guess. "Do you realize . . . ?" He couldn't go on.

She smiled coolly. "If you don't like it, tough. I don't always play by the rules, Wyatt, and you obviously don't, either. So why don't you just sit back and enjoy the flight."

Jared sighed. "Maybe I should be the one taking those tranquilizers."

She gestured toward her tote bag. "Be my guest."

He cocked one eye open and noticed the white lines around her lips. His grip on her hand gentled. "Funny, I wouldn't have imagined you to be afraid of anything, or anyone."

She turned her head and directed a deadly glare at him. "I'm not afraid of anything, including you."

He looked amused. "You didn't want to make this trip with me. While my ego isn't completely fragile it does feel a little dented to think that you'd prefer Joaquin as a guide over me."

Whatever reply Kate was about to make froze when the jet shook from the force of the engines and it began to push back from the terminal. Jared scanned her paper-white face and tightened his hold on her hand.

Just as suddenly his touch changed from friendly to something more intimate. He held her hand between his two, his thumbs rubbing lightly against her palm in a circular motion then gliding up and down along each finger. His fingers caressed her palm with a feather-light touch before interlacing with hers.

All Kate's attention was focused on Jared. His seemed to be equally directed to her hand, which lay relaxed between his. A strange tingling began in her toes and moved slowly up her legs and kept traveling until her entire body felt lighter than air. Convinced she had somehow become disembodied, she stared at Jared's face. He looked hazy and indistinct. Her breathing grew labored, and her eyes glazed with wonder. She was so caught up in Jared's tantalizing touch that she could have been flying without the plane and not have cared. The world faded away and only Jared remained in her sights. She noted his tan chinos topped by an off-white shirt and navy V-necked sweater. The faint nick on his chin where he must have cut himself shaving that morning. Not to mention the tantalizing clean scent of his after-shave. Time had no meaning. When he finally eased his hands away she felt strangely bereft. She slowly floated back to the present. For the first time in her life the plane had taken off and she hadn't even noticed!

She licked her dry lips. "Was that acupressure?" she whispered, her voice husky.

His wolfish smile revived those earlier tingles. ''Not really. Some might call it foreplay.''

Kate felt the heat wash over her body. For a man she was determined to keep at arm's length she was developing some incredible ideas about him, not to mention his body.

''Would you two care for something to drink?'' The attendant's cheerful question was a rude intrusion to the mood building between the couple.

''Coffee and orange juice, please,'' Kate requested huskily, not surprised to find her voice not working properly. Her entire body was still reeling from Jared's sensual touch.

Jared looked up at the smiling brunette. ''Just coffee for me. Black, please.''

Kate reached down for her tote bag and rummaged through the contents. Then their drinks were placed on the trays in front of them.

Jared frowned. ''What are you looking for?''

''This is going to be a long flight and I certainly don't expect you to hold my hand the entire time.'' She pulled out a small bottle of vodka and dumped half the contents into her orange juice. She cocked her head and looked at Jared for a moment. The second half of the vodka quickly followed the first.

''I prefer this over the tranquilizers,'' she muttered, downing the juice in several gulps.

Jared grabbed her tote bag and rummaged through the contents.

''Do you mind!'' She tried to snatch it, but he held it out of her reach. ''Ask the attendant if you want some.''

''God, what a mess! You probably haven't cleaned this thing out in the last ten years,'' he grumbled, digging through crumpled tissues and old credit-card receipts. "How do you find anything in here?"

"I have a lot of personal items in there that you have no right to see." Kate slapped his hands and retrieved her bag, quickly stowing it under the seat before Jared stole it again.

"I've always wondered what a woman crammed in one of those bags. It's nice to have that question answered," Jared drawled, settling back in his seat. "I just wanted to make sure you didn't have any more booze in there. I'd hate to have to pour you off the plane in front of my parents."

She almost suffered whiplash when she spun around to face him. "Your parents?" she asked in shock.

He nodded, unfazed by her reaction. "They're picking us up at the airport. We'll be staying with them while we make our final preparations for the trip."

Kate fell back against the seat, first cursing in Arabic, then Greek before switching over to an obscure language of a desert tribe. Jared listened with a great deal of interest and respect for her knowledge.

"I'm not exactly sure what you said, but I don't think it's physically possible."

Her smile was deadly. "It's possible if I break all your bones first."

He nodded, not unoffended by her threats. "Maybe you can teach me some of those phrases during the trip. That way I can at least understand what you have in store for me."

"Pull any more surprises like this one and you'll learn more than you could ever dream of."

"I WISH YOU HAD TOLD ME sooner that we were staying with your parents," Kate mumbled as they deplaned in Phoenix.

Jared looked all too innocent. "You never asked."

She grimaced. "That's the last time I'll leave the travel arrangements to you and Gramps."

"At least I was gentleman enough to give you the window seat."

She chose not to reply to that.

"I'd know your parents anywhere." Kate's eyes drifted toward a couple standing on the fringes of the small crowd waiting for the incoming passengers. She now wished she hadn't drunk the entire bottle of vodka because her world was acting a bit fuzzy around the edges and she hated the idea of meeting Jared's parents with less than her normal faculties. She had taken the time to use the jet's lavatory to freshen up but wondered if she shouldn't have just stayed in there.

Jared followed the direction of her gaze and lifted his hand in greeting to the couple. "Glad to see you're so observant in that befuddled state of yours."

"I am not befuddled." She bit out each word, shifting her tote bag over her shoulder.

He grinned. "Sure, you're not. After all, you only drank that entire bottle of vodka."

"Why don't you say it a little louder. I don't think the people in the next state heard you." She tried to disengage her hand from his grip, but he merely tightened his fingers. She looked toward Jared's father and knew she was looking at Jared thirty years from now. Dark hair turned silver-gray, character lines etched around the eyes and mouth and a ramrod posture as a legacy from his many years in the military. The pleasantly plump woman standing beside him had the same vivid sapphire eyes as Jared.

"Look at you!" Marilyn Wyatt chuckled, wrapping Jared in a tight hug. "Darling, you've gotten positively thin. Don't they feed you back there?"

"Sure they do, but they don't cook like you, Mom." He returned her hug then dragged Kate forward. "Folks, this is Dr. Kate O'Malley." He flashed Kate a rakish grin.

"Oh, J.C., she's lovely." She turned to Kate. "I've heard so much about you, my dear, that I feel as if I already know you. Welcome to our family." She threw her arms around the younger woman in an exuberant hug.

Kate's smile froze on her face, but her eyes snapped deadly warnings at Jared.

"I told them about our engagement when we first talked about getting married, honey." He wasn't fazed by her silent threats. "I think they're relieved someone is willing to take me off their hands."

"Yes, I can see."

"I'm pleased to meet you, Kate." Jack Wyatt was more circumspect as he offered his hand. "I have to admit I was afraid J.C. would come home with a real bimbo. I'm glad to see his taste in women has improved over the years."

"Yes, well, the noose isn't around his neck just yet." Her smile at Jared intimated she'd look forward to doing just that.

"Let's get your luggage and get out of here." Jack took charge. "We still have our flight to the ranch."

Kate paled. *"Flight?"*

Jack nodded, his attention diverted by his son. "No problem, the helicopter will hold all of us."

"Helicopter?" She stared long and hard at Jared.

"Oh, didn't I tell you?" He was clearly enjoying this as he reached over to take her tote bag from her nerveless fingers. "Since it's too far to drive to the ranch, Dad has a helicopter pad out there. Don't worry, we'll be there in no time."

"Yes, I'm sure." With grim purpose Kate held out her hand for her bag.

"I'll take it for you, sweetheart," he offered gallantly.

"Yes, but, darling, I need it *now*." She tugged on the strap so strongly she almost jerked him off his feet. He still didn't surrender it.

Jack looked from one to the other as if sensing the undercurrents flowing between them. "Is something wrong?"

"Nothing," Kate hastily assured him. "I just hate to weigh Jared down with that awkward bag of mine when I'm so used to traveling with it."

Jack glanced at Jared. "J.C.'s a strong kid. He can handle it."

"What a shame you're only staying two nights." Marilyn sighed, walking with Kate as they headed for the baggage carousel. "I would have loved hearing about your travels. I read your grandfather's book and found all those legends fascinating."

"He does know how to tell a story," she agreed, discarding her sweater and loosening an extra button on her shirt. She was grateful her houndstooth slacks weren't wool. While they left a temperature in the thirties that morning they had arrived at a desert heat hovering in the high nineties.

"J.C. mentioned that you've participated on your own archaeological digs?" Marilyn questioned.

She nodded. "I've headed up two and was second in command to two others."

In the end, Kate was grateful for Marilyn's cheerful chatter when they boarded the helicopter that was entirely too small for her taste.

"You all right back there?" Jared asked Kate as she and Marilyn settled in the rear seats.

Her smile didn't even come close to her eyes. "Just peachy." When the overhead blades began whirring, she felt the need for some primal scream therapy but repressed it in favor of thinking up how to punish Jared in the most primitive ways known to man. As each idea took shape in her mind she felt her mood lighten just a little bit more. By the time they reached the Wyatt ranch she felt positively euphoric.

"What'd you do, have a bottle hidden in your clothing?" Jared asked in an undertone as they walked toward the sprawling adobe ranch house. "You're actually smiling."

"Oh, I just thought up some lovely ways to punish you when this is all over. I've discovered it's much more relaxing than alcohol or a tranquilizer."

After the heat, the cool interior of the adobe house was a welcome change.

"I'll get us some cold drinks." Marilyn bustled toward the rear of the house. She turned. "I wasn't sure if you'd prefer one or two rooms?" She looked questioningly at the couple.

"Two," Kate said hastily.

"Pity." Jared's lips barely moved.

Marilyn nodded. "J.C., why don't you put Kate's bags in the room next to yours?"

"I'll do it now." Jared hoisted Kate's bags and gestured for her to follow him down a long hallway.

The room he showed Kate was spacious, with a large double bed and adjoining bathroom.

"We share the bathroom," he explained. "Don't worry, I don't leave messes in the morning." He placed her suitcase on a wooden blanket chest at the foot of the bed.

"Why did you tell your parents we were engaged?" she demanded once she was certain they couldn't be overheard.

"Probably because we are."

"*Were*. Past tense. Kaput. Over. You agreed with me that it was called off."

"We were engaged when I talked to them, Kate."

She looked suspicious. "You talked to them three days ago."

"So I forgot. Sue me."

"Don't tempt me."

She watched him lay her tote bag on the edge of the bed, mentally cataloging the enticing sight of a nice pair of buns. How did he suddenly turn so damn sexy? she asked herself in a silent fit of frustration. She hastily raised her eyes when Jared turned, but not quickly enough. He grinned at the bright streaks of color on her cheeks.

"And here I thought it was my mind you were interested in, O'Malley," he murmured, ambling out of the room. "Take your time pulling yourself together. We'll be in the den. It's at the opposite end of the house toward the rear." He closed the door after him.

Kate collapsed across the bed. "I was better off with Joaquin the Slime."

"ARE YOU SURE Kate knows the two of you are getting married?" Jack Wyatt asked, handing Jared a whiskey and soda. "She looked pretty surprised when your mother mentioned your engagement."

He chuckled. "She's still getting used to the idea." He drank thirstily. "Have you heard from big brother?"

"He called last week when he returned from Spain. He'd hoped to fly out while you were here, but a job came along that was too good to resist." Jack chose a comfortable looking chair upholstered in a nubby oatmeal-colored fabric. "I took care of your list of supplies. We'll fly you over there day after tomorrow. Mind telling me why you felt you couldn't discuss this trip over the phone?"

"This is Kate's show. I should give her the honor." He looked up and smiled when his mother entered the room pushing a tea cart. "Don't tell me you're afraid we'll starve until dinner?" he teased, reaching to snatch a couple taquitos from a serving dish. He dipped them in guacamole sauce before popping them in his mouth.

"I know from past experience that airline food is not filling," she argued. "Just save something for Kate. She's a lovely young woman, J.C. It's hard to believe she's involved in the same kind of work as you."

"Not exactly the same," he dryly countered. "Her work requires a passport while mine expired a long time ago." Jared wasn't about to confess that Kate's work had given him more than a few bad moments from the time he had first met her. Even more so recently when he couldn't help but wonder if the time would come when her wanderlust would flare up and she would yearn to follow that horizon. And since he had done more than his share of world travel during his father's years in the military he was more than happy to keep his perimeters to the good old U.S. of A.

"How are your classes going?" Jack inserted, sensing Jared's unease with the subject.

He grinned wryly. "All of them full."

"And most of them female," Jack guessed, his grin as potent as his son's.

Jared rolled his eyes.

"He's also well known for his tough exams and big blue eyes," Kate announced as she walked in and took a seat on the couch. Jared immediately abandoned his chair and sat beside her.

"Care for a drink?"

"Anything is fine as long as it's cold."

"And nonalcoholic," he murmured, moving away.

"I fixed some snacks." Marilyn gestured to the tray. "Feel free to help yourself."

"Mom is afraid we might starve within the next hour or so." Jared handed Kate a tall ice-filled glass of diet cola. He eyed her clinging tank top with an appreciative male gaze. She had pulled her hair up in a ponytail tied with matching ribbon. He hated to use clichés, but he had to admit she looked good enough to eat. If his parents weren't present he would be sorely tempted to take a bite. Even if only to see her reaction. It hadn't taken him long to find out how much he enjoyed unnerving Kate. He hadn't missed the way she stared at him when he bent over her bed and the way she blushed when he caught her. Faint color stained her cheekbones now and he knew she guessed what he was thinking. He grinned broadly, making her blush even more.

"I'm curious as to why you'd want to travel into the Superstition Mountains, Kate," Jack spoke up. "If it was J.C. I'd say he was looking for one of the old abandoned Apache camps for some unknown reason, but there's nothing old enough there to interest someone with your background.''

"True, my expertise is in ancient cultures and legends," she agreed. "But this is something very special. Actually, I'm doing this for my grandfather. Long-term recovery from a broken hip has left him unable to make this kind of trip.''

"Do you make these kind of trips often?" Jack asked.

She nodded. "Yes, I've made several, in fact. Although this is the first in this country. Most of my own work has been done in the Mideastern deserts and once in Afghanistan. That was one trip I wouldn't care to repeat," she admitted.

"Oh, my," Marilyn breathed, her eyes wide. "It sounds a great deal different from traveling with the military.''

"It is.''

"I'm sure you managed to always take that lethal knife of yours along," Jared drawled, eyeing Kate with a look that could have said anything. He wasn't about to let her know that the idea of her traveling through the mountainous country well known for its furious battles sent a shaft of fear through his body. Did she think she was invincible?

She smiled. "Like my American Express card, I never leave home without it.''

Chapter Six

"There are no Xs marking the spot, no piles of rocks at the cave opening, only a feeling that riches beyond one's dreams are close at hand," Kate mumbled, leafing through the photocopies of Jacob Waltz's journals she had brought with her.

While Jared's parents were friendly and an all-around nice couple, she was relieved to escape to the privacy of her room where she could look over the papers and truly relax. The pace of the past few weeks had left her feeling more than a little frazzled. A long hot bath helped her relax and now she sat in her nightshirt in the middle of her bed, sheets of paper scattered around her in a semicircle. She rubbed the end of her nose with her fingers and absently pushed her reading glasses back up. "The man was crafty, all right. Nothing here to give it away, just a lot of tiny clues that would take a Sherlock Holmes to figure out." She threw herself backward, sending the papers flying in every direction. At the moment she wouldn't have cared if they went up in smoke.

"Oh, Gramps, why couldn't you have come up with something easier?" she groaned. "Like finding the island of Atlantis?" She didn't move when she heard someone knocking at her door. "Come in." She lay there, listening to the sounds of the door opening then closing, footsteps muffled against the carpet and a weight settling on the edge of the bed next to her. Slightly callused hands touched her hands then handed her something very warm to the touch.

"Hot cocoa?" she asked whimsically, her eyes still closed.

"Even better," Jared assured her. "Coffee with a healthy jolt of Irish Cream. I figured that was more to your liking."

"Ah, Wyatt, you know the way to a girl's heart." Kate opened her eyes to find Jared studying her bare legs. "If you expect me to gasp with a maiden's embarrassment and demand that you leave my room you'll lose. I left modesty behind a long time ago."

"I'm sure you did," he murmured, concentrating on her toenails which were painted a soft rose shade. A frown creased his brow as he looked up her legs to her hands cradling the coffee mug. Then he grasped one of those hands. The long nails, previously painted a matching rose, were now unpolished, the nails clipped short.

"Manicures don't mesh well with archaeological digs, so I always clip them first," she explained, sensing his unspoken question. A smile crossed her lips as she edged backward until she sat upright against the headboard. She sipped the hot coffee and closed her eyes in bliss as the potent liquid trickled down her throat. "One year, when I was about twelve or thirteen, one of Gramps's assistants was the kind of woman who assumed archaeology was glamorous and didn't realize how much hard work was involved on a dig. She broke three nails the first day, tried to kill a rope with a hoe because she thought it was a snake and discovered her portable hair dryer couldn't be used since, of course, there wasn't any electricity. Needless to say, she left the next day.''

"While you worked alongside Shamus without a word of complaint," Jared guessed.

"He called me his human sponge, soaking in as much information as I could." Her coffee finished, she set it to one side, all the while using her position to study long muscular legs encased in faded denim stretched out by the bed.

"Tomorrow we'll choose our horses for the trip and pack up our supplies." Jared seemed reluctant to tear his gaze from her bare legs.

"Good, the sooner, the better." Kate began picking up the papers, but was stopped when he covered her hands with his. He shifted his weight and put his other hand flat on the quilt next to her hip, and she was effectively trapped.

"You do realize we're going to be in those mountains alone for many days." His voice was a husky murmur that sent warning tingles along Kate's nerve endings.

"Not exactly alone," she countered smoothly. "I'm sure there will be plenty of reptiles and coyotes to keep us company. You should feel right at home."

"Still," he continued undaunted, "that kind of time, alone under a desert sky, with no other human beings around, could bring about some temptations. If you know what I mean."

"I think so," she replied dryly.

"So, whaddya think? Shall we just get it out of the way right here and now?" His eyes skimmed the bed's surface. "That way we can make the trip without any tension affecting our work. Sound good to you?'' He flashed her a cocky grin.

Kate's answering smile was a great deal cooler. "No, it doesn't."

Shrugging as if her reply meant little to him, Jared stood and snagged her coffee mug. "Mom said to feel free to sleep late. See you in the morning." The door closed softly behind him.

Kate sat there, staring at the door for a long time as she gnawed on the side of her hand, feeling frustration surround her in waves.

She moaned. "I should have said yes."

"ARE YOU SURE you had enough breakfast?" Marilyn asked Kate as she refilled the coffee cup.

Kate silently scanned the serving dishes filled with waffles, eggs, bacon, sausage and biscuits. Not wanting to hurt the older woman's feelings, she had taken a bit of each and now felt convinced she'd eaten enough to last her for six months. She was suddenly more tired than she had thought, even though she had slept better than she had in days. She hadn't awakened until after the men had left the house.

"For someone who usually only has toast and coffee for breakfast, I had more than enough," she assured her. "Please, won't you sit down and relax?"

Marilyn chuckled as she took the seat next to Kate's. "I'm one of those people who's happier when I keep myself busy," she explained. "Oh, I know it makes me look a bit flighty at times, but it also strokes Jack's ego. That way he thinks he's the brains in the family." Her eyes twinkled with laughter.

Kate giggled. "Why, Marilyn, you're a lady of many talents, aren't you?"

"I try." Her gaze was a great deal more discerning than usual as she studied Kate. "So when are you going to put my son out of his misery and marry him?"

Kate choked on the coffee she was drinking. "Me put him out?" she gasped. "He's the one who took me out under false pretenses! Letting me think he was some kind of nerdy professor when he wasn't. There were days he acted so stuffy that he practically had me convinced he wore starched underwear! Then when I run into him in Mexico he comes across like someone out of one of those men's adventure books!" Now that she got herself started she found it difficult to stop. "Would it have been so difficult for him to tell me that he had to put on a different persona for the university and ultraconservative Dr. Phillips? I would have understood. After all, I've had to tone myself down a few times for the man." She quickly finished her coffee. "I have an idea I'm on a caffeine high. I always mouth off when I've had too much caffeine."

Marilyn stood and began gathering dishes. "I would think this would be the best time to confront J.C. with how you feel about this."

Kate picked up several serving dishes and followed Marilyn into the kitchen. "Not until I feel the time is right." She opened the dishwasher door, preparing to load it.

"You go on outside to the barn," Marilyn ordered, staying her hand. "These won't take me any time at all to do," she assured her when she saw the indecision on the younger woman's face. "Besides you want to choose your own horse, don't you, instead of having J.C. choose it for you."

"Only if I can help with the next meal," Kate insisted.

"Don't worry, you can. Now go on outside."

"WELL, SON, YOU SURE CAN pick them," Jack commented, looking out the barn doorway.

Jared followed his gaze. "What can I say, Dad? I take after you."

Both men smiled, appreciating the unrestricted view of Kate walking toward them in jeans and a soft pink and green plaid shirt. Her boots sent tiny puffs of dust upward around her heels as she walked across the yard. A California Angels baseball cap sat perched on her head. Her shirt collar was flipped up around her throat.

"Gentlemen," she greeted them. "I hope I haven't kept you waiting long."

"You were the lucky one," Jared told her. "Dad gave me the pleasure of allowing me to help his men muck out the stalls. We just finished."

Kate's smile held pure mischief. She wrinkled her nose. "Yes, there's no mistaking the distinct aroma of eau de stable, is there? It appears I came just in time. Now, what about our mounts?"

"This way." Jack led them toward the rear of the barn and outside to a corral where several horses walked back and forth. "I've always been interested in horse breeding on a limited scale and the ranch allows me to do just that. My horses are regular little mountain goats and also make good pack animals."

Kate studied each spirited horse's small delicate head and slender legs. They displayed inherent strength. "They have Arabian in them," she stated.

"You, of all people, know they're the best for desert travel," Jack replied. "J.C. and I chose these four from my stock and you can choose your personal mount. I can guarantee that any of them will carry you into hell, if necessary. Considering where you're going, you might need such a horse." His sapphire eyes, so much like his son's, sparkled with the spirit of shared adventure. "Makes me wish I was going with you. Many people have searched for the Lost Dutchman Mine over the years. From what J.C. has told me, you have a better chance than most of proving the legend a fact. Some people figure Jacob was nothing more than a bearer of tall tales, but that still doesn't stop them from looking for the mine."

"Everything I've read about him indicates he was pretty closemouthed about his gold," Kate said.

"He was, but all that did was add to the legend," Jack replied. "Some say it was deliberate. After all these years, who knows? There's been a lot of serious prospectors searching those mountains and they haven't found a hint. Maybe it's been waiting there for you to discover it."

Kate thought of the journals and maps her grandfather had gathered over the years. "Maybe it has."

"I'll be happy as long as we don't have to do a lot of digging," Jared spoke up. He turned to Kate. "Dad's going to have the horses and our supplies trucked over to the base of the mountains tonight so they'll be waiting for us and we'll use the chopper in the morning. I've already alerted the rangers we're riding in; they're pretty picky about people just riding through there on pleasure trips without letting them know. Dad's already picked up the latest maps of the area. We should take the time tonight to compare your maps with the new ones to see how much the land has changed over the years."

Kate groaned silently. Flying again. "You're right, we do need to study them carefully." She lifted her shoulders and allowed them to fall. "This is pretty new to me. I'm beginning to think it's easier to travel into a foreign country than explore within my own. I bow to your judgment since you're more familiar with the ins and outs. But if you ever want to travel along the Nile or the Middle East, call me. I'll have you set up in nothing flat."

Jared was relieved that Kate didn't object to his taking charge. After her first insisting she would be the boss on this project, he feared she would battle him at every turn. Still, he sensed this acquiescence of hers wouldn't last for long. Once they were in the mountains, she might allow him to lead since he was familiar with the area, but he knew she would assert herself every chance she got. He had an idea this trip was going to turn out to be very interesting. Especially after their discussion last night. She thought he hadn't noticed the way she watched him during dinner and afterward when he stopped by her room. Oh, he noticed, all right! And while the lady wouldn't admit it he easily read the hungry look in her eye. Now all he had to do was show her that this trip was only going to be the first of many for them and that J.C. and Jared together were a pretty good package deal.

After dinner they took over the dining room table. Kate's papers scattered across the polished surface, mingling companionably with the more modern maps Jack contributed. She absently chewed on the end of her braid as she traced a faintly marked trail.

"Jacob seems to have loved puzzles," she murmured with a slight frown as she compared a map of more than a hundred years ago with the latest one.

"The more I look at these the more I'm inclined to think that he was, indeed, a better storyteller than prospector. Maybe he only found a small cache up in the hills and the legend grew because he never flashed a lot of it around. Depending on the authors of what I've read, some say he bragged about his mine, others say he was closemouthed." She shifted in the chair, curling her legs under her body so she could reach across the table for another map. "Right about now I would prefer looking for some of the lost crown jewels of Nicholas and Alexandra than do this." She looked irritated with the changes in each map she scanned.

"Russia would be too cold this time of year." Jared handed her the sheet of paper just out of her reach.

"So I'll wear thermal underwear." Kate pushed her glasses up her nose as she strained to read the faint spidery handwriting. "Can you make this out?" She handed him the paper, pointing halfway down the page.

Jared squinted, held the paper at arm's length then brought it so close it almost touched his nose. After patting his shirt pocket and discovering he didn't have his glasses with him he slipped Kate's off.

"Do you mind!" she objected.

"Not at all." He slid them on. "Your prescription is close enough to mine that I have no trouble reading with your glasses. Something else we have in common. Good to know if one of us loses our glasses. I have a bad habit of misplacing mine. It's embarrassing enough that I have to wear them without losing a pair each time I'm on a dig."

"Not unless you've ever had an assistant who got hysterical because she lost one of her contact lenses in the sand while we were once digging through an old Roman city," Kate told him.

"I've had a few of those, too." Jared carefully replaced her glasses on her nose, his fingers lingering as he took his time adjusting the earpieces.

Kate's breath caught in her throat as she felt his fingers gently combing through her hair.

"Jared?" The name came out as a hoarse croak.

His fingers slowly traced the outline of her ear, around the shell and down to the lobe where a gold earring in the shape of a rose impeded his progress. They moved round and round the carved shape.

"Your parents are in the next room," she said between dry lips.

Jared shook his head. "They went to bed twenty minutes ago and since my brother and I reached twenty-one they've turned into sound sleepers." Now his fingers trailed down the side of her neck, pausing long enough to feel her pulse, which was increasing by the second.

Their eyes locked.

They stared at each other for several long moments.

"Are you sure you wouldn't care to reconsider last night's suggestion?" he asked in a hoarse voice.

The tip of her tongue appeared and slid across her lower lip. As he watched he could feel his blood pressure skyrocketing.

"Oh, you mean about our easing the so-called tension between us? Taking care of it before we're on the trail, alone, for days on end?" Her smile was the kind that could turn a man to Jell-O. Jared was no exception.

Unable to speak, he nodded, afraid to dare to hope.

"I don't think so."

JARED KNEW HE HAD TO BE UP long before dawn but sleep was much too elusive for him that night.

"That little witch," he groaned, staring at his bedroom ceiling, which was washed with various shades of gray from the moonlight spilling in from the open window. "At this rate I'll come out of those mountains a babbling idiot happy to live in a padded cell for the rest of my life."

He crossed his arms behind his head as he tried to think of anything but spending days alone with Kate. Had he made sure enough supplies were packed? Was all the tack in excellent condition? Was he taking too many clothes? Was he crazy to do this? Yes, yes, yes, and most definitely *yes*.

"I would have been better off falling in love with an English teacher," he muttered, rolling over and punching his pillow with more force than necessary.

Love was very new to Jared. And when it involved someone as unique as Kate, it turned out to be more than fireworks and violin music. It was rightly called frustration. Dr. Kathryn O'Malley with her infectious smile and zest for life brightened Jared's days and made his nights hell.

"Good going, Wyatt, you've got all the finesse of a bulldozer," Jared muttered. "Why didn't you just go ahead and jump her bones, to put it crudely."

He couldn't remember a day a certain long-legged blonde hadn't driven him to distraction. From that first time he saw her on campus, where he quickly engineered a meeting, he knew he was well and truly sunk.

"Maybe you should just go in there and tell her you love her," he suggested to himself. "Yeah, sure, and she'll laugh in your face because right now you're not exactly at the top of her list."

He stretched his naked limbs under the sheet. "Plan of action, Wyatt," he decided out loud. "You're not going to let her get to you on this trip. In fact, if you can drive her more than a little crazy along the way, so be it. It'll be good for her."

KATE WAS IN THE MIDST of a lovely dream where she was swimming naked in a pool of gold when a loud pounding on her door rudely intruded.

"Up and at 'em, O'Malley!" Jared shouted from the other side. "We're leaving in twenty minutes."

"There are easier ways to pull someone back to the land of the living," she groaned, pushing herself into a sitting position. She brushed her hair from her face and squinted at the bedside clock. "Heaven forbid, it's three o'clock. How could I have overslept?" She stood and stumbled her way toward the bathroom in search of a cold shower in hopes of shocking her body to life. "It's not as if I don't always get up at this disgusting hour."

"It's about time you got out here," Jared greeted her when she stumbled into the kitchen. He leaned against the counter drinking a cup of coffee.

"Don't listen to his grumblings," Marilyn advised Kate. She bustled around the room, filling a thermos with coffee. "You sit there and eat something. You have plenty of time whether he thinks so or not."

Jared pointedly looked at his watch. "If Kate isn't ready in five minutes I go without her."

"Fat chance," she retorted. "My clothes are already packed."

"Good, then if necessary you can eat during the flight," he told her.

She was certain he could see the way her stomach lurched at the idea of eating while flying in what she privately called a flying baby carriage.

He picked up a pair of worn riding gloves and a battered Stetson from the kitchen counter. "I'll wait for you outside."

Out of sheer perversity Kate took her time eating her meal even though she was eager to be off. Now that all her plans were falling neatly into place she wanted to begin the search, to find what Shamus considered so important. She intended to do whatever was necessary to find the mine.

"Good luck." Marilyn smiled at her. "Or perhaps I should offer that sentiment to J.C. I have an idea he might need it more than you will."

Kate looked confused.

Marilyn continued, smiling. "From what I understand he has an uphill battle to win you and this trip just might be his last chance. Don't make it too easy for him. I led Jack on a merry chase before I finally allowed him to catch me. I always felt it made him appreciate me more."

Kate felt embarrassed at the woman's obvious hope to have her in their family. "We wouldn't have gotten along anyway," she mumbled. "There's a lot we don't agree on."

"My dear, haven't you ever heard of the word compromise?" They were her parting words as she pushed the thermos into Kate's hands.

Kate gathered up her saddlebags and bedroll before walking into the chilly early morning air. She shivered inside her sheepskin-lined denim jacket as she crossed the yard to where Jared and Jack stood talking quietly.

Jared looked up at her approach. "Ready?"

She drew a deep breath. "Ready."

Luckily for Kate, the helicopter ride was mercifully short and over before she knew it. The machine set down on the ground in the pale gray predawn light. They found two men sharing a small camp fire with two saddled horses and a packhorse waiting for them.

As Kate looked up at the jagged outlines of the mountains she felt that familiar tingling in her veins, the same tingling sensation she felt before every trip. She was venturing into the unknown, looking for something that hadn't been seen by man for a hundred years. She picked up her baseball cap and settled it on her head. She then drew her riding gloves from her back pocket and pulled them on. She looked over at their mounts, prancing in the cool air, obviously sensing everyone's excitement.

Kate walked a short distance away, breathing in deeply, but nothing could still the blood racing through her veins. This was what she was meant to do: find proof of the past.

"I know this won't do you any good once you're well within the mountains, but you'll be able to use it when you come back out," she heard Jack tell Jared as he handed him a radio transmitter. "We'll be here to pick you up right away."

Kate spun around on her boot heel.

"Let's get this show on the road," she said crisply.

Jared looked over. There was no missing the excitement filling her eyes and face.

"Ready anytime you are, O'Malley."

Her face lit up like the sunrise. "Then, Wyatt, let's ride before the posse catches up with us."

Within a few minutes they were mounted, and with Jared leading the packhorse, they followed a well-worn trail. Ten minutes later they could hear the distinctive whirring sound of the helicopter taking its leave.

Jared looked at Kate. "It's not the mine and the gold so much as the legend you're after, is it?"

She adjusted the bill of her hat to better shade her eyes from the rising sun. "It's always been the legends that attract me," she replied, her thoughts roaming back hundreds of years to another time. "The idea of something out there that no one has seen for perhaps hundreds, if not thousands, of years fascinates me. It makes me want to be that first person to see it again, to see it shared with others." She turned her head, her eyes still glittering with thoughts of what would happen within the next few weeks.

"We can't file a mining claim, you know. The government stopped all filing of new claims in 1983," Jared explained.

"We can apply for permission to excavate for lost or buried treasure as long as we have factual data and Gramps has more than enough of that," she explained. "To be honest, I think he wants proof of the mine more than the gold itself."

"Their idea of lost or buried treasure doesn't include minerals, and gold is most definitely a mineral." Jared felt that old uneasy feeling settle in the pit of his stomach again. While Kate was growing more and more excited with each step they took up the trail, he was beginning to feel just the opposite. He silently wondered if this trip couldn't end up to be a great deal more than either of them bargained for.

Chapter Seven

"There's a legend that these mountains inflict a curse on anyone who challenges them," Jared remarked, guiding his horse up a particularly steep trail.

"Curses are nothing new to me," Kate told him, lifting her canteen to her lips for a sip of water.

"If we're lucky the water holes won't be too dry this time of year." He paused, looking from right to left, his face lifted to the searing heat of the sun. "But they're still not going to be easy to find."

Her gaze sharpened. "What do you sense?"

He shook his head. "Maybe something, maybe nothing. There's never a lack of prospectors looking for the same thing, so we may not be as alone as we think we are." He half turned in the saddle, his hand braced on the smooth leather. "I know I don't have to warn you to remain on the alert. Some people aren't too friendly up here if they think you might find what they've been looking for, perhaps for years."

Kate nodded, easily able to understand his warning. She had encountered the same problem many times before. "Man and his greed."

"Not to mention rattlesnakes, gila monsters, scorpions and other assorted reptiles," he added.

She looked around in the harsh forbidding land-scape and wished her grandfather were riding beside her. How he would love this! Shamus wasn't meant to be confined to the house when there was still so much for him to do. "Are most of the trails marked?" She adjusted her shirt collar to shade her neck as much as possible from the sun beating down on her.

"About a hundred and twenty-five miles or so are, but even they aren't as clear as they should be. They can change overnight because of landslides and flash floods. That's why visitors are so strictly monitored. People get lost up here on a regular basis and if the forest rangers have no idea they're up here, they'll die in no time."

"How long has it been since you've been here?" She was beginning to find out how little she truly knew about the man she had once seriously considered mar-rying. Looking at him riding in front of her, his jaw set in hard ridges, his eyes constantly on the prowl for anything unusual, he looked nothing like the amiable professor she had dated for almost eight months. Right then and there she decided that she would get a lot of questions answered during this trip.

"Actually, it was last fall when I was visiting my folks before the new semester began. A couple of tourists thought it would be a snap to hike in here and they promptly got lost. Dad and I helped the forest rangers search for them. It took us three days to find them and we almost got lost ourselves."

Kate winced, thinking of what three days in a harsh, unforgiving land could do to someone unfamiliar with it. "Were they still alive?"

"Barely. They were badly sunburned and thirsty as hell when if they had gone over a small nearby hill they would have found a water hole. They had no idea how to survive out here or that they could get water from a barrel cactus. All they were familiar with was the adage 'When lost, hug a tree.'" He reined in his mount and pulled a map out of his shirt pocket. He chuckled. "At least they didn't try to hug a cactus." He spared her a brief glance as he slipped on his glasses. "Your backside holding up?"

She grinned. "We've only been riding a few hours, Dr. Wyatt. Ask me again four days from now. Although riding a horse is infinitely more comfortable than riding a camel or elephant."

"Yeah, I heard camels don't have the best of tempers." He traced a squiggly line with his forefinger clearly lost in the intricacies of the map he held.

"They smell terrible, they spit and they bite." A devilish imp prompted her to ask, "Care to see my scar?" He'd been acting so impersonal all morning that she'd love nothing more than to shake him up.

Jared concentrated on the map he held. "Hm?"

"Of course, I was bending over all the time," she persisted, wanting to see if she could get a reaction, *any* kind of reaction from him. "I ended up with eight stitches in my backside."

"Um, that's nice," he murmured, looking off into the distance then back at the map.

Kate preferred to forget she had been accused many times in the past of acting just as abstracted in her work as Jared was now. "Actually, he bit off one entire cheek and I had to have a prosthesis," she said matter-of-factly.

Jared folded his map and slipped it into his shirt pocket. He picked up his reins and guided the bay along a narrow path to the right. They rode in silence for almost ten minutes before he spoke in the same matter-of-fact tone Kate had used earlier.

"It's amazing what the miracle of modern medicine can do nowadays, isn't it? Even those tight jeans of yours doesn't give a hint that part of you is built by Mattel."

It took Kate another ten minutes before she realized she was grinding her teeth in frustration.

"I'll make him crawl before this is over," she mumbled when she felt he was out of earshot. "He's going to learn just what frustration really is." She glared at his back, her eyes tracking the patch of sweat darkening his shirt. "Even if it kills me."

KATE DECIDED right from the beginning she wouldn't mind taking up the rear on this expedition. After a quick lunch break of jerky and trail mix with a few welcome sips of water, she offered to take the packhorse's reins for awhile and even hung back a little farther than necessary. She found herself studying Jared as they rode deeper into the mountains, most especially watching his rear end.

Funny that she never thought all that much about his body when they were first seeing each other. Of course, she hadn't seen him in tight jeans then, only well-tailored slacks or casual twills or chinos.

"Just think. If I'd followed my father's footsteps I could be off on a Pacific island studying the inhabitants," she commented.

"You think you'd prefer studying tribal customs instead of studying bones?" Jared asked.

Kate shrugged. "If I was with Dad we'd be studying tribal mating customs." There was no derision in her voice, only friendly affection for her father. "Dad still believes in 'make love, not war.' He's a true product of the sixties.''

"Yeah, I've heard that about him. Some say he's the exact opposite of Shamus.''

She chuckled, the sound musical in the still air. "Actually, I think they're more alike than they'd care to admit. They both march to their own drummer and they both defy convention when it pleases them.''

"And they both had a hand in forming the woman you've become," he finished, reining in his mount. He leaned forward so he could reach in his back pocket to pull out a bandanna. He took off his hat to wipe the sweat from his forehead, then replaced and pulled it low over his forehead.

Kate's mouth grew dry as she watched him and not because of the arid land around them.

When had he turned so utterly masculine? she asked herself. Not to mention damn sexy. How did she, a usually eagle-eyed scientist, miss this other side of his personality? She tried to swallow past the gigantic lump in her throat.

Keep your mind on the job, O'Malley, not on his tush, she silently ordered herself. *You're looking for a gold mine, not a hot and heavy fling in the desert.*

Except the woman who had the kind of vivid imagination to easily visualize a culture from centuries ago could just as easily visualize the dark-haired man sprawled against stark white sheets. And he wasn't wearing a pair of flannel pajamas, either. She shifted in her saddle. It was going to be a very long trip.

IT WAS GOING TO BE a very long trip.

Jared groaned silently. He knew it was impossible, but he could swear the light scent of Kate's perfume was surrounding him in insidious waves. He was positive she wore it just to drive him crazy. But then he knew he was crazy from the first day he met her.

What was it about Kate that fascinated him? Besides everything, that is. The way she constantly rose to a challenge, her effervescent personality, not to mention she was as sexy as hell. He closed his eyes, ignoring the trickle of sweat making its way down his forehead. He had to stop doing this, thinking of her as a desirable woman. Remembering her long bare legs under that skimpy excuse of a nightshirt. Her feminine side revealed by the brightly colored polish on her toes. He forced himself to remember her wearing more unisex clothing, the jeans, tailored shirt and the baseball cap covering that blond hair. It didn't help. Not when he recalled how well the jeans fit her body, how her shirt revealed as much as it covered and even the baseball cap seemed to emphasize her large green eyes and make her look feminine instead of boyish.

He thought of the archaeological digs she had participated in, then later directed, in the past. How many men had she captivated during that time? He didn't think he wanted to know. He wished he was British. Then he could see if thinking of Queen and country would cool him down, although he sincerely doubted even that would help where Kate was concerned.

"I wish I could continue the fiction that I'm a stoic person, but there are times when nature won't allow it," Kate spoke up, her voice devoid of embarrassment considering her request. "Would you mind stopping for a couple minutes?"

Jared pulled on the reins and dismounted. "Sounds good to me. You go left and I'll go right."

"We really should complain to the management about these primitive facilities," Kate said with a touch of humor laced through her voice when Jared returned to their horses a few minutes later. "When the travel guide spoke of up-to-date rest stops I didn't realize they were talking about up-to-date a hundred years ago."

"Considering some of the places you've traveled to I would think this isn't anything new for you." He opened his saddlebag and rummaged through the contents.

"True, but that doesn't mean I don't appreciate modern facilities." She took off her hat and ruffled her bangs, which clung damply to her forehead. She turned to her horse, stroking his mane as she searched through her own saddlebags. She pulled out several folded sheets of paper and opened them. "These old maps are useless to us. Everything has changed so much in the past hundred years that nothing here is the same. It comes down to a lot of guesswork for us."

"You must be used to these kind of puzzles. How many times have you looked for an ancient city that isn't where it should be because the maps don't agree?" Jared asked her, chomping on some trail mix and holding the bag out to her.

"Probably not as often as Gramps has." She picked out the raisins and tossed them to the ground.

"Those raisins are good for you," he pointed out.

She wrinkled her nose. "No, thanks, I always think of them as dried ants."

"I thought they were considered a delicacy in some countries."

"They are. I won't eat those, either."

Jared glanced at his watch. "With luck, we can get in a few more hours of riding before we reach where I want to make our first camp." If he could survive this first night in the middle of nowhere, he knew he could survive the trip with his sanity intact.

Kate grasped the reins and pulled herself into the saddle. "Lead on, MacDuff."

The remainder of the day was ridden in silence. By the time they halted to make camp Jared was wondering if he had done the right thing in insisting in leading this expedition of two instead of helping Shamus find a suitable guide. How could Shamus trust him with his granddaughter out here in the wilds when he wasn't sure if he could trust himself with Kate? As he took care of their horses, he found himself watching her nimbly start a cook fire. He reminded himself he wasn't going to let her get to him on a physical basis. Easier said than done.

"You have a choice, freeze-dried beef stew, freeze-dried beef Stroganoff or a freeze-dried chicken dish of unknown origin," she announced, looking up.

"Let's live dangerously and go with the stew," he replied, pulling his attention from her delicate profile.

She nodded. "How about freeze-dried coffee to go with it?"

"Why not." Jared crouched on the other side of the fire and watched her work. "I'll do my share of the cooking."

"Good, because we trade off or we eat trail mix a lot." She poured a small amount of water in a pan set over the fire and began stirring the contents. "This shouldn't take long." She frowned then turned away to pull her saddlebags toward her. After a bit of searching she drew out several small plastic bottles.

"What are you doing?" Jared noticed her sprinkling what looked like herbs into the pan.

"Giving a bit of flavor to something that we both know will be very unappetizing without some help," she explained, tapping the side of one bottle to drop a few more flakes into the stew. "I decided a long time ago if I had to eat anything that was freeze-dried the least I could do was add a few homey touches, so I always take some spices and herbs with me. Of course, there was one time when it turned out to be a very bad idea," she added wryly, putting the spices away.

He was intrigued. "Oh?"

Kate nodded. "Gramps was in Greece helping excavate an ancient city and I was meeting him there after recovering from a bad bout of flu. Customs didn't believe that I was carrying spices so I was held for a few days while they decided whether they truly were herbs or some kind of new drug."

The film *Midnight Express* immediately crossed Jared's mind and he repressed a shudder of horror at Kate experiencing a fraction of what the real life character suffered.

"You were in jail?" His voice was raw with feeling.

She shrugged, her head downcast as she concentrated on her cooking. "That's what they called it."

"Were..." He cleared his throat, fearing what the jailers must have thought having a pretty blonde under their power. "Were you bothered by the jailers?"

She looked up, a slight smile on her lips. "Let's say they tried, but they didn't get far. Luckily, a member of the American embassy appeared before things got too sticky. One jailer ended up talking falsetto for awhile and he wasn't too happy with me for being the cause."

Horrors of what could have happened flashed before his eyes. "Why do you take such chances?" he asked. "Didn't you realize what they could have done to you?"

"Of course, I did, but I couldn't afford to worry about it. I bet you don't worry when you're in trouble." Kate was surprised by the tension in Jared's question. "Do you mean to say that you don't take chances? What about that time in Mexico where some mountain tribe that had never seen a white man before seriously thought about sacrificing you to their gods and you convinced them that you were one of their gods? Wasn't that taking a chance? Your mother told me the story while we were eating breakfast yesterday. She said she was glad she heard it afterward because she would have worried herself sick until she knew you were all right."

"I wasn't in danger of being raped!" he shot back.

"You never can tell. I've heard that some of those native women can turn into real animals if they see a man they want," she said whimsically. "I wasn't all that worried. After all, I knew they'd finally figure out that paprika wasn't what one would care to push up one's nose and they'd let me go."

Jared threw up his hands in disgust. "And if they decided not to, no matter what?"

"If anything had happened to me they would have had to deal with Gramps and I wouldn't wish that on anyone." She set about doling the warm stew onto two tin plates, then handed one to Jared. She opened a plastic bag and divided the biscuits between them. "We should probably eat these tonight because I doubt they'll stay fresh very long."

Except Jared had little appetite. He knew that Kate's work had sent her into dangerous situations, but not until now had he realized just how much she seemed to thrive on the danger. He tried to convince himself that she was able to speak so matter-of-factly about it now because it was in the past, but he knew differently. She had been brought up to take care of herself in any situation and it appeared she had been able to do just that.

"It did teach me one thing," she went on.

"What was that?"

"I learned not to pack up my spices with me but to buy what I wanted when I got there."

Jared closed his eyes and counted to ten. "Does nothing ever bother you?"

She shrugged. "Not much. Well, I'm not too keen on eating foods that I would normally squash under my foot..." Her voice trailed off as she set her empty plate to one side. "Know what would be a perfect ending to the meal?" To Jared's ears her voice was husky, the kind of tone a woman used in bed.

He coughed. He wasn't going to allow her to get to him. He kept repeating that statement as if it was his personal mantra, but he didn't think it was helping very much. "What?"

Her eyes were half closed as she appeared to dream about something very intriguing. Or, in Jared's mind, very sexy. The tip of her tongue slid across her lower lip slowly. Could she be inviting him to kiss her? No, he must be strong!

The tone was pure honey to Jared's ears. "Something I feel very passionate about. Something that just sends tingles through my veins. Chocolate." He almost fell over in surprise. "I'm talking about rich milk chocolate with perhaps some caramel or peanuts, even coconut, I'm not fussy. Just as long as there's tons of chocolate surrounding it." She sounded like a woman in love.

Jared didn't know whether to laugh or cry. It took awhile for him to regain his wits and his voice. "You're lucky, O'Malley. That's a request I can grant." He reached into his saddlebags and withdrew a familiar brown bag. "Let's find out if they'll wait to melt in your mouth." He tossed her the bag.

With a squeal of delight Kate caught the bag and promptly tore it open. The brightly colored candies were a bit soft, but she was past caring and took several. With her head thrown back and her eyes closed in bliss, she most definitely looked like a woman in love with chocolate. Remembering her manners she held the bag out. "You should be honored. Gramps will tell you that most of the time I won't even share chocolate with him." She considered the bag. "You didn't bring any peanut ones with you, too, did you?"

"Don't push your luck," he advised wryly. He began to think his personal mantra could very well turn into a curse. Especially if she pulled something like this every night. "After all, I might have more stashed away."

Kate eyed his saddlebags with undisguised hunger.

"*Might* is the operative word, O'Malley," Jared reminded her, pulling his saddlebags against his hip in a protective manner.

She wrinkled her nose. "You're a cruel man, Wyatt. Tempting a woman then withholding your favors." Her smile was pure mischief, not to mention pure female.

He could already feel the heat coursing through his veins as his gaze was transfixed by that smile. Yep, his vow about her not getting to him was rapidly flying out the window. Yep, he should have found a nice reliable, *old* guide for her. That way he could have kept his sanity.

KATE LAY AWAKE long after she and Jared rolled up in their respective sleeping bags for the night. Sleeping out under the stars was nothing new to her. Sleeping out under the stars with Jared not more than six or seven feet away from her was very new.

"What happened to him?" she whispered to the air. "What happened to *me* where he was concerned? Good going, Kate, a lot of questions with no answers. And why are you just sitting back and letting him do the leading? You're the one in charge, not him. This is your expedition, not his. So quit acting with your hormones and show the man who's boss."

She rolled over onto her side, forgetting until it was too late that rolling over on that side meant she was facing Jared. He lay sprawled on his back, his soft snores reaching her ears. Pumped up with new resolve, she glared at him and promised herself to rifle his saddlebags first chance she got to find just how much more chocolate candies he might have hidden in them. Yes, sir, now that she had made up her mind, there was no stopping her.

Chapter Eight

"Shake a leg, O'Malley, the sun will be up soon and we've got a long haul ahead of us." A cheerful shout interrupted her peaceful sleep.

Kate rolled over on her back and forced open her heavy eyelids. After falling asleep not more than a couple hours ago, thanks to thinking about Jared, she was not feeling very sociable.

"People have been shot for having such a bright disposition first thing in the morning," she said, carefully enunciating each word. She sat up, pushing her hands through her hair. She could feel the strands that escaped her braid during the night caress her cheeks and knew she probably looked like a hag with tangled hair, no makeup—she never bothered with any when she was out in the field—not to mention morning breath. Jared looked disgustingly wonderful, even with one day's beard and a wrinkled shirt.

"I fixed breakfast. Freeze-dried scrambled eggs," he said.

"Oh, goody, my favorite." She pushed aside the top part of her sleeping bag and slowly got to her feet. Bracing her hands against the small of her back she arched her body in an attempt to relieve the nagging pains in various parts of her body.

Jared watched her, amusement lighting his eyes. "I thought you were used to roughing it?"

"I am," she said loftily, trying not to wince when one ache escalated when she twisted to one side. "I always do a few stretches in the morning to get the blood pumping." She looked down at her sleeping bag and debated about rolling it up now or waiting until after breakfast. After breakfast won. She gratefully accepted the tin mug filled with hot coffee Jared held out to her. "How far do you think we'll get today?"

"We're going to look someone up first."

"Visiting friends isn't part of the deal, Wyatt," she pointed out. "We have a search ahead of us that isn't easy considering what we have to work with and our time is limited."

"Which is exactly why we need to see and talk to a certain person first," he argued. "Someone we can trust."

Her eyes glittered. "I thought no one could be trusted out here."

"True, but we can trust this man to a certain extent."

Kate forked up some of the eggs into her mouth and forced them down. She decided they were about as tasty as sawdust. "A touch of dill wouldn't have hurt."

"Sorry I don't have your culinary expertise." He ate his own eggs as if they were to be his last meal. "Just be glad I'm willing to do my share of cooking."

"My, my, didn't we get up out of the wrong side of the sleeping bag this morning." She was pleased to discover his mood wasn't as cheery as she first thought it was. Perhaps his sleep wasn't any more peaceful than hers.

"Eat up, O'Malley, we've got a lot of miles to cover today if you want to get even close to Weaver's Needle by the schedule we set up. And you've still got to gather up your stuff."

Kate set her plate down and faced him with her hands braced on her hips. "Gramps may have been right that you should be the leader since you're familiar with the area, but that doesn't mean you have to act like a marine drill sergeant."

"My dad was in the air force, not the marines," he countered, looking her square in the eye. He stood over her, nose touching nose. "So get to it, O'Malley, or I'll leave you behind."

She opened her mouth, prepared to blast him, when something unknown closed it for her. As she faced Jared she felt something hot and primitive zing between them and was positive, for just a very brief second, that primitive sensation came from Jared. It was nothing more than a flicker in his eyes, but she was certain it was there. Her saner side pointed out it was probably nothing more than her imagination. She turned away because she wasn't prepared to deal with that kind of situation just now.

"Give me ten minutes," she said quietly, quickly stepping back.

She wasn't surprised when Jared said nothing. After all, what was there to say?

"I GUESS INDIAN TRIBES could hide in these mountains for years and no one would ever find them." Kate was the first to break the silence as they rode up the steep trail. She was glad she had thoroughly rubbed the sun block on her skin so it wouldn't burn under the intense sun. She made a mental reminder to reapply it in a couple hours.

"Rogers Canyon, deep in the mountains, has some well preserved Salados cliff dwellings," Jared replied. "The Pimas, Hohokam and the Apaches later invaded the area."

"Do you ever teach that time period to your classes?" she asked curiously.

He nodded. "I spend a quarter on Indian history, although I don't feel I have enough time to go into the kind of detail I'd like to. I wouldn't mind teaching it as a course itself, but Dr. Phillips isn't too keen on it. Old Toby knows a lot more about the history of the area than I do, and I've interviewed him extensively in the past and recorded as much as I could."

"Is that who we're going to meet with today?"

"Yes, you'll discover he's a law unto himself." Jared chuckled. "He's convinced the government is another name for the devil, modern conveniences are for wimps and the only decent drink is good Scotch. He's been a miner up here for about sixty years."

"Sounds as if he and Gramps would get along beautifully," Kate commented.

"They would." Jared halted and looked around, a frown creasing his forehead.

"What's wrong?"

He held up his hand indicating silence.

Kate opened her own senses, reaching out for anything that might be out of the ordinary. But the air was so silent it was eerie, not even a hint of a breeze to cool the heat that shimmered around them. Still, something didn't seem right to her. She had no idea just what, but she could feel it deep in her bones even if there was nothing tangible to back up her feelings.

"Something doesn't feel right," she whispered.

Jared half turned in his saddle to look at her. "What do you feel?" His voice was so quiet only her sharp hearing caught his words.

"Something's wrong, but I'm not sure what."

He nodded. "It's too quiet," he agreed. "Maybe Toby will have some insight. We've got another couple hours or so before we reach his cabin. He has an underground spring so we'll be able to get some fresh water. Do me a favor and stay alert."

Kate dug out her pistol from her saddlebag and pushed it into the waistband of her jeans under her shirt, nestling the metal against her spine. She was glad she had already strapped her knife sheath to her leg. As they started up the trail she couldn't help humming under her breath in a weak effort to break the tension rising between them.

Jared easily recognized the tune and laughed. "If you pull out a fedora and bullwhip I'm leaving."

"It seemed appropriate." She looked around, but couldn't see anything out of the ordinary. "Let's talk," she said suddenly.

"I thought that's what we've been doing."

"I mean really talk. Serious stuff. It's not as if we don't have the time. You know, we attended faculty functions and went out at least once a week, but we never really talked about how we felt about people and things."

"We talked. I just don't think we listened to each other," he said quietly.

"Is that what I did? Not listened when you talked to me about J.C.?"

Jared's back stiffened, even though her question wasn't accusing, but there was a hint of hurt in it. "No, that wasn't one of the things I told you."

"Will you ever tell me why?"

"When the time is right."

"Well, until then I think I'll call you J.C. all the time. It suits you now. So, J.C., how much longer to your old friend Toby's cabin?" She deliberately raised her voice.

Jared's mutter was decidedly profane.

She cupped her hand behind her ear. "What's that? I didn't quite hear you."

Jared repeated his words in a louder voice that bordered on defiance.

"Why, sir, you've sorely wounded my sensibilities using such nasty words." Kate affected a syrupy southern drawl.

"You don't have any sensibilities, so just shut the hell up so we can get to Toby's before dark," he snarled.

Kate silently decided once they returned to civilization she was going to write up a very suggestive advertisement and list Jared's name and telephone number in every personals column in a five-state area. And that would only be the beginning. Over the years she had learned some painful ancient curses that would come in handy.

Their several rest stops were made in silence, Jared stalking off and Kate making sure to take off in the opposite direction.

It was going to be a very long trip.

"TOBY'S CABIN LOOKS LIKE something out of a John Wayne western," Kate commented, as they paused on a small rise, overlooking a wooden cabin with an attached lean-to. It was almost dusk and her aching body felt as if it had been in the saddle for months instead of hours. She shifted her weight. At least her rear end had finally turned numb.

"It's older than we are," he replied, the ease in his manner indicating his earlier anger was forgotten.

"I thought no one was allowed to live in the mountains any longer."

"To be technical, no one is, but there's a few old-timers who really have nowhere else to go and in their own way they do some good, because they can keep their eyes on areas the rangers can't always patrol. The rangers stop in and check on them periodically and they also keep a close eye on each other. It's figured they aren't doing any harm, so they're allowed to live out their years where they've been the happiest." He indicated to their right. "There's a trail over here we can follow down."

They had barely reached the perimeter of the property when a mangy dog of indeterminate parentage ran out of the lean-to barking loudly at the visitors.

"All right, mutt, all right!" a raspy voice shouted before a grizzled looking elderly man shambled out of the cabin with a double-barreled shotgun cradled in his arms. "You better be a friend or expect to have your private parts shot off!"

"It's me, Toby, J.C. Wyatt," Jared yelled, holding his horse's reins tightly to control his unease as the elderly dog snapped at his legs. "You want to call off that sorry excuse of a watchdog of yours so we can dismount without getting a piece taken out of our butts?"

"Mutt, heel," Toby ordered. He peered nearsightedly in Kate's direction. "Who's your friend?"

"Kate O'Malley, Toby Waters," Jared made the introductions. "Toby, Kate's a teacher like me and wanted to see the mountains. So naturally, I wanted her to see the mountain's institution, namely you." He dismounted and walked over to the packhorse. He reached into one of the bags and pulled out a bottle, which he tossed in Toby's direction. The old man was swift in catching it with one hand while the other held on to the rifle.

"Women are nothin' but trouble," Toby muttered, walking inside the cabin, the bottle cradled lovingly in his arm.

"My God, it's Gabby Hayes in person," Kate muttered, also dismounting.

"Yeah, pretty much. Toby leaves his teeth out more than he leaves them in. He says they're too much of a nuisance," Jared replied, loosening his mount's saddle. "He's rude because he doesn't know how to be any other way. I think he believes it makes him seem more of a colorful character."

"He wasn't rude enough to reject that bottle of Chivas you gave him."

"I said he was rude, not dumb."

Toby appeared in the doorway. "You gonna stand out there jawin' all day or come in and tell me why you're here?" he shouted.

"We'll be in as soon as we unsaddle the horses," Jared replied.

"They can stay in the lean-to as long as they don't disturb Bertha." He disappeared into the dark interior.

"Let me guess, Bertha is his mule."

He nodded. "She's older than time and meaner than a rattlesnake."

Kate lowered her voice. "Why exactly are we here? Other than dropping off some booze?"

He kept his voice equally low as he pulled off the saddle and draped it over a nearby split rail. "To get information."

Caution darkened her eyes. "Jared, he can't know why we're here."

"I'm not going to tell him the whole story, but he will know what people are in the area, how many and how dangerous they might be," he informed her. "Toby knows more about the mountains than even the rangers and cartographers know. I want information that maps and the rangers can't give me. Information I can only get from Toby."

"How do we know we can trust him to keep his mouth shut about our reason for being here?"

"Toby knows secrets he'll take to his grave. I trust him and that's enough for me. If you don't like it, too bad."

Kate swallowed the heated words threatening to spill out. "Then we better finish up here and get inside to see if he's willing to share his Scotch."

The horses were rubbed down and stabled, and Kate and Jared walked toward the cabin. The moment they entered Kate couldn't help but notice it probably hadn't been cleaned since the day it was built.

"Interesting aroma," she said.

"Toby once said he had been married to a woman who believed in dusting a table every five minutes so he left her so he could have a place where he could live the way he wanted to," Jared said under his breath. "Nights when he wants more company than Mutt, he brings in Bertha."

"Now why am I not surprised?"

Toby eyed Kate suspiciously. "O'Malley's an Irish name. You don't look all that Irish."

"I've got the temper, the love for good whiskey and the talent for blarney," she replied. "My grandfather, Shamus, once said that's all that's required, especially the love for good whiskey."

Toby chortled. "Sounds as if you're a good match for J.C. here. Can you shoot?"

"I always hit what I aim at, although the staff at one shooting range got a little upset when I always hit the silhouette target below the waist. I always felt it was more effective than hitting someone in the heart."

Jared coughed and immediately reached for the Scotch bottle, drinking deeply without the benefit of a glass.

"Sure hope you brought more'n one bottle," Toby grumbled, snatching back the bottle and taking a quick swig, sighing happily as the potent alcohol hit his stomach. He turned to Kate. "Suppose you want your share, too?"

"Only if Jared brought a second and third bottle."

The old man grinned, his toothless mouth wrinkled in a grimace. "You might be all right."

Kate looked at the dog who was resting his muzzle on her knee. "Mutt seems to have accepted me."

"If he drools too much, just push him away. He's old and forgets he's not as lovable as he used to be. Least he don't have fleas."

Setting the dog to one side, she got up and prowled around. She found a tin cup in the corner of the cabin set aside as a kitchen and rinsed it out before pouring herself a few inches of whiskey. She returned to her chair where Mutt promptly dropped his wet muzzle on her knee as she listened to the two men talk about past visits.

"How's it been going lately?" Jared asked casually, passing the Scotch bottle to Toby.

"Quiet for now. Pretty soon the greenhorns will come on their hikes and get lost. Some die of heatstroke and thirst if not bit by a rattler or stumble over a gila monster," Toby rumbled. "Old Quint fell and broke his leg 'bout a month ago. Luckily, a couple rangers came by and found him the next day. The doctors said he can't stay by himself no more, so he's going to live with his daughter in Philadelphia. He figures she'll stop him from cussin' and drinkin', but least ways he won't be alone."

"Do you have any family besides your wife?" Kate asked.

He shook his head. "Nope, I figure we were both too mean to have kids. Oh, I had a brother, but he died ten years ago. It don't bother me, though. I like it here. I got my Social Security to pay for food and whiskey. Don't need nothin' else."

Kate thought of her grandfather and father, traveling the world, each studying history and cultures in his own way, not needing anyone. Both had been married, but their choice of wives hadn't worked out, so they had gone on alone. And how she continued the family tradition of traveling the world alone. Funny, it was beginning not to seem as fulfilling anymore.

Jared watched Kate seated in the rickety old chair, looking as comfortable as she had in Shamus's study. This was why she was so successful in her work; she could easily fit into any society. Her face was dirty, her nose sunburned and her braid was coming undone. She drank Scotch out of a battered tin mug and her booted feet were propped up on a scarred wood table that looked as if it would be reduced to kindling at any moment. A dog that looked as old as Toby drooled on her knee, the firelight played over her face and he doubted she ever looked as lovely to him, as she did then. Looking at her, he suddenly realized the idea of not letting her get to him didn't seem all that good.

Jared hadn't expected their trip to be easy and two days into the mountain backed him up on that supposition. Still, he couldn't have wished for a more able companion than Kate.

"Have you seen Harry lately?" he asked Toby, quickly explaining to Kate that Harry was one of the forest rangers.

"He stopped by about a week ago when he was making his rounds." Toby squinted into the firelight. "He asked me if I'd heard anything strange lately."

Jared's senses were on alert. "Strange?"

The older man nodded. "He said that Leo over near that one canyon told him he was hearing big birds in the middle of the night but only when there was no moon. He thought for sure Apache ghosts had come back to finish some old battle. Harry asked me if I'd heard anything like that, but like I told him, I sleep pretty deep at night and Mutt's hearing ain't what it used to be. Though I did see something weird one morning around dawn."

Kate leaned forward. "What did you see?"

Toby hunched his shoulders. "Don't make no sense to me, but one morning around dawn I saw a strange bird flying off a ways. I never saw a bird like that before. I could tell right away it wasn't a hawk or turkey buzzard. Nope, this bird was green and yellow. I never saw a green bird that size around here. Leastways, never a bird like that." He nodded his head to reinforce his statement.

Kate's eyes met Jared's in silent communication. Either the old man had drunk too much whiskey the night before or his eyesight was worse than they thought.

"Now don't you look as if I've lost my marbles, 'cause I ain't ready to be put away yet." Toby was irritated by Kate's skepticism. "I had my spectacles on when I saw that bird. And I tell you it was green and yellow. It was a bright green, almost the color of fresh grass."

"Sound like anything you've ever seen?" Kate asked Jared.

He shook his head. "I had hoped you'd have an idea."

"Ask me about the avian life in ancient Egypt and I can give you a boring dissertation."

"Egypt, you say?" Toby's interest was piqued. "You know all about those pharaohs and Cleopatra and such?"

"I've studied the tombs and their artifacts," she replied.

His toothless mouth stretched in a broad smile. "Missy, I could keep you here a long time asking you about the kings and mummies. Did all that mumbo jumbo they did back then really preserve their bodies?"

She nodded. "And to this day their methods are still pretty much a mystery to us. Examining a mummy is a tricky proposition because if great care isn't taken it turns to dust the moment it's exposed to the air."

"Well, if that don't beat all," he said, slapping his knee. His blurred eyes shining, he barraged Kate with questions that she happily answered.

Seeing they were well occupied, Jared quietly excused himself and walked outside, with Mutt ambling along behind him. He stopped at the split rail fence and braced one foot on the bottom rail, his crossed arms on the top one as he looked up into the night sky.

"Apache ghosts reliving their battles on moonless nights," he mused. "Green birds flying during the day. What else are we going to find out there? Jacob Waltz's ghost guarding the mine and shooting us on sight?" He looked at the cabin, the windows softly lit from inside. Bits and pieces of Kate's and Toby's conversation filtered out. It wasn't difficult for him to realize that she had captivated the ornery hermit, just as she had captivated him.

"You really saw that Pompeii that was buried by a volcano thousands of years ago?" Toby questioned Kate as they worked together to fix dinner.

"Well, it wasn't as buried as some of the nearby cities so it was easy to excavate the buildings," she explained.

He leaned forward. "I once read there's dirty paintings on the wall that the guides won't let the women see."

She chuckled. "They're not as dirty as some would have you believe. Actually, most of the paintings were found in the local brothels and they're considered more of erotic art. And for an extra fee, the guides would let anyone view them."

Toby shook his head in wonder. "Now why would a pretty young thing like yourself want to dig around in the dirt looking for dead bodies and broken pots and such?"

"I enjoy it because I can't envision any other kind of life," she said simply. "My grandfather sought out ancient civilizations and legends and I caught the fever early. Just as you prefer living out here with only a dog and mule for company, I prefer to dig around looking for dead bodies and broken pots." A small smile touched her lips. She had no idea Jared stood in the doorway hearing her words and the conviction ringing in her voice. The expression on his face was as bleak as the middle of winter.

"You're searchin' for old Jacob's mine, ain't ya?" Toby asked, just before they parted for the night.

Jared laughed. "The Lost Dutchman Mine is as much a legend as you are, Toby."

He shook his head. "So was that Italian knife Kate's grandpa found. And that South American war idol Kate discovered was a legend, too, until she proved it was real. Yep, you're lookin' for the mine," he stated. He cocked his head in Kate's direction. "If anybody can find it, you two can."

KATE AND JARED chose to lay their sleeping bags outside that night near the lean-to.

"Ah, the coyote choir is serenading us again," Kate murmured sleepily, unzipping her sleeping bag.

"Which is why we're out here to keep an eye on the horses," he replied.

"Toby doesn't seem to worry about Bertha."

"He doesn't have to. She's too tough even for the hungriest coyote. A coyote sneaked down here one night looking for an easy meal and Bertha took a chunk out of his hide. They've pretty well stayed away since."

Kate wiggled her way under the down folds. "You were right, Toby would get along with Gramps. They're a lot alike."

"Toby sure took a shine to you."

She smiled. "Because I cooked dinner?"

"No, because you drank straight Scotch without a whimper, because you didn't turn up your nose at his cabin and because you didn't try to clean the place up. You looked at the man, not the surroundings. It's things like that that's important to him."

Kate chuckled. "I'm not sure that was all of it. I wonder if it couldn't have been my willingness to talk to him about Greek erotic art and mummies that captivated him more."

"That and because you promised to tell him more about an ancient Egyptian curse that will turn his ex-wife into a sand flea."

Kate turned on her side, cradling her head against her hand as she stared at Jared's silhouette against the night sky. "You're right, that had to have turned the trick."

Chapter Nine

Kate didn't know what exactly jolted her awake. Only that her eyes flew open and she didn't have to turn her head to know that Jared was missing from his sleeping bag.

She squirmed around until she found her boots, which she'd pushed to the bottom of her sleeping bag when she got in. She quickly shook them upside down before tugging them on; just because they were down there didn't mean something hadn't crawled in. She slid out of the warm depths of her sleeping bag. She shivered in the chilly air as she tugged on her jacket and picked up her gun. Surveying the area she noticed that Toby's front door stood open.

"There's only one explanation—aliens came down and abducted them for research. I sure feel sorry for the aliens." She made her way up a small rise where two shadowy figures and a dog lay on the ground. When one of the figures turned, she held out a hand. "Don't shoot, I'm one of the good guys."

"What are you doing here?" Jared demanded in a low growl, grasping her hand and pulling her down beside him.

"Probably the same thing you are," she replied in a low voice. "What's up?"

Toby touched Jared's arm. "Hear 'em? This must be what Leo said he heard."

Both Kate and Jared lifted their heads, their expressions like those of animals catching a scent that spelled danger and trying to guess the direction.

"I know what I think it sounds like. How about you?" Jared asked in her ear, his breath warm on her skin.

Kate nodded, only too aware of the male body lying close beside her. Jared wasn't wearing a shirt and she could feel his bare chest nudging her arm. She wondered if he wasn't cold in the chilly desert night air. All she had to do was turn her hand upward and she could touch those same muscles, caress, stroke, incline her head to— She shook her head in quick denial. Her common sense said this was not a good time. Her body reminded her that all she needed to do was get rid of Toby and it would be an excellent time!

"If I didn't know better I'd say it was a helicopter. I thought you told me it was illegal to fly over these mountains?" She silently damned her voice for coming out so husky. She hoped Jared would think she was still half-asleep and not think she was having altogether unbusinesslike thoughts. Little did she know those immaculate oxford shirts had hidden a chest any sane woman would lust after.

"It is, but if the stakes are high enough for something...." Nothing more needed to be said.

She frowned. "But from what direction?"

Jared shook his head, looking frustrated. "Your guess is as good as mine. The surrounding mountains make it next to impossible to give an idea, not to mention where it even comes from."

"It has to be what Leo heard," Toby interjected.

Kate tipped her head to one side and held up her hand indicating silence. "Listen."

The faint music floating through the air was eerie to the three listeners, as were the softly spoken chants that followed.

"Spirits of warriors," Jared muttered. "The kind no one wants to tangle with because they will battle anyone who dares to cross their hallowed ground. There are so many curses connected with these mountains a lot of people don't dare investigate." He seemed to hold his breath for a moment then chuckled and shook his head. "Whoever is sending out those chants doesn't know their history."

"What do you mean?" Kate asked, feeling the chills chase across her spine at the sound. Many times she had heard similar sounds that meant just the same thing; the dead were protecting their own and no mortal man dared to interfere without loss of his own life.

He turned to her, his teeth flashing white in the dark of night. "I'll tell you one thing. Those so-called Indian chants aren't from any Indian tribes I'm familiar with. They sound more like something out of Hollywood's central casting."

Kate grabbed his arm. "So what we're hearing is someone trying to scare away what few residents there are and any tourists who might happen to stumble into the wrong area."

"Exactly." He began to expound on what to listen for in an Indian chant until Kate cut him off.

"Remember? I usually slept through any history class that dealt with a time period within the past thousand years," she reminded him.

Jared grimaced. "If you'd been in my class you wouldn't have slept."

"No, I probably would have done my homework for one of my other classes." Kate looked up. "Listen, the chanting stopped. And it appears the helicopter disappeared at the same time."

Jared frowned. "Yeah, as suddenly as it started, too."

The three made their way down the hill to Toby's cabin where he suggested some coffee.

"Did Harry mention when Leo first heard these sounds, Toby?" Jared asked, sorting through the collection of maps he'd dug out of his saddlebags.

"Nope, just that he heard them, but I have an idea it's been more than once or Harry wouldn't have asked me about it," he replied, setting a battered coffeepot on the wood stove.

"If it's more than once, there has to be an excellent reason for someone to basically sneak out here and set up something so elaborate. What could be so important that someone would go to the expense of using a helicopter to fly into the mountains, not to mention risk getting caught. And why use a tape recording of Indian chants in hopes of scaring off the people?" Kate asked.

Jared looked up. "The only obvious answer is gold. If someone found the Lost Dutchman Mine and didn't want to share their find with the government the only way to mine it would be in secret—at night. Packing in supplies by mules would be risky, what with the rangers keeping track, so flying them in would be their only alternative. And doing it on moonless nights lessens their chances of getting caught," Jared said grimly.

Kate leaned forward. "If so, then we have to get there before it's too late."

"You really want the gold that bad?" Toby asked.

She shook her head. "Not the gold. Just proof of the mine's existence."

"Why would your grampa be interested in somethin' around here? 'Pears he only looked for treasure in other countries, and from what you told me, it was only real old treasure."

"Yes, but this particular story has interested him for many years and he always meant to come out here and explore the area for the mine but too many commitments kept him from following through. Now he can't do anything too arduous, so I do it for him," she told the old man.

Toby shook his head. "Thing is, there's more than just the mine." He studied both people sitting at the table before turning to Jared. "She know about the curse on the mine and in these mountains? A lot of people have died 'cause of those old curses."

"No curse would stop her," Jared admitted. "She'd just counteract it with one of her own. My money's on her."

"When my grandfather was in his late twenties, he searched for a rare Aztec ceremonial dagger," Kate spoke up. "When he found it he was told that he would never be a man again if he dared to take it from its rightful place. To date he's never sung soprano nor has any woman in his life complained about his masculinity. We respect curses, because they're usually a part of a people's religion, but we can't allow them to stop us from our work."

"Ever have any curses put on you?" Jared asked her.

"Not so far, but that's probably because I've learned enough to defend myself."

Jared shuddered. "I'll behave."

THE SUN BARELY PEEKED over the mountains when Kate and Jared saddled their horses.

"Maybe you need me to go along with you," Toby offered, watching them. "I know these mountains better'n even you, Jared."

The younger man smiled and shook his head. "Thanks for the offer, Toby, but I really could use you here. If there's trouble I'd like to know we can hightail it back here. You were smart enough to build in an area that's difficult to ambush. We may need it."

Toby stared at them, looking more than a little sad that he just might be missing out on the action, but slightly mollified by Jared's suggestion. "If there's no trouble you be back here in six days or I'll come after you," he warned.

"If we can't get back in time we'll find a way to send you word," Jared promised.

"You better." The older man wagged a finger in Jared's face. "And you take care of this lady. She might seem capable, but she's still a woman."

Kate smiled at Toby's old-fashioned dictum and hugged him for his obvious caring. Toby blushed and blustered but didn't push her away.

"Now don't forget you promised to find some real good curses for my ex," he reminded her.

"I'll search through my notes and find the best ones for you," she vowed with a wink, then kissed him on the cheek.

"You two make a real nice couple," Toby told them. He scowled at Jared. "You're gonna marry her, ain't ya? Don't you try and compromise that girl's reputation."

Jared shot an amused glance at an embarrassed Kate. "I won't."

"You'd better not, Wyatt. This trip is purely business. Once we return to the university we plan to go our separate ways."

Toby shook his head, exasperated with the two stubborn people. "Keep hold of her, Jared. Kate's nothing like that old battleax I once hooked up with." With nary a wave of the hand, he stalked off. "Next time, bring some of that Johnny Walker with you," he called over his shoulder. "I'm due for a change."

"He'd be better off with a new liver," Kate whispered to Jared as she slid her boot into the stirrup and pulled herself up into her saddle. Jared secured an extra saddlebag behind her. Considering what they had heard in the early morning hours, they had decided it would be better to leave the packhorse behind.

"He wouldn't agree with you. Plus he doesn't get alcohol as often as he likes to have people think he does." He mounted his horse and led the way up the rise they had scouted from the previous night.

"Something tells me we just might be heading in the direction of our midnight visitor," Kate commented.

"If we're lucky we are." Jared looked around before settling his hat over his eyes. "That frighten you?"

"Nothing scares me," she insisted.

"Yeah, I figured that, except I think there's one thing that does scare you." He kept his tone deliberately light.

She arched an eyebrow. "Oh, really, and what might that be?"

"Me."

Kate dared not argue that point. She feared it would be one argument she'd lose.

Realizing she'd forgotten to apply her sun block before they left, she dug a tube out of her saddlebag and dabbed it on her forehead, cheeks and nose then smeared the almond-scented cream across her face and lips.

Catching the exotic scent in the air, Jared turned his head. "Most suntan lotions I've used smelled like coconut, not almonds."

"This is something I picked up overseas and have used for years," she replied. "You're welcome to use some if you think you need it. It also keeps the skin from drying out."

His eyes scanned every inch of her skin, noting the light gold tone and the three freckles dotting her nose. The sun block was excellent but not perfect. He didn't mind because he was intrigued by the freckles. "So that's how you've managed to work out in the sun for so many years and not end up looking like leather."

Her breath caught in her throat from his studied gaze. "I've picked up a few tricks here and there. This was something a French archaeologist Gramps used to work with told me about. She had the most beautiful skin you could imagine and I couldn't understand how she could work outdoors for so many years and not look years older." Her fingers trembled as she held up the tube. "This was one of her secrets," she said huskily.

Jared kneed his mount to move closer to her. Kate held out the tube, thinking he meant to take it from her. Instead, he ran the back of his hand down her cheek perilously close to her slightly parted lips.

"If I used it do you think my skin would end up as soft as yours?" he whispered.

"You, ah, you might need more than one tube," she finally managed to say, her gaze snared by his.

Jared's fingers lingered on her chin. "Might be better to save it for you." He plucked the tube from her nerveless fingers and squeezed some onto his fingers then rubbed it carefully over his face.

By the time he moved to ride in front of Kate, she was certain all oxygen had left her lungs.

She wondered how long she would last before she gave in and attacked the man. At this rate, it wouldn't be long at all. Her sweaty fingers gripped the reins so tightly, her knuckles turned white.

"He's making me crazy," she muttered.

She was determined to not let Jared get to her during this trip. She was finally learning why it was so difficult to do. Just as her grandmother and mother succumbed to the O'Malley men, she was falling for a Wyatt who proved to be just as dangerous.

"Kate, we're going to have to be doubly alert from now on." Jared's quiet voice reached her ears. "That pig sticker of yours in easy reach?"

"Yes, and I also have my pistol under my shirt against my back," she replied in an equally low voice.

He cursed under his breath. "Let's just hope we won't need any of them."

"Jared, I've been in dangerous situations before. I know how to take care of myself," she told him.

He only nodded. He already knew she could take care of herself.

THE DEEPER THEY RODE into the mountains the more uneasy Jared grew. He had ridden here since he was a teenager, but he had never felt as uneasy as he did now. The prickling sensation along his shoulder blades refused to go away. The fact that he had Kate along didn't ease the situation one bit. He knew she could take care of herself, as she enjoyed reminding him, but that didn't stop him from worrying just the same. No matter how well she could defend herself, she was still a woman and the prime target for any creep in a battle.

"I don't suppose you'd consider returning to Toby's cabin and waiting for me there," Jared said.

"Not really. If there's something out there, I want to be there to see what it is." She pulled the bright blue cotton bandanna from around her neck and twisted it across her forehead, tying it in back. "After all, who knows, maybe some warriors from West Hollywood did a bit more traveling than we thought."

"You're right. You did sleep through your history classes."

"Just American history."

"I hope your instructor flunked you," he grumbled, furious with the idea that any student would so blatantly disregard a class. "I know I would have if you pulled that in my class."

"Oh, I bet you would have, if said student sat in the front row wearing a very sexy miniskirt," she teased.

Jared pulled on the reins and half turned, his face dark with anger. "Are you saying you used your instructor's fascination for your legs to pass a class?"

Her mouth dropped open in shock. Then just as suddenly she recovered and stunned laughter replaced her first emotion. "I can't believe you would even think I would do such a thing. I knew you were serious about your work, but this is ridiculous. Not to mention my instructor was a woman with a husband who resembled Wally Cox.''

He pulled off his hat and ran his hand through his hair, the damp ends sticking to his fingers. "Look, I'm sorry. I don't have an excuse except that it's hot, I'm mad as hell because I'm afraid I could be getting us into more than we bargained for. And we might run into something we can't get out of."

"Because of the helicopter and so-called Indian chants we heard?"

Jared nodded. "It doesn't feel right, Kate. None of it makes any sense."

"And if that helicopter is making the rounds where we're going, we could end up in even more trouble," she guessed.

He grimly wished he could persuade her to return to Toby's cabin before it was too late.

"You got it."

"Then it's a good thing there's two of us to watch each other's backs," Kate told him.

Jared didn't feel optimistic.

As THEY SET UP CAMP that evening, it was understood they would remain on the alert for anything unusual.

"There's something about freeze-dried chow mein that goes beyond the realm of nutrition." Kate sighed, dipping her fork into her dinner. "Sorry, I didn't have any herbs that would help this. Although now I'm seriously wondering if a few cups of oregano wouldn't have improved it."

Jared sipped his coffee. "I have to admit you've been able to make these meals a great deal more palatable with those herbs and spices you brought along. There've been times in the past I actually held my nose while trying to eat this stuff.''

Kate put her plate to one side. ''Why do we do it, Jared? How many years have we traveled off to the middle of nowhere to search for something no one has seen for perhaps centuries? We battle the elements, sometimes lack of food, people who don't want us there, not to mention curses heaped on us,'' she added whimsically. ''Still, we continue looking for that next rainbow. Why?''

''It's simple, we have nothing to hold us at home,'' he said. ''We have no one to love, to share our lives with, to show us there's more to life than ancient statues and cities, so we bury our innermost feelings in our work and use it as a substitute for the real thing. That's why.''

''You really know how to get to the heart of the matter, don't you?''

''No, I just believe in speaking the truth.'' His gaze captured hers. ''Which you need to do, too.''

Kate felt caught within the spell of Jared's deep sapphire eyes, the irises highlighted by the orange-red brilliance from the small camp fire he had built. She felt the itch in her palm to reach out and caress his cheek, to find out just how a several-days-old beard felt to the touch. She cradled the hand with her other palm, rubbing it furiously as if to rid it of the traitorous feeling.

''We needed to talk like this before,'' she said softly, feeling confused by all the strange feelings flowing through her body. ''Perhaps we would have understood each other better from the beginning.''

''We understood each other well enough to discuss marriage. You, the ultimate rebel, decided to marry this uptight conservative. To do that we must have understood something.''

Kate shifted uncomfortably, feeling his words too close to home. ''When you have an extremely liberal family you have to either keep up the image or go the opposite way. I guess I was trying to do both.''

''Just as the son of an air force major has to keep up appearances,'' Jared said. ''No long hair, no offbeat clothing, no lewd behavior, good grades in school, be prepared to pack up and move at a moment's notice.''

''And you didn't like it,'' she guessed.

He shrugged. ''I saw a lot of the world, but I also made a lot of friends and ended up leaving them when Dad was transferred to another base. Pretty soon it was easier to just not make friends. When I began to study local history and customs more than learning about my own country's, I started ordering books on American history and got hooked on the subject.''

''Is that why you don't care to travel outside the United States? And you probably can't understand why I do enjoy it when I grew up pretty much the same way you did,'' Kate went on. ''There's one difference, Jared. I love learning local legends and customs. I've studied people that are no longer on this earth and taught others what I learned. I've walked through homes that were lived in thousands of years ago, studied their art, their clothing, their way of life and I can't imagine doing anything else.''

''Your grandfather finally stopped to teach full time,'' he said quietly.

''Only because of his health,'' she insisted. ''Gramps would have preferred dying in the field than having to remain home all the time. It's only because he's been able to write his books that he's kept going. Archaeology is his life. Just as it's become mine."

If her words hurt him, he didn't betray it by a flicker of his eye. "Then why did you consider stopping field work to teach full time?"

She couldn't look at him. "You know why."

Jared stood and moved to sit beside her. "Pretend I'm not smart, and give me a clue," he coaxed, running his fingers down her arm.

Kate breathed deeply. "I think we're getting off the subject, Jared. We were talking about our childhoods. So, talk to me, what countries did you live in?"

"More than I cared to. Come on, tell me why you were willing to stop your fieldwork." His eyes narrowed. "Or was that what you thought I wanted to hear?"

Kate shifted her position so she faced him. "You want honesty, I'll give it to you. I'm not sure if it was nothing more than talk or not. We both know Gramps only had to mention he had something special for me to look for and I was ready and willing. This trip is a perfect example. So I guess I wasn't all that willing to settle down after all."

His jaw tightened. "You're right, a perfect example. An answer to your prayer on how to postpone our wedding."

"Meeting your alter ego was also part of it. And I'd like to remind you a wedding wasn't mentioned, only an engagement," she said hotly. "There's a big difference."

Some undefinable emotion flashed across Jared's face then disappeared just as quickly.

"You sure have a fixation with old J.C.," he murmured. "Maybe because he's so much like you." He leaned over her, dropping both hands to the ground to effectively trap her within his embrace. "Tell me something, Kate, if J.C. was here with you instead of Jared, would you be using two sleeping bags or one?" His coffee-scented breath warmed her skin. "Would you be more receptive to J.C. if he was here with you right now?"

She couldn't tear her eyes away. If she didn't know better she would have sworn his face had sharpened with need, his eyes hooded with desire. One thing she did know. This was not the same man she had started the trip with.

"Don't be silly," she croaked, then coughed to clear her throat. "You're one and the same."

"Am I?" His voice had deepened, husky with what Kate could only think of as raw lust. "Are you honestly sure about that?"

Kate was positive of only one thing: her blood pressure shot up thirty points just because of the way Jared looked at her chest, though there was hardly anything sexy about the checked cotton shirt she wore. Yet just the way he was looking at her sent some interesting signals along her nerves to her brain. Her tongue appeared and dampened her dry lips.

"Is this some kind of joke?" The moment she asked the question she knew it was a big mistake.

Jared lowered his head farther. "You tell me."

The moment his mouth covered Kate's she knew this was not a joke. No, if anything, Jared—correction, J.C.—was most serious. And just about the best kisser she had ever encountered.

Chapter Ten

Kate was certain she had died and gone to heaven. The kisses she had received from Jared before had been brief, almost impersonal pecks on the cheek or lips. Now she knew they had been more than impersonal; the rat had been holding back!

Jared definitely knew what he was doing. He nipped at Kate's lips until they parted enough for his tongue to slide inside.

"Relax," he murmured, nibbling his way along her jawline.

"That's easy for you to say," she gasped when he pressed his mouth over her pounding pulse point.

"Aren't you enjoying my . . . attentions?"

She planted her hands against his chest, but she couldn't come up with the strength to push him away. Not when it felt so good. Instead, her traitorous fingers investigated the hard ridges and planes covered by soft cotton.

"This is not a good idea," she breathed.

"What isn't?" His mouth explored a small patch of skin by her collarbone. "This?"

One hand rested just above the swell of her breast, perilously close to her hardening nipple. It didn't venture farther, which only served to drive Kate crazier. Her plan to not give in to Jared was rapidly dissipating.

"So which is it you prefer, darlin'?" he whispered, now feasting on her ear.

"Which what?" She was almost lost.

"Which man? Stuffy ole Jared or renegade J.C.?"

It took a moment for the question to sink into her muddled brain.

Kate's eyes flew open. While she felt as if all her willpower had flown out the window, Jared looked remarkably composed. It didn't take long for her heated blood to chill. She placed her hands against his chest and using every ounce of her strength she pushed hard.

She caught Jared unawares and he fell back hard on his buttocks. "Now what's wrong?"

She sat up straight. "You're a college professor, you figure it out." Her formerly warm voice turned icy cold.

"Pretend I'm dumb. Enlighten me."

She poked a finger in his shirt front. "You were testing me. Even before you kissed me you mentioned J.C. So you pretended to be J.C. and acted like him to see how I'd react."

Jared threw up his hands. "So I did something stupid. Sue me!"

Kate closed her eyes and counted to ten. "The best thing I did was call off our engagement." She stood and walked away from the camp.

"Don't go too far. No telling what could be out there," he called after her.

"Nothing can be worse than what's right here."

Kate stalked off, furious with the low-voiced laughter that followed her.

"As if I don't know the routine," she fumed, scanning the area. "I wish I could turn him into a dung beetle."

There was a small part of her, lurking under her fury, that grew a bit more hurt with each passing second.

"This trip is a disaster," she muttered to herself, resting on a rock. "We're already starting to fight, we probably won't even find any evidence of the mine and if we're lucky we'll get out of here before I shoot him in his mercenary heart." She suddenly moaned. "And as much as I want to murder him I love him."

She had no idea how long she sat there, feeling more miserable by the moment and wishing she could understand the tangled thoughts racing through her mind.

For the first time in her life, Kate wasn't able to get her way. Not that she had ever been spoiled, just that she was a strong-minded woman who worked hard for what she wanted and usually got it. While a part of her wanted Jared another part of her wasn't sure what she wanted. She forced herself to think of their expedition.

She sat alone for a while longer before finally realizing she wasn't accomplishing anything and returned to the camp fire. What she found was their dishes cleaned up and put away, the fire banked and Jared ensconced in his sleeping bag. Kate stood there watching him, furious that he could sleep so peacefully when she felt her insides pull together in painful knots.

Anything could have happened to me out there and he sleeps like a baby, not even worried about me, she silently fumed. Without thinking twice, she lightly kicked him in the side.

He rolled over and sat up, his gun in his hand. "What the hell is wrong with you?" he demanded, once he realized who his attacker was.

Kate walked over to her sleeping bag and sat down. "I can't sleep as long as you lie there snoring like a freight train."

JARED WAS ASTOUNDED that Kate could maintain a cool silence for almost twenty-four hours. He had been positive she would finally break down and say more than, "More coffee, please," or, "According to the map we'll need to go northwest here." Still, he should have known better after what Shamus had told him.

"That girl is about as stubborn as ten mules put together," Shamus had boomed. "She once got so mad at me she vowed she wouldn't speak to me for five days. I bet her she couldn't do it. She didn't speak to me for six days just to prove she could do it. And this is a girl who purely loves to talk!"

"Kate, we're going to have to talk things out sooner or later," Jared said after breakfast, desperate to break the cool silence between them.

She eyed him the way she might look at a stranger. "Why?"

"Because this silence between us is ridiculous." He cursed under his breath as he caught her cutting glance slicing through his body. "Okay, wrong choice of words. Still, we can't continue the trip this way. I had hoped we could use this time to really get to know each other."

She wasn't ready to give in. "I thought that was what we were doing back home."

"Hey there, is this a private party or can anyone join?"

At the sound of the strange voice, Jared and Kate jerked around, startled. They saw two bearded men astride two tired-looking horses.

"Mornin'," Jared greeted them with an easygoing smile.

"Mornin'." One of the men spoke to Jared, but kept his eyes trained on Kate. "You're the first human beings we've seen around here in quite awhile. Most people don't come out here on a camping trip. He studied their horses with narrowed eyes. "You from around here?"

"Nope, actually we're history teachers from back east," Jared said cheerfully, putting his arm around Kate's shoulders. "The wife and I decided to see the desert the way it should be seen. The way people saw it a hundred years ago. We figured we would have a lot of stories to tell our students this way."

The second man stared at Kate. "Never knew a married woman not to wear a wedding ring," he said in a slow voice.

"I prefer not to wear any jewelry when we travel," she replied smoothly. "That way I don't worry about losing it."

"Fine looking horses for people on a teacher's salary." The first man spoke again, his voice gravelly to the ear. "Not the usual rental nags we see around here."

"Yeah, we were lucky." Jared grinned, not really giving him an answer. "We're Jared and Katherine Carter. And you?"

"It don't pay to go too deep into these mountains, mister," the first man said, the words sounding ominous in the quiet morning air. "They're dangerous enough for those who know them, much less a couple of tenderfeet like you two. People every year ride into these mountains and never come out. If I had a pretty little wife like yours I'd want to be real careful where I go."

Jared nodded. "Oh, we got the latest maps from the rangers," he blithely assured the man. "We're hoping to get lots of pictures of the scenery and all these interesting cacti to take back home. Say, have you been out here for long? Perhaps you could tell us some good places to camp."

The man's unshaven face seemed to turn to stone. "Like I said, I'd be real careful if I were you. Phoenix or Tucson might be more to your liking. If you want history, take a drive down to Old Tombstone. You'll get plenty of the atmosphere you tourists like out there. There's been some talk of an old Indian curse around here killing off innocent folk just because they're where they oughtn't to be. As for myself, I don't think it's just talk." With his warning ringing in their ears, he clucked to his horse and urged his friend to follow. Kate was relieved when the second man rode away, as he had been mentally undressing her the entire time.

"You deserve an acting award for portraying the most greenhorn teacher I've ever seen," she said once both men disappeared over the hill. "At least you didn't call me 'the little woman.' Good thing, too. I would have hit you if you dared say it."

"Actually, that would have been my next phrase." He kept his attention centered on the direction the men had gone.

"Those two sleaze bags aren't your run-of-the-mill prospectors, are they?" she commented, looking in the same direction.

He shook his head. "Far from it. Did you see how their saddlebags were loaded down? Not to mention the shotguns they carried? Heavy-duty stuff. Those men meant business. They also meant to scare us off."

"And if we were the naive teachers you portrayed us to be, we would now be packing up and heading for civilization," Kate guessed.

Jared turned his head. "Right."

"What now, Wyatt?"

He began putting out their fire. "We'll take a different route to reach the Needle."

She helped by picking up the cooking utensils. "Is that the direction they were coming from?" She began loading one of the saddlebags.

"No, that was the direction they were heading for." Jared's words were crisp as he picked up his saddle and headed for his horse. "From now on, it's little or no fire and we may even want to consider standing night watches. We'll keep our guns in easy reach at all times and don't even think of having a tantrum and running off at night. We can't afford for them to find you away from me. Mr. Personality's friend looked as if he wanted to give you his reform-school pin."

Kate shuddered. "I realize conserving water means I probably don't smell as good as I should, but I'd say those two hadn't even looked at bathwater for the past twenty or thirty years." She wrinkled her nose.

Jared fixed her with a smile of approval. "You're taking this pretty well, considering the characters you've met so far."

"Are you kidding? I've met some that would make those last two look like little angels. Some of Shamus's contacts aren't of the best sort. Then there's Joaquin." She finished saddling her horse and after checking the cinch, picked up her saddlebags. "Do you think we'll find any rangers in the area to report those guys to?"

"Report them for what? Suggesting we see another part of the state? For not acting neighborly?" He shook his head. "All we can say is that we met up with a couple of strangers that weren't exactly friendly. There's no concrete proof that they're the bad guys. Or that there's even any around here."

Kate knew that line of reasoning only too well. She had heard almost the same words from Shamus a few times in the past.

"Well, Wyatt, let's show these guys we Easterners are made of tough stuff and don't scare off so easy," she drawled.

"That's my lady," he murmured, leaning over to drop a swift kiss on her lips. "Thanks for giving me an excuse to kiss you."

Kate's fingers itched to grab hold and prolong the contact, but she forced herself to hold back. She tried to remind herself this was not the time for kissing and groping, but it wasn't easy.

"Think they might have something to do with those Indian chants and nighttime helicopter rides?" Kate swung herself into the saddle before she gave in to her baser instincts.

"Could be," he said grimly. "But I wasn't about to ask."

Jared knew he was setting a killing pace that day, but he couldn't stop himself. As it was, if he had his way he would be leading them out of the mountains, not farther into them. He had met unsavory characters up here before, but they hadn't been anything like those two. He hoped to run into one of the rangers soon to see if he had any information on the men who'd visited their camp.

"You know, Jared, I'm used to hardship and all, but even Shamus took a break at least once a day," Kate called out.

He pulled on the reins. "Sorry."

Kate slid out of the saddle and grabbed her canteen. She drank sparingly then dampened her bandanna with a bit of water and used it to wipe her face.

Jared watched as she tipped some water into her cupped hand and offered it to her horse.

"You've been great about all this. It hasn't exactly been a picnic, but you haven't uttered one complaint."

She smiled. "You should try working with Shamus sometime. He can be a regular Simon Legree when he's in the field. When he's engrossed he forgets about all sorts of natural functions such as eating and sleeping." She stifled a yawn, turning to face him. "I just bet he's sitting at home going crazy wondering what's going on. Since he's been housebound he hasn't been easy to live with."

Jared took his hat off and used it to shade his face as he looked at the blue-white sky. "We better get going. I don't like us being out in the open for too long."

"I don't think they believed your story, anyway." Kate put away her canteen and swung herself into the saddle.

"Why not? I thought it sounded pretty reasonable. There's been plenty of teachers who've thought it would be exciting to experience history firsthand." He looked a bit offended.

She shook her head. "Our boots and clothing don't look new. As Mr. Personality pointed out, our horses aren't your run-of-the-mill rental nags and for all we know, they could have observed us for awhile before approaching us. Even our camp was too well organized for a couple of tenderfeet. It's obvious we know what we're doing."

He grimaced, seeing the truth to her words. "It's a good thing they didn't see that we were armed." He glanced around. "I'd really like to get a look at the maps, but not here. There's some caves a couple miles north of here. Let's head over there."

Kate nodded. "I won't argue against a little shade."

They didn't take long to reach what appeared to be nothing more than an opening in a mountain.

"Let me check it out first," Jared advised, dismounting and handing his reins to Kate. He grinned. "You have anything against spiders and all sorts of creepy crawlers?"

"I'm not fond of them, but they don't send me screaming."

Jared pulled out a heavy-duty flashlight and paused at the cave opening before slowly entering.

"Lions and tigers...." Kate chanted under her breath, looking over her shoulder.

"It's fine," he pronounced, appearing in the opening. "In fact, bring in the horses. There's enough room for them and that way no one can see us before we see them."

"And come to their own conclusions," she finished for him.

The moment Kate entered the cave opening she felt the temperature drop a good twenty degrees. Jared dropped to the ground, pulled the folded papers out of his shirt pocket and directed the lit flashlight onto the scrawled writing and lines. "I just know those two came from the Weaver's Needle vicinity," he said.

"Do you think they're also looking for the mine?" She dropped down beside him, her shoulder brushing his.

"Could be, if they haven't already found it. We might be better off spending the night here." His brow furrowed with thought. "As I told you before our main problem is the fact that the land has shifted so much over years that landmarks from years ago aren't around any longer or have changed drastically. With luck, we should be there in two days or so."

"You think we should just give it up, don't you?"

"No, but I want you to keep in mind that a lot of people have tried finding that mine, many of them dying in the attempt. There's no guarantee that we'll have any success just because Shamus has maps that no one else supposedly has," he replied, slipping his arm around her shoulders and drawing her close.

"It's bad enough that I have to be logical about this. I don't care for anyone else to have the same viewpoint. Shamus wouldn't give up this easily. I don't intend to, either," she protested.

Jared shook his head. "I don't think you realize the ramifications, Kate. Those two men were armed to the teeth and those weren't friendly warnings they gave us. There could be something going on out here they don't want us to know about. Shamus would understand if going back meant your safety. He doesn't expect us to get killed for some damn mine!" He gripped her arm in a punishing hold, his features sharply etched by the merciless beam from the flashlight now lying on the ground.

"I'm not going back, Jared." She slowly enunciated every word. "If you want to, fine. Just leave me the maps and I'll go on alone. I have a compass and I can take care of myself."

His hold tightened. "Can you? What if those two creeps had come up on you at night while you were sleeping? That one guy looked as if he wouldn't have minded having you for breakfast.''

Her eyes glittered with fury. "I've already proved to you that I'm able to handle anything that comes my way.''

Quick as lightning, Jared grasped both Kate's wrists. "It wouldn't take much for me to break these," he said. "Then what would you do? How would you defend yourself then?''

Their eyes locked. Fury changed to something else just as elemental as they remained as still as statues. Senses sharpened with intense need and respiration was heightened. Skin tones flushed with deep color and moisture dotted their skin. Jared's hold unconsciously tightened.

"Let me go." Kate's lips barely moved.

He didn't release her right away but continued staring at her face, still flushed with a wild rose color.

"You said you could handle yourself. Make me." He issued his challenge between set lips.

Before he could blink an eye, Kate's head dipped down and her teeth grazed the back of his hand. She looked up.

"Don't worry, I've had my rabies shots.''

Jared opened his hands and moved back a fraction. "Yes, but what about distemper?''

The moment between them wasn't lost, merely postponed.

KATE WASN'T SURPRISED they didn't stay the night in the cave. Not after that last supercharged moment between them. She knew she was wrong in goading him. There was so much tension building up between them the past few days she had a feeling it would soon come to a head. She just wasn't sure whether the resolution would be acceptable to them both. A speck on the horizon caught her wandering attention.

"Jared, there's a rider coming up south of here," she said in a low voice.

"I see him, too. Luckily he's on our side."

The rider approaching them was dressed in a khaki shirt and faded jeans.

"Hey, J.C.," the man called out in a laughing voice. "You're pretty far from the hallowed halls, aren't you?"

"Harry," Jared greeted him with a smile. "How's it going?"

"Never changes." He eyed Kate curiously.

"This is Dr. O'Malley." Jared made the introductions. "Kate, Harry Lawson, one of the rangers for the area. Kate's here to study one of the abandoned Apache camps."

He tipped his hat. "A pleasure, ma'am. So you're a professor like J.C. here."

"Yes, I guess you'd put it that way." She smiled.

Harry turned to Jared. "Did you see Toby on your way in?"

He nodded. "We stayed the night. He, Bertha and Mutt seem to be doing well, although he did say that Leo was hearing some strange things," Jared said all too casually.

Harry grimaced. "Yeah, he's convinced the Indians have come back to reclaim their land and he'll end up scalped one night. He's decided to move to Phoenix to be with his son."

"What brought all this on?"

The ranger shook his head. "Who knows? He claims he's seen their ghosts and heard their chants. Thing is, no one else has heard them. I talked to Toby once about it, but he said he sleeps too deeply to hear anything. The only strange thing he's seen is an unusual green bird one morning, but he couldn't give me any kind of description.'' He shrugged. ''Is that why you're up here, because of Leo's reports of Apache ghosts? That sure would be up your alley, J.C.''

''We thought we might look into it while we're here.'' Kate was the one to answer.

Harry turned his attention to Kate—the kind of attention a healthy man gives to a lovely woman—which a disgruntled Jared easily noted.

''Maybe so, ma'am, but someone as pretty as you still needs to be careful out here. At least you've got J.C. to protect you and I don't know anyone better in a crisis situation,'' he said. ''Except for Leo's reports, things have been too quiet out here and that doesn't make any sense. I feel something's going on. I just can't find any proof.''

''Well, if we hear of anything we'll let you know,'' Jared spoke up.

''Where exactly are you headed?'' Harry asked Jared, ignoring his not too discreet dismissal.

''From what I understand we're heading for one of the camps at the base of the inner mountains,'' Kate explained, flashing a winning smile that dazzled Harry and thoroughly irritated Jared. ''Since you know the area as well as, if not better than, Jared, perhaps you wouldn't mind joining us.''

''Yes, he would,'' Jared muttered.

''Actually, I'm on my way back to the headquarters,'' Harry explained, looking warily at Jared who looked fit to kill. ''Do me a favor, J.C., keep a close eye out for anything unusual.''

"Human or ghosts?"

The ranger didn't crack a smile. "Either. I'm not so sure that Leo's stories are just the ramblings of a lonely old man. Charley said he thought he heard what sounded like some kind of plane one night last month, but he couldn't pinpoint the location. Plus he couldn't say for sure that's what he heard."

"Have you seen many strangers traveling through lately?" Jared asked, his irritation with the man gone.

"We have tourists all the time. A lot realize right off there's more to the mountains than they figured on and they go on back to civilization. Others are more experienced and come in for camping and exploring. Thing is, we can't keep an eye on anyone who doesn't check in with us first." He gathered up his reins. "I'll stop in to check on Toby on my way out. You two be careful." He tipped his hat again to Kate. "Nice to meet you, Dr. O'Malley."

"It was nice meeting you, too." She smiled and nodded. "And we'll be careful."

Jared waited until Harry rode out of sight before turning to Kate. "I must say that little scene was a bit sickening," he said without preamble. "The smile you gave him was so syrupy I'm certain I got three cavities just watching."

She glared at him. "It kept him from asking too many questions about where we were going, didn't it? There are times when a little bit of femininity goes a long way."

Jared rolled his eyes. "Meaning?"

Kate smirked. "Right now he figures you're guiding a professor into the mountains to look at the remains of an old abandoned camp. It's better than his thinking otherwise."

"True," he conceded grudgingly.

"Then what's your problem?"

"Nothing, but it wouldn't hurt if you'd give me one of those smiles once in a while," he grumbled, turning away.

Kate exhaled a frustrated breath. She decided she would never be able to understand the opposite sex. It was much easier to figure out thousand-year-old cultures. At least they don't make you crazy.

"When you deserve one, you'll get it."

Chapter Eleven

"Why didn't you tell Harry about our two visitors?" Kate asked when they stopped to make camp in the early evening.

"Mainly because I didn't have all that much to tell him. What should I say? That two squirrelly looking guys intimated we'd be better off out of here? That's nothing new. There's men who roam these mountains all the time and act as if the sun and too much whiskey fried their brains years ago," he explained. "Besides, we have no idea where those men are now, so he wouldn't have a chance to track them down and find out why they wanted us gone."

Kate looked around the area Jared had chosen for their camp. Protected on three sides, they would have the advantage if any unwanted visitors tried to surprise them. She sensed that was the reason he had picked this area.

"There's a small spring close to here that generally has plenty of good water available," he told her as he unsaddled his horse. "You may not like the restriction but I'd feel better if you didn't go down there by yourself."

She didn't care to run into those men by herself and readily agreed with him. "Perfectly understood. Although the chance to have more than a lick and a promise sounds wonderful. Would that be possible?"

"You bet." He grinned. "I was getting kind of tired of using those little moist towelettes of yours, myself."

She returned his grin. "You have to admit they've come in handy for us so far. And the lemon scent is so refreshing on warm days like these," she said in a proper New England matron's accent.

"They're something I never would have thought of bringing along," he admitted.

"I came up with them a few years ago. I always seemed to feel the need to freshen up when water was scarce. Then I once watched a young mother clean up her toddler with some of the towelettes. I found out where I could buy them in bulk and now I always carry them with me."

Jared stared at Kate until she shifted uneasily under his regard. "For a woman who doesn't wear much makeup you look pretty good at the end of the day."

She felt herself blushing. "It doesn't do any good to wear any in this kind of heat because it would only melt," she said, turning away. "Trouble is, blondes usually look too washed out without any color. I'm just glad I can tan without burning too badly."

Jared walked over and circled her arm with his fingers and slowly turned her to face him. "Kate," he said softly, "you look more than fine to me. You should know that by now. In fact, you look about as good as any woman I've known."

Her lips twisted wryly. "And I'm sure you've known many."

"Probably more than I'd like. But that's past history. I'm just concentrating on the present and you're the only one who counts." His eyes silently pleaded with her to believe him.

"Jared, we both know this isn't the time," she whispered, her eyes reflecting regret.

He released her and stepped back. "Unfortunately, you're right. We can't take any chances of allowing ourselves to be distracted with those guys roaming around."

"I wish...." Kate wanted to reclaim the words the moment they left her lips.

"Wish what?" Jared prompted.

She couldn't say it. She couldn't say she wished this moment could be all theirs. But she had her vow to remember.

Spinning, she picked up her saddlebags and walked away.

"Where the hell do you think you're going now?" he demanded, angry she would just walk away as if nothing had happened. As if she hadn't started a provocative statement she wouldn't finish.

"None of your damn business!" she shouted, her frustration boiling over. She stalked off in the direction of the water hole Jared had mentioned earlier.

"Damn fool woman," he muttered, watching her go.

"Arrogant beast," she threw over her shoulder.

Jared cursed pungently under his breath. "Shamus should have spanked her more as a kid. Then she wouldn't have turned into such a pain in the butt."

He stubbornly refused to follow her, telling himself she could just protect herself. He counted every second of the thirty-three minutes she was gone. When Kate returned, her damp hair was combed neatly, she wore a clean shirt and she appeared to be in a much better temper. She went ahead with dinner preparations while Jared excused himself to make use of the spring for his own clean-up.

Kate found it difficult to concentrate on her chores when thoughts of Jared, naked to the waist if not all the way, kept intruding.

"Make up your mind, O'Malley. Do you want the man or not?" she asked, adding a bit of water to their freeze-dried stew. She laughed under her breath. "That was a stupid question."

"What's a stupid question?" Jared's voice startled her from behind.

She turned her head. "Why they can't make freeze-dried food more palatable," she replied easily.

Jared dropped to the ground across from her. "How come you never talk very much about your father? All I know is that he teaches cultural anthropology at Berkeley, he believes in the philosophy of the sixties and enjoys studying the mating customs of remote tribes and sometimes even participates in them."

"That's Dad in a nutshell."

"Is that why Shamus applied for custody of you? Because he felt your father was a bad influence?" he asked curiously.

Kate put the pot to one side. "To understand the story you have to understand the two men. In many ways they're very much alike, though they'd be the last to agree. Both are very passionate about their work. What I remember from those early years was a lot of sitar music, the sickening sweet smell of pot, incense in the air and voices talking about love and peace. Gramps once told me there were twelve people living in a two-bedroom apartment when he flew out to San Francisco to see Dad and check on me. I was happily running around naked and had a rainbow painted on my cheek. In fact, that was what they called me. They felt Kathryn sounded too establishment and I needed a name more in keeping with the times. I had six mothers who took turns taking care of me after my birth mother left, so I never had a chance to miss her. I listened to music played by groups who are still popular today and I thought all women wore flowers and beads in their hair and all men were gentle and spoke philosophy all day. It was many years before I realized that the reason most of them were gentle was because of the pot they smoked, not because it was their true natures."

Jared shook his head as he took her hand in his and traced the lines in her palm with his thumb. "It must have been quite a culture shock for you."

"It was," she admitted. "A man I had only seen a few times in my life told me I was going to live with him and I couldn't understand why I had to leave the only home I knew. Dad later told me he allowed Gramps to take me because deep down he knew Gramps could do more for me than he ever could. I also think it had something to do with the little redhead he was seeing at the time and he didn't want a child messing up a budding relationship," she said without rancor.

"So because of Gramps I attended school on a regular basis, I wore clothing and shoes and I discovered snow." Her voice dropped. "And I also discovered books about faraway lands and people who had lived on this earth thousands of years ago. Gramps decided I was too old for fairy tales at bedtime, so instead he read Greek and Roman mythology to me. When I was ten I wrote a paper on the Trojan War for my history class. My teacher gave me an F because the class dealt with

American History—'' she grinned at him ''—but she didn't reckon on Gramps.'' She chuckled. ''He stormed in there and informed her there wasn't one wrong statement in my report and she should applaud a student who went into such detail.''

Jared grinned. ''It sounds as if that wasn't the only time.''

''It wasn't,'' she replied. ''Gramps had his own ideas of what a child should learn. One teacher was appalled to learn he was taking me to Egypt one summer and I would have to miss the first three weeks of the fall term. He told her I wouldn't lack for teachers over there and I would learn more than I could in a classroom and I did. Graduate students tutored me in various subjects, as did full professors. One thing I never lacked during my formative years was a proper education.''

''No wonder you earned your doctorate at such a young age.'' He laced his fingers through hers, laying his hand on his thigh.

Kate nodded, trying not to think of the muscles flexing under her hand. ''Some tried to accuse me of having help or using my influence with Gramps and he promptly set those people straight. I took his classes and he was deliberately harder on me than his other students, but I didn't mind. Dad said he was sorry I hadn't followed in his footsteps, but I don't think he was surprised that I chose archaeology.''

''From what I've heard your father hasn't changed very much over the years.''

''Not really, although each new girlfriend seems to be younger than the last one. His latest is twenty-one. She thought Woodstock was the name of a musical group.'' She chuckled. ''But I think he's beginning to see the error of his ways. It's getting more difficult for him to keep up with those sweet young things.''

''Rainbow O'Malley,'' he murmured. ''It has a ring to it.''

She wrinkled her nose. ''When you're six it's cute. When you're in your teens you're very grateful it isn't printed on your birth certificate.''

''You're a contradiction, Kate,'' Jared mused, raising her fingertips to his lips.

''Because I started out as a flower child and ended up an archaeologist?'' She stared at his teeth nibbling on her fingers.

''You have to admit the two don't go together.''

''True. Just as you spent your younger years traveling the world, acting the part of a military officer's straight-arrow son. Now you prefer to stay close to home and you're not as conservative as you let all of us believe.''

''I even fooled Shamus,'' he said. ''And that was no mean feat.''

''Not to mention Dr. Phillips's reaction to those tight jeans of yours,'' she teased. ''The poor man must think you're going through a midlife crisis.''

Jared stretched out on the ground, bracing himself on one elbow. ''Yeah, he probably thinks that would be a wonderful excuse, but deep down, he's acknowledged it's more my true self than those three-piece suits I usually wore. Since my classes were always filled to the max and my name added some prestige in the history circles,'' he said without ego, ''he was ready to forgive and forget. I reminded him that times change and he has to be ready to change with them. He wants people to think he's a forward thinking man and you and I are giving him a crash education. What also helped shift his thinking was the hint I dropped that we might have an important historical find.''

She pulled her hand away. "You told him what we're looking for?''

Jared looked at her as if she should have known better. "I told him Shamus was the brains behind this project and he would have to learn the main details from him. Needless to say, he backed off right away. Do you honestly think I would tell him the truth? The man would have called a press conference with the major networks within an hour. Give me some credit, will you?''

She nodded in silent apology. "I'm sorry, I blew it. It's just that you've said we're getting close to Weaver's Needle so I'm feeling more antsy. It's a bad habit of mine. Actually, I'm better than I used to be. Years ago I used to chew my nails, then I moved on to chain smoking until I had to spend six months with an anti-smoking fanatic who wouldn't even let me keep a pack of cigarettes with me. By the end of the six months I sincerely thought of shooting the man many times.''

"He might have thought of doing the same to you," Jared glibly pointed out.

Kate made a face. "Ha, ha, very funny.''

He grinned. "I thought so.''

"Just for that, I shouldn't tell you about an important clue I think I found," she said smugly.

He shrugged. "You'll tell me because you won't be able to keep it to yourself.''

Miffed that she would give in, Kate walked over to the saddlebags to dig through them until she found the slim leather wallet that held their papers and maps.

"While you were cleaning up I was remembering something from last night," she murmured, unfolding the maps and sifting through them until she found the two she was looking for. She studied each carefully, then marked her place with her fingertip. "Look at this." She gestured with her other hand. "Most of that area looks as if it's changed drastically over the years, but this one trail hasn't and it appears to dead end at a cave." She looked up, hope etched in her face. "And if you look at this section right here, you'll see a mark for a cave on the other side of the mountain. What if they connect? What if that was how Jacob kept one step ahead of anyone trying to follow him? Perhaps the cave isn't very easy to find even with it marked on the map. Sometimes that happens."

"There's nothing here to say it connects, Kate," he pointed out.

"Maybe no one has ever tried to see if it did. Maybe all anyone has done is look in one end or the other and not bothered to investigate further. Most people, unless they're truly serious, won't go too far into a cave unless they've brought along the proper equipment."

"Which we haven't."

She smiled. "Maybe we won't need any. I admit it's a hunch, but my hunches haven't failed me yet."

Jared took the map from her. He folded the two maps until he could place the two sections side by side. "One of those gut feelings that refuses to go away?"

She watched him closely. "Yes."

He slowly shook his head. "It could be nothing but a wild-goose chase, Kate. This might be nothing more than an ink splotch."

"It's in the area we're heading for anyway. What will it hurt for us to check it out?" she insisted, touching his arm. "Please, Jared? Surely you've had hunches in the past that haunted you until you did something about them.'' Her gemstone-colored eyes pleaded with him.

He heaved a deep sigh. "You're right, I've had them. Some turned out to be right. Others were so wrong it hurt, but I never ignore my hunches. Although I'm still not sure we'll find anything there. A cave that goes through a mountain doesn't mean it's also a mine."

"It doesn't mean it's not, either."

Jared knew he was lost. "We'll head up there first thing tomorrow."

"Oh, Jared!" Kate leaned over and hugged him. "You won't regret it. I promise."

"You just remember that if we get stuck somewhere and can't get out."

THE EERIE-SOUNDING SCREAM jerked Kate awake just as the sun broke over the mountaintops.

"What the hell was that?" Jared's irritated voice sounded from his sleeping bag, which was placed close to hers.

Kate sat up and looked around. "I'm not sure." Her voice was hushed. "I may not know much about the animal life in this area, but I don't imagine that sound is indigenous to Arizona."

Jared poked his head out from the folds. "What do you mean?"

She shook her head, then replied out loud when she realized he might not be able to see her action in the dim light. "I don't know, but one thing I can tell you is I've heard that sound somewhere before and it hasn't been while we've been here."

Another scream sounded before it appeared to be muffled by something.

"It's not human," Jared decided. "Wolves sure don't sound like that, nor do coyotes."

Kate uttered a curse of frustration. "I know I've heard it before," she said. "I just wish I could remember where." She pushed her hair away from her face.

"Maybe it was a hawk."

Except Kate wasn't convinced. "Maybe, but I don't think so." She pushed away the folds of her sleeping bag and scrambled to her feet.

Jared looked at her questioningly. "What are you doing?"

"It's no use going back to sleep for only another hour or so. I'm going down to the spring to wash up," she replied.

"Kate, I don't think you should go down there alone." He looked around with an uneasy expression on his face.

"I have my pistol with me." Kate gathered up her personal items. "I'll be back soon." She smiled wryly when she looked over and found him snoring softly. "You don't need to worry about me."

As Kate filled the canteens and dampened her hair so she could braid it, she searched her mind the way someone searches through a computer for information. She always hated it when something was just out of reach, the way that elusive sound was. While sounds were deceptive in the mountains and could easily come from the opposite direction from where a person thought he heard them, she had a pretty good idea the scream came from the area they were heading for.

By the time she returned to camp Jared was up and had breakfast cooking.

"I have a bad feeling about what's going on," she announced, dropping the canteens to the ground. "But we're too close now to go back."

He nodded gravely. "Okay, sweetheart, we'll just go on."

KATE LAY SLEEPLESS THAT NIGHT. This time she wasn't trying to figure out where she had heard that type of scream before. She was too busy trying to figure out the shrouded figure lying close by.

One thing she had been blessed with was an analytical mind and she was now grateful for that because she had a lot of things to analyze. Such as finally settling her feelings for Jared.

"I have something to tell you, Jared," she whispered to the night air. "I wasn't as angry with you as I let you think I was. I was more hurt than angry because you never told me about the other part of your personality. We were seriously talking about marriage and yet you never mentioned J.C. The fact that you didn't think you could tell me hurt me and I wanted to hurt you back. That's why I've acted so nasty toward you. That's also why I told you our engagement was off. I felt confused. I didn't know who you were anymore. I didn't know who *I* was, either."

Feeling the chill of the night air hit her shoulders, she pulled the covers over them and shifted her position a bit. "I didn't date all that much during my teen years, so my understanding of the male mind is fairly limited. After all, you have to admit Gramps is a man unto himself and I doubt any woman has ever fully understood him. Even me.

"You have to understand that from the age of nine I spent almost all my summers on digs with people much older than me. Nine months out of the year I spent with my peers, the other three I spent with people who smiled and tolerated me because of Gramps. I'm sure they saw me as nothing more than a polite nuisance. As a teenager I had a painful crush on one of Gramps's graduate students who only thought of me as a cute kid with braces. And as an adult, I spent more than three months at a time on digs instead of attending parties and going out on dates. Kiki was the social animal.''

Her voice lowered. ''So do you see why I'm not very good at anything but seeking rare treasures? You may be in the same field I am, but you're much better at the social level. You even handle Dr. Phillips's boring parties better than I ever did. I think that's why I always tried to shock people with my short skirts and bright colors, because I didn't know how to act. Also because I used to hope deep down they wouldn't invite me back. I should have known better. Besides, Gramps would have stepped in if I had gotten too outrageous and no matter what, I could never do anything to hurt him.'' Her voice broke.

''Oh, hell, I'm not even doing this right. What I'm trying to say is...'' She paused, sounding very weary. ''Maybe I'm better off not saying it aloud. At least I got all this off my chest.'' She slid inside her sleeping bag and closed her eyes. Within seconds she was asleep.

Jared's whispered reply fell upon deaf ears. ''Don't worry, O'Malley, I know exactly what you wanted to say but couldn't. As for me, love, ditto.''

Chapter Twelve

Kate wiped the back of her hand against her forehead, unsurprised it came away wet. She was convinced the temperature was twenty degrees warmer than the previous day.

"One thing about the desert is that it never changes," she said. "You roast during the day and freeze during the night. You get bugs in your boots, sand and bugs in your food, and sometimes between your teeth. And if you're real lucky you won't find a rattlesnake taking up residence in your boots or sleeping bag. How come Gramps never researches archaeological finds in Hawaii or Fiji? I bet there's a lot of rare idols out there. I'd even settle for Palm Springs if my room has air conditioning."

Jared grinned. "I'll settle for a hotel swimming pool if you'll wear a bikini for me to ogle."

"In your dreams," she countered, feeling more relaxed than she had in a long time. She was just grateful he hadn't heard her late-night confession. She had no idea what she would have done if he had, but she knew it wouldn't be a pretty sight.

"Okay, then I guess I'll have to wish for a shower instead," Jared said. "I wouldn't mind standing under it for about an hour."

"Yes," Kate breathed, thinking about a long shower, too. But she wasn't standing under it alone. The vision of Jared, naked and wet, was too much to consider when the temperature was already near a hundred.

"When do you think we'll reach the cave?" Kate croaked, then quickly coughed to hide the agitation her thoughts sent through her system.

He shrugged. "With luck, late today. If not, sometime tomorrow. I'm not sure."

"Jared, you do understand why I'm pushing so hard to go there, don't you?" she asked.

He nodded. "You have a hunch. Believe me, Kate, I understand. I've had plenty of them in the past. Besides, I've had a couple hunches during this trip, too."

"We're a lot alike."

He turned his head. "Yeah, I guess we are. We're both individuals, loners, involved in our work, not to mention we're both stubborn as hell. That's probably why we get along so well."

"Do you really think we get along well?" She was pleased he thought so.

"As well as two stubborn people can. I think we're managing pretty well on this trip, aren't we?"

"When we're not arguing," she pointed out.

"We're getting better with that," he persisted. "Come on, admit it."

An impish light appeared in her eyes. "Admit what?"

Jared reached out and grabbed hold of her bridle. "I seem to recall Shamus once mentioning that you're ticklish," he said with a devilish grin. "He told me that was how he got past your stubborn streak when you dug in your heels.''

Kate leaned forward, crossing her arms on the saddle horn. ''You like to live dangerously, don't you?''

''It makes the time go by faster.''

''You're turning out to be a very dangerous man, Jared Wyatt.''

''You don't need to worry.''

She met his gaze head on. ''Did I say I was worried?''

Jared leaned over until his lips barely grazed hers. ''Your lips may say no, but your eyes say yes.''

If either remembered their respective vows of not allowing the other to get to them they ignored the mental warning.

''Tell me more,'' she invited on a breathless note. Her vivid eyes sparkled.

''Your eyes are like cut emeralds, your skin is as smooth as pearls and your lips like pink rubies.''

Kate arched an eyebrow at this last piece of flattery. ''Is there such a thing as a pink ruby?''

His breath misted against her lips. ''Yep.''

She was intrigued with his description and especially with him. ''Have you ever seen one?''

''Yep.'' He was deliberately vague.

Now she was curious. ''Where?''

His gaze on her lips didn't waver. ''In my grandmother's engagement ring that was passed down to me for my bride.''

Kate's lashes slowly lowered to cover the expression in her eyes. ''Oh.''

Jared released her bridle and drew back. Enough was said for the moment.

KATE STUDIED JARED as he looked over the map. She took in his faded blue chambray shirt with several buttons undone, the damp dark hair matting the deep gold skin of his chest. He looked too good for words.

"If you're willing to ride a couple extra hours after dark we can shorten our travel time tomorrow."

"It will be dangerous traveling when there's no moon," she said. "Especially since we don't know where our friends might be lurking."

"We'll just be even more careful from now on." He continued to study the map.

Kate hesitated. "Traveling at night might give us the protection of darkness, but we also run the risk of stumbling unaware onto something we might not want to."

"I know that. The thing is I'm getting more than a little curious about our two visitors, chants from Indians that don't exist in this region, strange birds flying overhead and men who look as if they belong more in a dark alley than up here. It's turning into a mystery that I'd like to solve." He anticipated her argument. "I don't believe in looking for trouble, Kate, but if there's a chance to get some answers about what's going on out here I won't back down."

"I'm not one to back down, either," she replied. "Still, I don't think it would be a good idea for us to travel after dark."

He nodded. "Noted. But I want to get up to those mountains as soon as possible, so we won't be out in the open as much as we are now."

That old familiar tingling sensation skittered across Kate's nape. Danger was too close for comfort. She felt it deep in her bones.

"Then we'll ride as long as possible tonight, too," she said quietly. A slight nod was Jared's answer.

Kate pulled the brim of her cap down to shade her eyes and flipped her shirt collar up to cover her nape from the punishing sun.

Tension between them grew high as the day progressed. Both knew danger could very well be around the corner and they were powerless to escape it. The idea of turning back never occurred to them.

"I'VE BEEN TOLD I have excellent night vision, but this is going a bit too far," Jared grumbled, this time following Kate.

She turned her head. "You suggested we should travel tonight."

"Evening, yes. All night, no." He pulled on the reins. "Come on, Kate, my stomach is grumbling. Let's stop and make camp. I'll even do the cooking."

She turned her head and smiled. "It's your turn to cook anyway."

He waved his hand. "A mere technicality. Come on, O'Malley. It's a gorgeous moonless night. Let's make use of it." He dismounted.

Kate did likewise. "Too bad there isn't a full moon, so my lupine ancestors could surface. You'd love my alter ego." Her teeth flashed white in the dim light. Jared began patting his pockets. "What are you doing?"

"Looking for my silver bullets."

Kate walked over and punched him in the arm, hard.

"Hey!" Jared winced and rubbed his hand over the wounded area. "I happen to bruise easily."

"Do not make jokes about silver bullets." She used a throaty East European accent.

Jared pulled off his gloves and raised his hand, resting it lightly against her cheek. "Funny, I don't feel any fur," he murmured.

"That's because there's no full moon," she breathed, concentrating on the feather-light touch of his knuckles brushing against her skin. She lifted her face, studying the dark shadows surrounding his face. His skin was warm, the fingers, when he turned his hand, slightly callused. Without being aware of her actions, she tipped her head slightly to one side, allowing him further access.

"No urge to bite?" he whispered, stroking the curve of her throat with his fingertips.

She closed her eyes, enjoying the shivering ripples traveling through her body from his touch. "Not yet."

"What would I have to do wrong to merit your teeth on me?" His voice was low and husky. He trailed his fingers across her lips, which parted slightly at his touch, her tongue tasting the salt on his skin.

Her lips curved. "Who said you would have to do anything wrong?"

Jared groaned at her provocative challenge. "I promise to behave, then you say something to cause me to forget." He sighed. "Come on, little witch, we've got a camp to set up and if we don't do it now we might forget it altogether."

Smiling with satisfaction at unbalancing him again, Kate moved away and gathered up the two sets of reins and led the horses to one side. She could still feel the warmth of Jared's hand on her cheek as she performed one of the chores they had been companionably sharing for so many days.

What if they finally gave in to their baser instincts and forgot all about setting up camp right away? She doubted the outcome would have been what she so easily imagined. After all, they were civilized people, not primitives who would roll around on the ground while tearing each other's clothes off. She swallowed a heavy sigh. Right now the idea sounded too appealing for words.

LITTLE DID KATE KNOW that Jared's thoughts closely paralleled her own. While he got the fire going and began preparing a packet of stew, he fantasized what would have happened if he hadn't decided to act the gentleman.

Distracted, he jabbed a spoon into the thick mixture. When a drop of the hot stew spattered the back of his hand, he cursed and jumped, rubbing the wounded spot.

"What happened?" Kate appeared at his side.

"I burned myself." He grimaced.

She nodded and looked over his shoulder. "What's for dinner?"

He gestured toward the bubbling pot. "That famous culinary masterpiece of mine— stew."

Kate bent from the waist and reached for the spoon, stirring it carefully. "Looks delicious."

"Barely edible is more like it." Jared tried not to look at the extra button on her shirt she had loosened since the last time he had seen her, revealing skin that was gleaming with perspiration. "It should be ready in a few minutes."

Kate nodded and looked up. "Fine with me."

Jared groaned inside. Something was going on that he didn't understand and he wasn't sure if he dared ask, just in case he was wrong. Something caught the corner of his eye and he looked up.

"What are you doing?" As if he couldn't tell just by watching her pull her shirt tail out and unbutton the last four buttons, tying the ends together in a neat knot under her breasts.

"Cooling off. I can't believe how hot it's stayed tonight," she replied, unconcerned that she was displaying an interesting few inches of bare flesh. "Usually it's been so cold I've been grateful for my jacket."

Two can play at this game, he decided, reaching for his shirt and pulling it over his head. "Yeah, you're right. At least, the sun is down so we don't have to worry about a sunburn." He rolled the shirt into a ball and rubbed it across his chest, easily drawing Kate's gaze to the broad expanse of bare skin.

"The stew." Her voice was faint.

"Hm?" He turned toward her, secretly pleased to see the flags of bright color staining her cheeks.

Kate coughed to clear her throat. "The stew. It's burning," she said in a stronger voice.

Jared looked down at the simmering pot. He stirred the pot's contents and straightened up. "It's just right." He turned his head. "Ready anytime you are."

He could have sworn he heard a strangled sigh drop from Kate's lips. Why hadn't he tried some of this teasing before?

"I'll get the plates." Kate walked away with jerky movements.

Jared didn't bother to put his shirt on as they ate their dinner.

"You know, no one would see you if you wanted to take your shirt off, too," he suggested in a friendly tone.

"I realize no one would, but I'm quite comfortable, thank you." Her tone matched his.

Jared narrowed his eyes. "Why do I have the feeling I was just insulted?"

Kate looked at him with wide-eyed innocence. "I have no idea why you would feel that way. I merely agreed with you that *no one* is around here." She presented him with a sugary sweet smile as she dipped her spoon into her stew.

He sighed. "You really know how to hurt a guy, don't you?"

"I agreed with you, Jared. Doesn't that please you?"

He altered his position, feeling uneasy with her change in manner. "Not the way I'd like to feel pleased," he said, sensing the game shifting over to her side.

Kate felt very pleased with herself at turning the tables on Jared. It hadn't taken long for her to realize what he was doing. What had taken long was her shoring up her defenses against his masculinity. It wasn't as if she hadn't seen a man's naked chest before. In fact, there were some beaches in Europe where she had seen even more. And she wasn't a simpering virgin. But there was something about Jared's chest that gave off some very interesting vibrations. She only wished she had the time to investigate Jared in greater detail. This expedition was turning out to have more surprises than they expected.

"If it hadn't been for the heat, I would have been tempted to bring along my portable CD and tape player," Kate remarked, after the dishes were cleaned and put away.

"What did you do when you were in the Middle East?" Jared asked.

"I kept a tape player in my tent," she replied. "And some of the workers brought along musical instruments for nighttime sing-alongs. I remember one of Gramps's graduate students got me hooked on cross-word puzzles.''

Jared couldn't help but notice the light in her eyes. ''Is that all he got you hooked on?''

''Who says the student was a he?''

''That gleam in your eye.''

Kate smiled. ''I was a very vulnerable sixteen and he was a lordly twenty-three. I was crushed when he explained to me, in lofty tones, that if he tried anything with me Gramps would have not only flunked him but probably broken him into many small pieces. I was convinced my heart was broken and I'd never find anyone to replace him.''

Jared smiled. ''I recall a few of those kind of crushes.'' He stood and walked around the fire to where Kate sat. ''So who replaced him?'' He dropped down behind her and slipped his arms around her waist, then pulled her against him. ''Relax and tell Uncle Jared all about it.''

She studied the star-dotted sky. ''I had a few minor ones in high school, nothing special. ''You know, the usual kind—the captain of the basketball team, the class president and the head of the honor society. What about you?''

''Homecoming queen, prom queen, head cheer-leader,'' he said promptly.

''And I bet you dated each one.''

''Of course, it was a psychology project.''

Kate turned her head. ''Psychology project?'' She allowed her skepticism to show through. ''Oh, come on.''

''Sure, learning the difference in temperaments and such,'' he said blandly. ''One was a blonde, another brunette and the last a redhead. And one was built like a centerfold, one looked like Twiggy and the third was your typical athlete.''

She punched his arm. "Talk about a male chauvinist!''

"Nope, just a kid with overloaded hormones.'' Jared tightened his hold until she rested completely against his chest. "Come on, tell me more about Kate O'Malley as a teenager,'' he invited.

"Nothing much to tell. I wore braces, I was taller than a lot of boys and skinny as a rail. I understood more about the male sex of thousands of years ago than the males in my own time period,'' she told him in a low voice. "I wore glasses and had dishwater blond hair and wore jeans and sweatshirts all the time. I was about as attractive as Frankenstein's bride.''

He tweaked a stray strand of hair. "You've definitely improved over the years.''

She shook her head. "Not without help. Gramps was seeing this very nice Italian anthropologist who taught me a great deal about men in general. She urged me to get contact lenses and change my hair style. She took me clothes shopping and talked Gramps into letting me attend some self-improvement classes one summer.''

"And?'' Jared prompted.

She couldn't keep the self-satisfaction from her voice. "And I never lacked for dates during my senior year. I started filling out and I wore a strapless gown to my senior prom. As far as I was concerned, that was my greatest accomplishment.''

"I wish I had known you back then.''

Kate shook her head. "If you'd known me then, you would have been chasing after Kiki. Trust me.''

Silence loomed comfortably between them for a few moments.

"Are you finally deciding I'm not such a bad guy after all?" Jared murmured in her ear.

"I never did think you were bad," she replied. "I just had to come to terms with you and your alter ego."

He stilled. "Have you?" His voice held hope.

Her whisper hung in the air between them. "Yes."

Jared rested his chin on top of her head, his hands warm against the gentle curve of her stomach. "I'm glad."

She relaxed against him, content in his embrace as they shared the evening. "So am I."

KATE WAS UP just before dawn broke over the mountains. After her confession to Jared the night before, she had slept deeply and woke up feeling more refreshed than she had in a long time. Eager to start her day, she left her sleeping bag and glanced briefly at a sleeping Jared before going to get cleaned up.

Jared didn't stir until the scent of coffee floated through the air.

"What happened?" he mumbled, sitting up and rubbing his eyes.

"Our wake-up call didn't come through," she replied brightly, handing him a filled mug of coffee and a plate of scrambled eggs. "We really should complain to the main desk. The service at this resort is appalling."

"Yeah." He grunted as he pulled himself into a straighter position. It was clear to Kate he wasn't fully awake yet—unusual for someone who normally awoke fully alert while she was usually the one who needed time to rejoin the land of the living.

"Anything wrong?"

"Nothing a few weeks in a real bed wouldn't cure. Sleeping bags aren't as comfortable as they were ten years ago." He sipped the hot coffee and tackled his eggs.

"Don't you really mean to say you're not as young as you were ten years ago?" Kate couldn't resist teasing.

"Something like that, yes, although I probably would have used more tact," he said dryly. He glowered at the tiny smile on her lips. "I'm glad to see that you think it's funny." His head jerked upward when he found her standing over him and staring intently at his head. "What are you doing? Ow! Hey, that hurts!"

"I'm looking for all those gray hairs you must have if you're so old you can't handle a few nights in a sleeping bag. Ah, here's one!" she declared, triumphantly holding up the offending strand. She peered intently at him.

Jared put his mug down and quickly dragged his sleeping bag up to cover his bare chest. "If you even dare to look for any here, I won't be responsible for my actions."

Kate's head jerked up, her expression that of an animal scenting the unknown in the wind.

"What?" Jared whispered, easily reading her face.

"Something's nearby." Her lips barely moved.

He knew enough not to look around or make his actions obvious. Acting as if there was nothing wrong he picked up his mug and finished his coffee. "Can you tell the direction?"

"No, it's just something I sense. As if we're being watched."

Jared held up his plate and mug. "Why don't you take these for me so I can get up. Let's just pretend business as usual and pack up. I think we better consider an alternate route to our destination.''

"Fine by me."

They took their time as they packed up, but both felt uneasy pricklings the entire time as if danger was close on their heels.

Kate felt reassured by the warmth of her knife resting in its sheath against her calf. She didn't feel comfortable allowing her hand gun in sight so she kept it rolled up in her sleeping bag for the time being. She noticed Jared did the same with his pistol.

"The Indians are getting closer, Wyatt," she murmured, as they mounted.

"Then we have two choices—ride like hell for the cavalry or hope we can stay clear of them," he told her. "What sounds good to you?"

He knew her answer before she spoke. "What do you think? We won't give them any trouble if they don't give us any."

Jared nodded, feeling the stirrings of excitement in his blood. "Sounds fair to me."

Chapter Thirteen

Kate was used to danger. She remembered a band of desert bandits in a small Arabian country who decided a team of archaeologists weren't welcome in their land. Not to mention a previously unknown tribe in the Amazon who still believed in cannibalism. Her group had to do some fast talking to leave the area before they became part of a holiday feast. Shamus taught her that fear only weakened a person, while courage in the face of fear gave one strength. He also taught her not to take chances if she wanted to remain alive. Right now, she seriously thought about running like hell in the opposite direction.

More and more she was glad Jared was with her on this trip.

"Think our friends are anywhere near?" she asked, pretending interest in a barrel cactus standing tall off to her right.

"Could be. I admit I wasn't too fond of them in the beginning, but I wouldn't mind seeing their pock-marked faces right now if I could be assured they don't have the brains of a gnat."

"I know I wouldn't have asked them to tea." She strove to look relaxed in the saddle while she felt anything but.

"True, they probably would have stolen the family silver. Still, there's no guarantee they're the ones we sensed earlier," he told her.

Kate leaned forward in the saddle. "Jared, do you still think they might have found it ahead of us and their warnings were to keep us away?" she asked in a low voice.

He shrugged. "Hard to say. I figure we'll find out soon enough."

"That makes me feel secure," she said wryly.

"You know, if we are being watched, an occasional giggle out of you wouldn't hurt," Jared suggested. "Or a little wifely fondling." He lifted his eyebrows several times in comic parody.

"I never giggled even as a teenager and I'm not about to start now, but I will look more scholarly by wearing my glasses more often," she said haughtily. "I'll even throw out a few ten-dollar words in a loud voice. Latin terms always sound impressive to the layman."

"I prefer the wifely fondling, myself."

"In your dreams, Wyatt."

"Dreams have been known to come true, O'Malley."

WAS THIS THE TRAIL Jacob Waltz took to his mine?

Did he believe in a roundabout route to elude his enemies?

What if there wasn't a cave? What if that dark speck on the old map was nothing more than a spot of old ink? What if this was nothing more than a hoax and

Jacob's tales of his mine nothing more than tales? What if?

More importantly, what if Shamus was wrong? What if this was one of those rare times when his information was incorrect?

Kate didn't even want to contemplate that idea. It still haunted her because she did fear that. She was afraid all their searching would be for naught and she would have to return to her grandfather with the news there was no proof of a mine in the area. No, she'd remain in the mountain for years, if necessary, as long as she could find the tiniest clue to substantiate Shamus's research.

"You said bands of Apache once lived up here?" she asked Jared in the shadow of the mountain they would explore further the next morning. She found herself so excited they were close to their goal she couldn't keep still.

He nodded. "These mountains were a perfect hideout for them because the white man wasn't too eager to get caught in an unknown area and the Apache had a pretty nasty way of dealing with intruders. Of course, there have been a lot of violent deaths in these mountains for many years. Many of them were labeled suicides, but I wouldn't be surprised if most of them weren't murders. That's when people start talking about the curse of the mountains."

Kate felt a chill enter her bones despite the intense heat. She resisted the urge to wrap her arms around her body.

"Isn't it funny how we've lectured about ancient curses and barbaric practices, but when it hits too close to home...." She shook her head, unable to go on.

Jared nodded, able to empathize with her. "They say scientists don't have active imaginations, but I can remember a few times when I felt as if an ancient Indian curse was about to descend on me no matter how careful I was with an area I was exploring.''

''I remember Gramps and I once recovering a dagger that had belonged to a Druid priestess,'' Kate murmured, her thoughts clearly elsewhere. ''Legend had it that any unbeliever who dared to possess the dagger would live in darkness for eternity. Eight months later, we were caught in a cave-in in an Egyptian tomb. For a while I was positive we wouldn't get out of there alive. When we were finally dug out, we were told the searchers felt a strange compulsion to look in the opposite direction and if they hadn't used dogs, we would have never been found. It's things like that that have you firmly believing in ancient curses and giving them a lot of healthy respect.''

Jared walked over and enfolded Kate in his arms. ''Relax, Kate,'' he murmured. ''I just want to hold you, okay?''

''Do you hear me protesting?'' she replied, snuggling in his arms. She hid a smile. ''I never thought I'd go after a legendary mine with a sexy history professor.''

''So you think I'm sexy, do you?'' He sounded amused.

''You know you are, so don't ask me to elaborate.'' Kate's reply was grumpy as if she hated to admit it. She rubbed her cheek against his shirt front. ''How come a man who's all sweaty and dusty and grungy can still be sexy? It isn't right. The cologne I put on this morning wore off probably five minutes after I applied it, I smell as bad as the horse and my hair is loaded with grit.''

''But you're sexy to me.''

She tipped her head back to get a better look at his unshaven features. "Ha! You're not even wearing your glasses."

"I only need them for reading and right now you're closer than most books I read."

"What would J.C. say at this moment?" she asked with a purr in her voice.

His voice lowered to the husky drawl that sent chills along her spine. "That there's nothing sexier to a man than an earthy woman."

It took a moment for his meaning to sink in.

"An earthy woman!" She stepped back, her eyes spitting fire. "I'm sure what you really mean is a woman covered with dirt!"

Jared instantly pulled her into his arms. "I mean a woman who's not afraid to get dirty, who's willing to pitch in and use her hands, who doesn't give a damn if she's seen with a dirty face." He touched a speck of dirt on the tip of her nose. "I mean a *real* woman, Kate O'Malley, not some pretty doll whose makeup is always perfect and who's nothing more than a decoration meant to be taken out to fancy places and shown off at parties so that other men will envy a man for having a beautiful woman on his arm."

They never noticed that they were sitting on the ground, facing each other, their hands clasped.

"We have a chance of making it, Kate, as long as you're willing," Jared said quietly. "I know I'm willing."

She knew immediately he didn't mean their trip, but something a great deal more meaningful—their lives.

"I've never backed down from a challenge yet, and the way I look at it you're the greatest challenge I've encountered." She managed a wry smile. "You're right,

Jared. Something is happening between us. Just be prepared for some surprises when we return to civilization."

He grinned. "I'll be counting on it." He looked around. "I think we better get our camp set up. As much as I hate the idea we better consider cold food for tonight. No use in advertising our presence, just in case."

Kate nodded. She understood Jared's need for caution. She'd rather not let anyone know they were there, either. And if it meant eating cold food and doing without a fire, so be it. Who knows, perhaps she could talk him into combining their two sleeping bags—for extra warmth, of course.

"I WOULD GIVE MY EYETEETH for an electric blanket right about now," Kate muttered, pulling a sweatshirt over her head. "It's amazing how much heat a small fire can give off."

"It's more than that, the temperature has dropped a good ten degrees since the sun went down," Jared replied. He also wore a warm sweatshirt. "Last night's heat wave was obviously a freak of nature."

"I knew I should have brought some thermal underwear," she muttered.

"Don't worry, I didn't bring any, either."

Kate threw him a sly look. "Perhaps we should share body heat," she said, sounding just a touch coy. "It's helped a lot of people survive freezing temperatures."

Jared didn't react. "Keep your hat on. Most of your body heat escapes through the top of your head."

"Then I'm sure a great deal more than heat escapes from that empty excuse for a head you have," she said under her breath, pulling the edges of her sleeping bag around her like a blanket. "I hope I don't wake up a Popsicle."

"The morning heat will thaw you out in no time," he helpfully informed her.

"The man is an expert at driving a woman to the depths of insanity." She curled up inside her sleeping bag, ready to do nothing more than sleep. "No court in the land will convict me if I decide to murder him."

"Tell them you were suffering from PMS. I understand that works real well." Jared spoke with laughter underscoring his voice.

"Put a sock in it, Wyatt."

"You're reverting to your old ways, O'Malley. And here I thought this trip would help you find the truth."

"I did. I'm beginning to hate all this roughing it."

SLEEP WAS ELUSIVE for Kate that night. She felt she was too close to her goal and the last thing she wanted to do was sleep the night away even if the temperature was so cold she thought her nose would freeze and fall off. Her only consolation was the idea that Jared had to be freezing just as badly.

Kate wasn't sure what awakened her at dawn, but she knew it had something to do with her search. Just as suddenly as she had fallen asleep the night before she was awake with a blinding alertness. Confident there was enough light for her to see just past her hand held in front of her face, she crept out of her bag and pulled on her boots after thoroughly shaking them to dislodge any nasty creepy crawlies that might have taken up residence during the night. Once her knife and gun were in place, she slipped out of the campsite and headed for the base of the mountain where her senses led her like a radar beeper.

"It has to be here," she whispered, looking up the steep dirt grade. "I can feel it."

She began walking in one direction, but the buzzing sensation in her head seemed to abruptly still. When she changed directions, she could feel that old familiar buzz return. Her mental divining stick was working as well as ever.

If Kate hadn't been examining a boulder with strange markings etched across the face she would have missed it. It wasn't so much a cave opening as a slit set into the mountain partially hidden by a boulder. She touched the rock, already warmed by the morning sun.

She closed her eyes, willing herself to feel vibrations from years ago, desiring the power to do so. Although eager to explore farther she knew better than to enter the cave alone. She would have to return to the campsite and wake Jared. She was ready for some serious exploring.

Kate barely moved two feet away when a rain of dirt and rocks alerted her to danger. She ran to one side, narrowly missing a rock bouncing directly toward her.

Once out of the danger zone she stopped to catch her breath and ensure herself the rock slide wasn't manmade.

"The curse of the mountains," she murmured, sensing the slide wasn't accidental. "It's too late to scare me off now. I can't go back until I find out if this is the mine."

Fired with resolve, she hurried to the campsite. Kate ran toward Jared's sleeping figure then skidded to a stop a short distance away.

"Jared." Her voice was low, imploring him to wake up. "You have to wake. Just don't move. Please, for both our sakes, don't move a muscle." She kept her voice calm and even. "Just remain very still."

"What is it?" His body barely moved as he spoke.

She was grateful he was instantly alert. "Diamondback rattler," she said tersely.

His muttered reply was equally terse and very profane.

"He must have been attracted to your body heat because he's lying on top of your bag near your legs." Every movement was made in slow motion as she carefully reached for her gun. Kate didn't take her eyes off the sinuous reptile who watched this intruder with suspicion.

"Kate, I can't lie here all day."

"I can get him."

Jared's mouth opened as if he was about to shout, but he quickly snapped it shut. "Kate, I've been able to figure out where it is and, no offense, I'm not too comfortable with your solution."

"No offense taken." By now she had her gun in her hand and she was slowly raising it, the barrel sighting the coiled rattlesnake. The snake, sensing her purpose, coiled tighter, the rattles sounding like dry rushes in the still air.

"You have a better idea?" she asked between dry lips. She already knew his answer, but what choice did she have? If Jared even breathed wrong the suspicious rattler would definitely strike. While they carried the standard snakebite kit, the diamondback's bite would set time against them. She couldn't afford to think right now. What if she missed and hit Jared instead? What if she missed and the snake bit Jared before she could get a second shot off? What if— She cordoned off the questions and forced herself to concentrate on the task at hand.

"O'Malley, my love, all I ask is you remember those days at your shooting range and you try for a little lower," Jared said in a low voice, sounding as calm as a man with a lethal snake coiled practically in his lap could sound. "Because if you miss I could end up a soprano."

"No great loss, I've heard you sing."

Jared groaned as if in pain.

Kate held the gun in the shooting stance, one hand cradling the other, and sighted on the snake.

"Die, sucker," she breathed, gently squeezing the trigger.

The shot echoed in the empty air, seeming to gather in volume instead of dying away. As soon as he deemed it safe enough, Jared practically leaped out of his sleeping bag.

"That was too close for comfort," he whooped, running up to her. He braced his hand on her shoulders and bent to look at her. "Kate, you okay? Kate?" He reached out and pried the gun from her hand. "Kate, I'm safe. You did it. You killed it."

She stared at him through sightless eyes. "If I had missed...." She couldn't go on because her throat closed up from the great emotion flooding her body.

"If you had missed, we would have been denied the chance of having children the fun way," he quipped.

Kate's eyes blazed to life. "You bastard! Your life hung in the balance a minute ago and now you're making jokes! Don't you feel anything?"

"I know I'm glad to be alive and grateful you're an excellent shot." Jared smiled gently. "Kate, it's all over. Don't fall apart on me now."

Furious with his blasé attitude, Kate hauled back and hit him in the stomach as hard as she could.

Air exploded from his lungs. "What the hell was that for?" he demanded, once he could speak.

"You dumb idiot, you could have been killed if I had missed! I could have hit you or missed that snake and he would have gotten you!" she shouted, waving her arms around. "Doesn't your sorry excuse for a life mean anything? You could have died! What if I hadn't woken up earlier and decided to take a walk? What if I hadn't come back in time? It's bad enough I was almost buried under a rock slide a few minutes ago and if I had been trapped, there would have been no one here to save you from that snake! Then where would you have been? Don't you understand one damn thing I'm saying to you?" Her voice was tearful, her words disjointed, but all the emotion came through loud and clear. To say she was upset with the events of the past few minutes was an understatement.

Any angry retort he might have spoken died when he saw the tears shimmering in her eyes. The adrenaline that kept Kate going while she had shot the rattlesnake now left her with a vengeance.

"Kate, you shot the snake, you left me intact and I am a very happy man. As for that rock slide you mentioned we'll go into that subject later." He tightened his grip on her shoulder when she tried to pull away. "Kate, you saved my life. And I love you for it."

She froze. "I—"

Whatever she might have said was smothered by the hard pressure of Jared's mouth on hers. With her emotional level still running high from the morning's events, Kate was powerless to resist. Her mouth opened under his silent coaxing and her tongue sparred with his in a fierce duel as his body moved against her in a very inviting motion she eagerly reciprocated. The danger that had zinged through their veins only moments before now turned into a fierce desire to experience life in an elemental way.

"Jared," she gasped when she finally came up for air.

His smile was a combination Jared and J.C. "Shut up, Kate. We're finally doing what we should have been doing all along." His mouth returned to hers with a deep hunger as he explored every inch of her mouth.

Kate had no arguments. Not when Jared's mouth was doing things that she vaguely wondered were illegal, but she didn't care. In fact, as far as she was concerned he could keep on doing them!

"You're right, Jared," she breathed. "We should have been doing this all along." She pushed her hands under his shirt tail to caress his warm skin.

She moaned when she felt one of his hands find her breast under the cotton camisole she wore instead of a bra. She wound her arms around his neck and pulled him to her mouth where she pressed kisses everywhere she could reach.

It took a bit of maneuvering on both their parts to wind up on top of Kate's sleeping bag. Within seconds they were engrossed in discovering all the areas of each other's bodies they had missed before.

Pent-up longing burst forth as they helped each other loosen clothing and push garments to one side, each pausing to kiss or caress a newly uncovered area.

"Beautiful," Jared pronounced, covering one nipple with his mouth and pulling on it gently, curling his tongue around the dark pink crest.

Lost in sensations he aroused, Kate gripped his shoulders. "Jared, I'm not sure I can take much more," she gasped, raking her fingers through the dark mat of hair covering his chest. Her fingers found a nipple and quickly coaxed it to life.

"Yes, you can." His hand stroked downward under the waistband of her jeans and underwear, his fingers splayed across her bare belly. Breathing sharply through her nose, Kate arched upward, digging her nails into his skin.

Jared's croon of delight at Kate's unreserved responses soon changed to moans as she did some intimate exploring of her own. Her mouth rained kisses across his bare chest, while her fingers stroked his taut abdomen, slowly moving downward to find him fully aroused.

Jared kissed her slowly, his tongue lining the delicate bow before dipping inside to savor her taste. He didn't need his senses to realize his hunger increased every second he had her in his arms.

"I love you, O'Malley. I love you so much it hurts," he told her.

She called out his name in response, in a voice filled with longing.

Jared shifted his body until he lay between her legs. He entered her slowly, his eyes intent on her face the entire time. Kate's hips arched upward to meet him halfway. Seeing her eyes glowing with love was enough for Jared to surge forward and bury himself deeply inside of her. Their eyes remained focused on each other. Words were beyond them now; they spoke with their bodies instead. The tension that had built between them for so long soon exploded, leaving them fulfilled, yet eager for more.

"I always felt we'd be great together. I just had no idea how great until now," Jared said sleepily, rolling onto his side and pulling Kate against him.

She rested her cheek against his chest. She trailed her hand across his chest, the fingers tangling in the damp hair. "If a ranger showed up now we'd probably be arrested for indecent exposure." Her fingers followed a path downward.

He pulled half the sleeping bag from under them and draped it over their bodies. "There's not one thing indecent about this."

Her trespassing fingers stilled when they reached a part of him that was returning to life. "Then let's not be indecent again."

"Now, are you going to tell me about that rock slide that you said nearly buried you?" Jared asked once he'd regained his breath.

Kate grimaced. "I woke up early and couldn't get back to sleep, so I thought I'd do some exploring around the base of the mountain." Unable to stop herself, she reached over and traced the shape of his mouth with her fingertip. "I found it, Jared." Excitement coated her words.

His features sharpened. "What?"

"The cave opening. The one I found on the map."

"Are you sure? You didn't try to go inside, did you?"

"As sure as I can be." She shook her head. "I didn't enter because I know it might not be safe and because I wanted you with me. Besides, we're in this together, aren't we?"

Jared looked as if he wished to continue their conversation on a physical level, but he knew Kate's thoughts were elsewhere. If he cared to be honest with himself, his were, too. He was vastly curious to take a look at that cave.

Kate barely gave them time to dress before she dragged him off to the area she had explored.

"I think there's more loose rock overhead, so be careful," she cautioned as they approached the narrow opening. To lend credence to her words, a small rock bounced downward, landing at their feet.

Jared looked at the rock and looked up as if expecting more to follow.

"Curse of the mountains," he murmured. "We could just go back. We could turn around and be at Toby's cabin in a few days. The old-timers are right, Kate, there's too many curses in these mountains. The rock slide, the rattler deciding to set up housekeeping on my sleeping bag. I can't believe these are purely coincidence when there are powers here no one has ever been able to understand. Let's not push our luck too far. I don't want to take the chance of losing you now."

He turned away for a moment, looking up the steep mountain where several rocks looked as if they would fall at any moment. Just as they'd done twice already in one day. He wished there was a strong wind, hell, even a tiny breeze, to account for this. But the air was still, the land quiet. There was nothing to account for it, except the curse of the mountains. He turned to Kate. Whatever traces of unease he felt disappeared as he looked at her face, bright with expectation.

"You don't want to go back any more than I do," she stated, placing her hand on his arm. "Not when we've come this far. There's something in there, Jared. You feel it as much as I do, don't you?"

There was no hesitation in his reply. "Yes, I feel it. For once, I wish I didn't." He turned his head, staring at the slit as if he could see beyond the blackness spilling out of the entrance. The tension in his features indicated he felt the same prickling excitement she did.

"Look, Jared, we've come this far. You know we can't go back without having a look inside. We both want to know if there's anything there. We need to find out if it goes all the way through the mountain. Besides," she added on a mischievous note, "it's dark inside," she murmured in a soft, inviting voice. "And private. Not to mention it will be too cool for snakes to take up residence."

His lips curved. "And could be filled with bats."

Kate waved her hand in dismissal of something she considered trivial. "Then we'll give them directions to a dark Romanian castle where they'd feel much more at home than in an Arizona desert."

Her eyes were lit up with the excitement of treading the unknown. "Are you game?"

He grinned, the same reckless excitement kindling his spirit. "What do you think?"

Chapter Fourteen

Jared pulled out the flashlight he had brought along with him and switched it on as he stood in the mountain entrance. He turned and studied the boulder standing guard.

"This would have made a great cover," he said, running his fingers down the stone's rough surface. "But it would have taken more than one man to push it in front of the opening."

"Meaning Jacob Waltz couldn't have done this by himself or he never came this way," Kate interjected. "At the same time, maybe you're wrong about the boulder being used as a cover."

He nodded absently as he scanned the illuminated interior for traces of animal habitation, glad he didn't find any. "True." He walked slowly inside with Kate on his heels. The yellow light swept back and forth in a slow arc. As they delved inside they found it barely wide enough to walk two abreast.

"Do you feel it?" Her soft voice was sharp with barely leashed excitement.

Jared nodded. There was no missing the prickling sensation along his nape. He had felt it many times just before he stumbled upon the object of his searching.

Except something else was tempering the stirring in his gut. He hoped he was wrong, but something didn't feel quite right about this cave.

"Feel how smooth these walls are," Kate whispered, placing her palm against one of the sides. "You'd think water dripped down them for centuries to create this. It has to be how this was all created."

"Yeah." He studied the walls, running his hand across the smooth surface while looking for any sign that humans had been here in the past hundred years. His attention was diverted when Kate moved around him. "Don't go too far."

"I won't. At least, it doesn't branch out in different directions, so we don't have to worry about getting lost. I should have brought string or something with me to mark our way." Kate moved slowly down the narrow passage. "Gramps once told me about the time he looked for the Ark and found a cave like this."

Jared chuckled. "The Ark of the Covenant?"

She shot him an exasperated look. "No, Noah's Ark. You've got to stop watching those movies, Jared." She stumbled over something that crunched noisily under her foot. She promptly crouched and held up her hand. "Jared, hand me your flashlight."

He settled next to her and flashed the light over what tripped her. "Look at this."

A skeleton. Kate leaned closer to study it. Propped against the wall, it was garbed in what looked like nothing more than rags. "This looks like a bullet hole in the skull," she observed, tracing the jagged hole bored in the middle of the skeleton's forehead. "In fact, here's the bullet." She reached down and picked up a smashed piece of metal.

Jared picked up a gun lying near the bony hand. "If I don't miss my guess, this appears to be a Colt peacemaker. Must have been some battle in here." He shone the light around. "And it looks like a friend stayed behind to keep him company." Another skeleton lay nearby. "Both male, probably murdered. They've been here for a long time. I'd say their clothing is probably from the late 1800s."

"Jared." Kate snatched the flashlight out of his hand and crawled around the skeletons. Laying it on the ground, she dug into the dirt. "Look!" She held up round disks then picked the flashlight up and shone the light over her find.

"Well, I'll be damned!" He took the metallic circles from her. "Twenty-dollar gold pieces."

"And this." She held up a scrap of canvas. "It reads Wells Fargo." She sounded breathless. "Jared, are you thinking what I'm thinking?"

"A bag of twenty-dollar gold pieces."

She dug around more. "Three bags."

"All right, three bags of gold pieces in bags marked Wells Fargo, two skeletons with bullet holes in them." His voice carried excitement. "Looks like a fall-out among thieves when they stashed their loot here. With luck it shouldn't take much research to find out where the gold was stolen from. One thing we know for sure— if they were shot by a third party, their so-called partner never made it back for the gold."

She sat on her heels. "Then this isn't Jacob Waltz's mine." She was disappointed.

He curled one arm around her shoulders and pressed a kiss against her temple. "Honey, the minute we walked in I could tell it wasn't a mine. Don't forget we haven't searched the rest of the area yet. We're right by

Weaver's Needle. And we've got the maps. We'll find it, don't worry. Just remember, you did make an important find.''

She briefly laid her head against his shoulder. "I had hoped this was the entrance to the mine."

She sounded so disappointed he wanted to comfort her but knew this wasn't the place. "Your radar wasn't all that off. You set it to find gold and you found gold," he consoled.

A far-off clattering noise startled them.

"It came from there," Jared commented, looking in the opposite direction from where they entered.

"Then there must be two entrances." Kate stared ahead but was unable to see too far. She stood up. "Come on."

He grabbed her hand, standing fast. "Kate, we don't know what's there."

"And we won't know unless we go find out," she argued, pulling on his hand.

Except Jared's senses were screaming danger. He shook his head. "I don't like it."

Kate loosened her grip on his hand, but he refused to let go of her. "J.C. would go."

"I'm beginning to get tired of that guy," he grumbled.

She flashed a smile of triumph. "Then you'll go with me?"

He sighed. "Meaning if I don't you'll go without me?"

"You got it."

He heaved a deep sigh. "All right, but let's take it slow. We don't need any surprises right now."

"We've both got our guns with us," she pointed out.

"Kate, there's barely enough room in here to swing a cat much less pull out our guns in a hurry in case of a fight."

She looked frustrated. "Jared, those skeletons have been here for probably a hundred years or so. I don't think their friends are laying in wait for us. Now, you do what you want, but I'm going to find out what's there. We'll be fine. Trust me."

"Fine, but if we get killed I'll never forgive you."

They moved stealthily for about ten minutes before they saw a faint light ahead. Jared immediately switched off his flashlight.

"There is another opening," Kate whispered. She cocked her head to one side. "I think I hear birds."

Jared listened. "They don't sound like birds from around here. It doesn't make sense."

Kate crouched, keeping to the cave's wall as she inched her way forward.

"I'd feel better if I were in the front," he told her in a low voice.

She held up her hand as human voices drifted their way. "I wonder if those creeps we ran into a few days ago might not have friends in the area." She kept her voice at a low pitch.

Jared expelled a deep breath. "I have a bad feeling about this."

She reached back blindly for his hand. "Nonsense," she said, even as a sense of doom invaded her mind.

They crept forward slowly, watching the morning light grow stronger before them and hearing the sounds become more strident.

"No wonder that screech sounded familiar," Kate murmured in Jared's ear as they stared at two rows of wire animal cages stacked four and five high along the sides of the cave. She half turned toward him. "I heard it enough times when Gramps and I were in South America." She gestured toward one of the middle cages. "That yellow and red bird is a scarlet macaw. And there's a hyacinth macaw over there. Both are protected by law and it's illegal to import them. I'd say we stumbled upon a smuggling operation."

"Then let's get the hell out of here before someone finds us," he ordered in a low voice, pulling on her wrist. "We'll ride out of here immediately and get hold of a ranger. They can take care of this."

"We need more proof than just seeing them." She tugged her wrist loose.

"Kate, get back here." In his anger, he found it difficult to keep his voice low.

She ignored his order and went another few paces until she was hidden behind the last set of cages. She winced at the strident screeches assaulting her ears. "Hey, guys, I'm here to help," she muttered at one very angry blue-front Amazon parrot.

"Well, look what we have here." A rough-looking voice sounded from above.

Kate looked up to find a bearded giant standing over her.

"Hi, I'm new in the neighborhood and I just thought I'd stop by." She flashed him a bright smile as she slowly straightened.

Jared, seeing her in trouble, swore fiercely under his breath. He'd have to rescue her again.

"Where did you come from?" the bearded man demanded, reaching down to grab Kate's arm.

"Excuse me, but I don't like to be touched." She smiled sweetly just before stomping on his booted foot and lifting her knee.

"Al, get in here!" the man yelled, catching a glimpse of Jared as he tried to evade Kate's lethal knee.

Jared had no chance of going to Kate's rescue when he was too busy defending himself from another rough-looking character who ran in and began punching before asking questions. By the time the scuffle was over, Jared felt pain in his belly and the beginning of a black eye, and Kate's hair lay tumbled around her shoulders and a bruise darkened one cheek. Undaunted, she scowled at her captor who held her arms behind her back in a painful grip.

"These must be the two snoops Zeke told us about," Al told the other man as he held Jared in a viselike hold.

"At least we know where that gunshot we heard earlier came from," the other man said, pulling Kate outside. "You're dangerous, honey. I think I better frisk you real slow." His dark eyes gleamed.

She looked ready to kill him. "Not if you value your life."

He laughed. "Sweetheart, you did your best in there, but I can do a hell of a lot better." Ignoring her curses and Jared's threats, he patted Kate down, taking his time when he reached her inner thighs. He laughed with triumph when he found her knife strapped to her calf. "Very clever. I would have missed it if I hadn't thought you'd have something more than that peashooter of yours. Never saw a knife like this. Real fancy." He examined the symbols etched along the handle.

"An ancient Moorish curse is placed on that knife. If it's used by anyone but its true owner, the knife will turn into an instrument of death against that person," Kate declared.

The man laughed. "Curses don't scare me." He nodded toward Al. "Why don't you tie these two up while I go down and talk to the boss to see what he wants us to do with them." He ambled off with the knife cradled in his beefy hand.

"An ancient Moorish curse?" Jared muttered, once they were trussed up and thrown in a corner of the cave where Al could keep an eye on them.

She shrugged. "It sounded good at the time."

He lay his head against the wall. "What do you recommend now?"

Kate tested the ropes binding her wrists and soon discovered all she did was cut off her blood supply. "I'm thinking."

"You're really something, you know that? All we had to do was creep the other way and they never would have known we were here," he said. "But you just had to go on and check it out for yourself, didn't you?"

"They say they heard the gunshot when I killed the rattlesnake and they probably would have turned up to investigate it sooner or later," she pointed out logically.

"We would have been gone by then."

"We wouldn't if we hadn't found all this," Kate reminded him. "We'd be on the other side searching for a cave and they would have found us." She studied their surroundings. "I read somewhere that parrot smuggling was pretty profitable, but why are they here? Most of them cross the border into California or Florida. Why choose these mountains? And how are they getting them in and out without anyone seeing them?"

Jared pushed himself up onto his knees and looked outside. "Easy. Look out there and you'll have a lot of your questions answered."

Kate looked. "A helicopter," she breathed. "That's what we thought we heard at Toby's, and we were right." Her face glowed.

"No one would expect to hear one around here."

"And if the night is moonless..." Her voice dropped off.

"So these are our unexpected visitors." A tall man, dressed impeccably in neatly pressed jeans and a cotton shirt with its sleeves rolled up to his elbows, walked up to them. His accent had a slight European smoothness to it. "Two of my men said they met teachers a few days ago and it appears you two fit their description. Strange, I never knew teachers to carry the kind of guns you two had on you. Perhaps you're with the authorities." His eyes hardened.

"I can't understand why you'd think we were authorities," Jared said calmly.

"We're archaeologists," Kate explained. "I'm Dr. O'Malley and this is Dr. Wyatt. We've been searching for an abandoned Apache camp and site for their holy rituals." She presented him with her most winning smile. "To be honest, I can't imagine why you would be holding us prisoner when we can't be of any danger to you."

He looked amused. "Walt also said you are a dangerous woman. I can see what he means. I have heard of your work, Dr. O'Malley, and of your grandfather, Dr. Shamus O'Malley. You are both well known in your field of expertise and I have heard, rightly it seems, that you are a woman used to facing danger because of your occupation. Please do not try to fool me with the appearance of a simple woman."

Jared glared at the man. "Now that you know our names, perhaps you would be willing to share yours with us."

The man merely smiled. "I think not. I am only sorry I met the lovely doctor under such, shall we say, hazardous conditions. I have always been interested in learning how you discover such rare riches."

"I assume you want to know for your own gains," Jared mumbled.

"We honestly could care less what you're doing here," Kate told the man. "We have enough to worry about with our own work."

He shook his head. "You are an honest woman and would deem it fit to inform the authorities of our presence. I'm sorry, Dr. O'Malley, you are a lovely woman, but I'm afraid...." He gave an elegant shrug.

His unspoken words hung heavily between them.

Jared looked past the man at Al and Walt who were engrossed in sliding flat plastic bags into slots set into the bird carriers. "No wonder you can't afford to have us around. You're not just smuggling birds, but drugs, too. Which is it? Cocaine or heroin?"

"A little of both," the leader said easily. "I admire a plain-spoken man and since you will be dead before we leave here with this last shipment I do not mind telling you. I own a chain of pet stores across the country and a shipment of exotic birds is not necessarily unusual when I can show the authorities the proper paperwork. The drugs are a more profitable sideline that no one would ever consider to be hidden in bird carriers. As you can see I am nothing more than a simple businessman. Now if you will excuse me I have work to do. I suggest you two make yourselves comfortable while you're with us. I'm afraid we will not be able to provide you with a proper last meal as we will be leaving just after dawn, but it will not matter in the end, will it?" With a slight bow he left them.

"Birds who haven't been quarantined spread one disease and the drugs spread another," Kate muttered, glaring at the retreating back. "I wish I had my gun. Or at least my knife."

"And I wish you hadn't been so damn curious." Jared wiggled, cursing violently under his breath as his bonds proved too snug to loosen.

"We needed solid proof for the rangers," she pointed out.

"Well, there's going to be plenty of proof now," he ground out. "Our dead bodies! If anyone finds us, that is. Those two guys back in the cave haven't had any recent visitors. Even Walt and Al obviously haven't gone back."

"All right, I made a mistake. What do you want? My abject apology or merely my blood?"

"Both," he snapped, turning his back on her. "See if you can do something with these while they're not watching us so closely. I don't know about you but I don't intend to end up as vulture bait because you had to barge in and indulge your curiosity."

"Barge in?" her voice rose. "If you felt that way why didn't you just take off for help when that idiot grabbed me?"

"Because I wasn't going to abandon you." He bit out each word. "I only hope that my genes are the dominant ones because if our kids turn out anything like you I'll lock them up until they get some common sense."

"Then I'll do my best to make sure they're pure O'Malley." Her anger dissipated as the meaning of his words sunk in. "Do you really want children?" she asked in a soft voice unlike her earlier strident one.

He looked sullen. "Of course, I do. Just as long as they don't take after you."

"Oh, Jared, I'm sorry." Her voice softened even more. "I really did get us in a lot of trouble, didn't I? I'd understand it if you didn't want to marry me after all this."

Even with his hands tied tightly behind his back, Jared had no trouble turning and pressing a hard kiss on her mouth. "Kate, I never thought of marriage for myself until you came along. Marriage to you could end up to be my greatest adventure."

She nibbled his bottom lip. "Oh, yes. The trouble is, our continental-sounding friend might have something to say about our future plans."

"We've each been in rough scrapes before. If we put our heads together we should be able to come up with a workable plan."

"Considering our suddenly shortened life expectancy, I think we better come up with one as soon as possible." She looked off, noting the way Al's eyes greedily roamed over the areas her torn blouse revealed as he moved around, picking up bird carriers and transporting them to the waiting helicopter. "How can they keep them here with so little food or water?" she murmured. "Most of them will die."

"I doubt these guys care as long as the drugs make it through." Jared looked disgusted. He jerked his head toward the helicopter. "Look at the undercarriage. If I'm not mistaken those are loudspeakers. Probably the source for those so-called Indian chants."

"You're too smart for your own good, buddy," Al spoke up.

"Too bad you aren't." Jared smiled. "The chants you tape-recorded aren't exactly authentic to this region or any other region, as a matter of fact."

Al's scowl told them he didn't understand Jared's words, but he understood enough. He walked over and backhanded Jared in the face. "It won't matter after tonight. At least we'll still be alive even if you won't. Who knows, we might even keep the lady here for a while. She'd make real good company, I bet." He sneered.

Jared growled and jerked forward.

"Don't, Jared," Kate entreated. "He's only trying to goad you into a fight."

"You two sure like to use big words," Al said. "But big words won't keep you alive." With that he ambled off.

"Once it's dark I'm getting out of here one way or another," Jared muttered. "But I'm going to take care of him first."

"Then we better concentrate on loosening these ropes," Kate replied. She shifted around until she faced him. "Jared, did I ever tell you I love you?"

His harsh features softened. "Yeah, but don't let that stop you. When we get out of here, we'll go into further detail about what you can do to make it up to me."

"I swear all you think about is sex," she muttered, not sounding one bit angry.

"Tell me you haven't been thinking more about ravishing my body on this trip than finding the mine," he challenged.

"No comment."

KATE FELT SO ANGRY and frustrated with their situation she wanted to scream. At the same time she felt ready to break down in tears. Evening dusk had left the narrow gorge in deep shadows and the cries of frightened birds rent the air and pierced her eardrums.

"I wish I could let them all loose," she whispered, trying to appear composed on the outside while feeling vulnerable inside. The only bright spot was her feeling her ties loosen just a little bit.

"But you can't, honey," Jared gently reminded her.

"I know, but I can hope, can't I?" She uttered a sigh of frustration. "We've got to get out of here, Jared."

"Tell me something I don't know. Thing is, if they're waiting until dawn, we'll have to do the same. Riding in the dark at the speed we'd need to is too dangerous. Luckily, this place is getting as dark as a tomb so they can't see that we're working on the ropes."

Kate winced. "If you don't mind, I'd prefer you use another analogy."

"Sorry. Still, it should be too dark for them to see us clearly."

She shifted around, drawing her knees up against her chest. "Oh, Jared, we're so close to the mine I can feel it." She groaned with frustration and pain from the ropes on her wrists and from the lack of proper circulation. "I just know it's right around here. We would have found it."

"It's not going anywhere, Kate," he assured her grimly.

Kate kneeled and craned her neck trying to see as much as possible when new activity sounded near the camp fire. "It appears our two local thugs did some searching and have our horses. So how do you expect us to escape now? On foot? We won't get very far that way. Not to mention they've got the chopper to search for us when we do get away." She dared not think that their escape might not come about if they couldn't get their ropes loose.

"Then we'll have to disable the helicopter first, won't we?" Jared asked quietly. "And there's no reason why we can't get our horses back."

"If this was a movie we'd have a much easier time because we're the heroes and we're meant to get away." Kate uttered a sigh of triumph when she felt the ties loosen enough that she could slip her hands through the bonds.

"We're still the heroes and they're still the bad guys, so we'll wing it from there." Jared winced. "This guy sure tried to cut off my blood supply, but I'm nearly there."

"He probably steals antiquities, too," she mumbled, rubbing her wrists to restore the circulation. "This guy has to be brought down, Jared."

"Good idea. Just as soon as we find some reinforcements."

"Too bad he didn't give us his name," she rambled on. "We might have been able to trace him. Although his admitting he has a chain of pet shops might be of some help."

"It depends whether they're nationwide or just in one state."

She shook her head. "If this operation is any indication he's pretty serious." She turned to Jared to help him get loose. "Okay, we're free and have the choice of running out the other way to our campsite where our horses are no longer waiting for us or we can overpower these guys, who happen to have some pretty powerful guns slung over their shoulders. Plus those other two guys we met several days ago are a part of this and could show up at any time." She paused to take a much-needed deep breath. "So tell me, how do we handle this?"

Jared stared into the distance, rubbing his jaw with his hand, which sported angry rope burns around his wrist. "You know how to fly a helicopter?" He suddenly laughed. "Sorry, I forgot who I was asking."

"Your father owns one and you're telling me you don't know how to fly one?"

"Never seemed to have the time to learn."

"I wish you had made the time," she muttered, crawling around. "Where did they put our guns and my knife?"

"The big guy has your knife hooked on his belt."

She groaned. "I wish it did have a curse attached to it. That knife wasn't cheap and it was difficult to get." She sat back. "Maybe I could entice one of them inside and you could jump on his back and knock him out."

"Are you kidding? I'd only end up with a second black eye."

"Then you come up with something," Kate snapped.

"We'll sneak out around dawn while they're busy packing up their campsite. They'll probably make sure not to leave any trace of their presence. While they're doing that, we'll be making our famous getaway." Jared's gaze sharpened. "Get back, pretend you're still tied up," he ordered suddenly, scooting until his back rested against the cave wall.

Kate wasted no time in returning to her original position. "Oh, great, it's the jolly bearded giant," she grumbled.

"We should use you two to help us in the morning," Walt told them, as he stood in the cave entrance.

"Are you going to give us any dinner?" Kate asked.

The man's belly laugh boomed through the small area. "You two are something else, you know that? You're gonna die in the morning and all you care about is food. Sure hope you enjoyed the sunset cause you sure won't be around to see much past the sunrise." With that he made his way down the shallow incline toward the small camp fire.

Kate inched her way next to Jared. "Funny, but when I thought of us sleeping together, I hadn't thought of us sleeping together like this."

Jared chuckled. "Neither did I. Get some sleep, Kate. We've got to keep up our strength for tomorrow. From his reaction they don't intend to offer us dinner."

She wrinkled her nose. "After I smelled the chili on that guy's breath I knew there was no way I would eat something that deadly. I'll put up with hunger." She closed her eyes. "Jared."

"Hm?" He sounded half asleep.

"Let's try Club Med on our next vacation."

"ARE YOU SURE this is going to work?" Kate whispered, clutching Jared's shoulder. Her sleep had been fitful and when the time came for their escape she began to wonder if their crazy scheme would be successful.

"It has to. It's the only chance we've got. Wait a few minutes before you follow me," Jared said in a low voice as he began to move away.

"If you don't know how to fly a helicopter how do you intend to disable one?" Kate asked, grabbing hold of his shoulder to stop his escape.

He turned his head and grinned. "Hey, I watch all those action shows on TV. No problem."

"Then I suggest we call for one of their stuntmen to do the job for us."

Jared placed a hand on each side of Kate's face and drew her forward for a warm, lingering kiss that quickly heated their blood. He pulled back slightly before they lost track of where they were.

"You ready, O'Malley?" His whisper fanned over her lips.

"Ready when you are, Wyatt," she murmured, gripping hold of his belt.

He stood and pulled her up with him.

"Then let's party."

Chapter Fifteen

Kate watched Jared crouch and run toward the helicopter using cactus and boulders to hide his flight. Just as Kate was ready to leave, something caught her eye. A portion of the wall where the birds had been stacked was covered with what appeared to be scratches. She strained her eyes in the gray light to see if they made any sense then used her hands to trace them.

"Oh, my God," she breathed. "Jacob Waltz *was* here!" She quickly bit down on her lower lip before she screamed with joy. "This is the proof we needed." Suddenly remembering something, she ran into the cave toward the skeletons, scooped up a couple of gold coins and dropped them in her jeans pocket. When she returned to the mouth of the cave she found Jared looking up with a furious expression. "Something tells me this isn't the time to read all this."

She stole into the pale dawn light, crouching so she wouldn't be seen by the three men sitting around the camp fire eating their breakfast.

"You sure took your sweet time getting here," Jared hissed in her ear.

"I had something to do." Her eyes glowed with excitement.

He gave her a look that said he wasn't about to ask because he doubted he would like the answer. Kate's grin told him that she could barely contain her news.

"Not now, O'Malley, we've got to get out of here." He correctly guessed her thoughts.

She nodded, understanding. Her news could wait. "What if the birds give us away?" Kate kept her mouth close to Jared's ear so her voice wouldn't carry.

"They're yelling so much no one will be able to tell if it's because of us or just because they're upset," he said. "While I'm working on the helicopter I want you to go for our horses."

"Are we going to have a signal to announce we've each accomplished our tasks?"

"You just get the horses and get them over to the chopper. I'll take it from there."

Kate surveyed the land, noting the location of the horses. "At least those idiots left them saddled after they rode them back. I wouldn't want to make that wild ride we're in for bareback."

Jared studied the men he would have preferred to battle face to face, except he knew this wasn't the time. Not if he wanted them to get out of there alive. At least if the helicopter was put out of commission he knew they wouldn't have much of a chance to escape. He prayed he could find help for them in short order.

He heaved a deep breath. "Okay, any questions?"

"Just the wish that we had a nice heavy-duty machine gun at our disposal." Kate kissed him on the cheek. "After this our wedding will be pretty anticlimactic, won't it? Meet you at the chopper, big guy." She crouched and started to creep toward the horses when she suddenly stopped and looked to her right.

"Jared." Her whisper was frenzied. What she read in the cave now made more sense.

"Get your butt in gear," he ordered.

"Jared, look." She pointed toward the mountain.

He gripped her arm. "I don't care what you see. Just get those horses and get back here before they discover we're gone."

She shot him a dark glare. "Believe me, you're going to be sorry when I tell you later and you wished I'd told you now."

"I doubt it. Now go!"

Muttering curses under her breath she crept off.

"Life with her is going to be real interesting," Jared muttered, as he made his way toward the helicopter, grateful the men had left it unattended. Keeping his eye on them, he crawled along the side of the chopper and reached up to open the door. Holding his breath, he looked inside and reached for the appropriate wires. He used his elbow as a club to smash the instruments. "Thanks, guys, for covering up the noise I'm making," he said to the screeching birds crated in the rear of the helicopter. He scooted to the rear to wait for Kate.

From his vantage point he could see her covering the two horses' muzzles to quiet their nickers of welcome. "Come on, O'Malley," he muttered. "Time is growing short and if those jerks discover us too soon we won't have a chance in hell of getting out of here." As he watched her lead the horses closer to him, he waited with bated breath. "Okay, baby, come on. Just a few steps more." As soon as Kate was close enough he sneaked over and grabbed one set of reins. "Let's get the hell out of here." He pulled himself into the saddle.

"Fine by me, but you'll be sorry you didn't hear my news." She nestled her boot into the stirrup and pulled herself up. "Uh-oh, I think our hosts have realized we're leaving early."

They kneed their horses into action as the three men ran after them.

"Into the helicopter, you fools!" the European shouted. "We'll catch up with them that way."

"That's what you think!" Jared laughed as they clung to their horses' withers in hopes of dodging the bullets flying their way.

They didn't look back as they raced out of the narrow canyon and across the wide expanse.

"Jared!" Kate shouted. "We've got company!"

He looked over his shoulder and saw two men on horseback racing after them. "It's the two we were worried about," he yelled. "When did they show up?"

"Sooner than we hoped, obviously. She urged her mount to run faster. "It would be nice if we find the cavalry just over the next hill. Right about now, I'd even settle for Toby and mean old Bertha."

They kept an even pace, with their pursuers close on their heels. Kate squinted in a vain attempt to keep the flying sand out of her eyes as they rode their race to safety. She continued whispering encouragement in her horse's ear. Sharing his mistress's urgency, he put on a fresh burst of speed. Kate didn't need to look around to know that Jared was riding alongside her.

She ducked her head as a bullet whizzed a little too close for comfort.

"They're catching up!" she shouted, grimacing as sand flew into her mouth.

"Just keep up a steady rhythm," Jared advised. "That's our only chance of keeping ahead of them. Our horses are bred for the desert. Theirs aren't."

All Kate could do was hope and pray as they made their escape. While the two didn't catch up with them they kept close enough to make her worry.

The sun beat down fiercely on their backs, she felt a terrible thirst and she was convinced the color on her nose rivaled Rudolph's. The sand flew up, getting in her nose and abrading her face.

And I thought I knew what being in danger was, she thought. *Let's get out of here, Jared, and I'll happily teach full time until I'm a hundred years old. If Shamus dares suggest another exploration I'll personally see to it that he never has another Cuban cigar or bottle of Irish whiskey for as long as I live.* She ducked when another bullet flew past her ear. "How can they aim so well?" she screamed.

"Pure luck. Moving targets are more difficult to hit," he told her.

"Then they spend a lot of time in a shooting gallery, because they're doing better than I expected they'd do." Kate felt grimmer by the moment. "By the way, I want you to know that Jacob Waltz scratched a map on the cave walls. We didn't see it before because the bird cages hid it. He probably figured no one would know what it was about, but there's enough proof there for us. I also went back and got a couple of those gold coins. So the trip isn't a total loss. And I found the other cave opening when I got the horses. Ten to one that's where the mine is. It's hard to see unless the sun is hitting it directly the way it was early this morning."

Jared almost jerked on the reins when he heard her news. "What?"

"You wouldn't let me tell you before! So you'll just have to wait to hear the rest of the story when we get out of here." She felt a tiny bit of satisfaction in knowing it would drive him crazy. But that was all right. She had read enough of the scratches on the cave wall to know what they meant and she had seen the cave opening highlighted by the morning sun. She knew it had to be the one they were looking for.

When Jared suddenly pulled on his reins, Kate had to haul her horse off to the side in order not to crash into him.

"What are you doing?" she demanded.

He spat out a pithy expletive and nodded toward an unseen spot in front of him. "We've got a minor problem," he announced, tight-lipped.

Kate looked to discover the earth sloped abruptly away in front of her to a sheer drop. She repeated Jared's curse. She half turned in her saddle, seeing the swirling dust their pursuers kicked up as the distance between them was eaten up at a rapid rate. When she turned back she watched Jared studying the drop in front of them.

"This is just great. One thing we don't have is time, Jared. Pretty soon they'll be close enough to make our lives hell," she said swiftly, her tone indicating her urgency.

When he turned to her, his eyes gleamed like brilliant-cut stones.

"What do you say, O'Malley? You game?"

She looked puzzled as she tried to figure out his meaning and when it dawned on her she widened her eyes with amazement. "What? Are you crazy?" she shrieked. "Have you ever done anything like this? Riding down a drop like that could kill us!"

"Which is what those guys will do if they catch up with us. I don't see where we have much choice, Kate. Do you have a better idea?"

Kate looked around and realized just how boxed in they were.

"If it's a choice between a bullet and a broken neck I'll take death on my terms." She laughed, the excitement flowing through her veins like bubbly champagne. "Hell, Wyatt, you only live once and if we're going out, we may as well go out in style." She leaned forward, speaking softly in her horse's ear.

"Arabic?" he guessed, keeping one eye on the two men spurring their horses on as if they guessed they finally had their quarry trapped with no chance for escape.

She nodded. "I asked him to fly like the wind and set me down gently. I wouldn't try this except with a horse with a big heart and the courage to attempt something crazy."

They looked at each other, fully aware of their fate if this last-ditch ploy didn't work.

"I love you." Jared's voice was rough with emotion.

Kate couldn't say anything. Her throat was too choked up with all the words she wanted to say, but she allowed her eyes to say what she couldn't.

Jared looped his reins around his hand and with an earsplitting rebel yell, he urged his stallion over the edge. Within seconds he was out of sight.

Kate's answering yell echoed in the air as she guided her own horse downward. For a split second she felt as if she and her horse were floating on air.

Epilogue

"I can't believe you two survived a ride virtually down the side of a cliff. You were lucky you didn't break your necks," Kiki exclaimed. Into four glasses she poured champagne—her contribution to the impromptu party celebrating Kate and Jared's return to civilization and, more importantly, their recent marriage. They'd been home for two weeks and Kiki finally heard the entire story of their trip. "You go searching for a gold mine and instead find skeletons, bags of stolen gold and drug runners."

"Considering it was either that or get shot we chose the lesser of the two evils," Jared said dryly.

"It wasn't your typical expedition," Kate admitted.

Jared rolled his eyes at her understatement. "It's nothing I'd care to repeat."

"I feel as if this is my fault." Shamus shook his head. "If anything had happened to either of you I don't know what I would have done."

"Gramps, you've been in lots of danger in the past," Kate reminded him. "None of us had any idea all this would happen. We were lucky that not long after we reached flat land we found a ranger and that those two men didn't try to follow us. They probably figured we would break our necks. Luckily, Jared had disabled the helicopter and they didn't have any horses back there, so the authorities were able to get in quickly and take them into custody.

"They were so excited to find the bags of drugs hidden in the parrot cages. It turned out these men had a pretty large operation that had been going on for several years because no one had the idea of searching the mountains." She looked disgruntled as she remembered something. "But they wouldn't let me have my knife." She looked at Jared as if it was his fault. "He wouldn't even let me tell them it was mine to begin with!"

"Did they keep it as evidence in the case?" Kiki asked.

Kate shook her head.

"I made her keep quiet regarding her ownership of that thing when the police said it was illegal to own." Jared frowned at Kate. "That's something we've got to work on, Mrs. Wyatt. You seem to feel you can twist the law to suit yourself. If you had gotten caught with that knife on you I swear I would have stood back and pretended not to know you."

Kiki laughed throatily. "You two have been married, what, four days and you already act like an old married couple. I love it!" She beamed, holding up her champagne glass in a silent toast.

"Spend several days out in the desert with Kate and you'll find out what true punishment is." He yelped when Kate pinched him. "I didn't mean it, sweetheart."

"Ah, but I did, darling," she crooned, leaning over to kiss him. She sat up. "Now for the important news." She faced Shamus. "In the two weeks Jared and I have been back here we've been doing a lot of figuring and we want to assure you that the mine isn't forgotten."

"No, I'm not letting you take any more chances," he argued. "You two could have been killed and I don't want anything to happen to either of you."

"He wants us around until he gets his great-grandchild," Jared said.

Shamus shot him a censuring look. "That would be nice, but I've come to realize that it isn't fair to have Kate go out there and risk her life. She's been in danger before but nothing like this. I appreciate what you two did, and the fact that you did come back with information on that unsolved Wells Fargo robbery is a feat in itself."

"Gramps." Kate reached over and touched his hand. "You don't understand. We found proof of the mine."

He stared at her, unable to believe his ears.

"*You* found proof," Jared corrected. "While I'm risking my butt out in the open you're going back for those damn coins and checking out chicken scratches on the cave walls."

"Quiet," she ordered.

"Four days married and henpecked already." He sighed dramatically.

Kate turned to Shamus. "I found several lines scratched on the cave walls, Gramps. They appeared to be a poem to the sun and the initials at the bottom were J.W." She smiled when she saw she caught his attention. "It was obvious the scratches had been there a long time and I didn't have much time or adequate light to read them properly, but I tried to memorize as much as I could and when we got back to the ranger station I wrote down what I remembered." She handed him a sheet of paper.

He read the neatly typed words then looked at his granddaughter. "And?" he breathed, his green eyes glowing with hope.

"When I sneaked out to steal our horses I happened to look at one section of the mountain where a shaft of sunlight was directed. I saw an odd-shaped opening," she continued in a low voice. "Gramps, I'm pretty sure that was why the poem to the sun. The sun would point out an opening that probably isn't ordinarily seen. And I just bet that's where we'll find his mine," she concluded with triumph.

"So you two really did it!" Kiki squealed, jumping up and refilling everyone's glasses. "You actually found the mine!"

Jared held up his hand. "We're not entirely sure it was the mine. After all, we weren't able to check out the writing on the cave wall or the opening."

"The man has no sense of adventure," Kate spoke up.

"I married you. That's adventure enough, thank you," he retorted, but his eyes reflected the love that had been growing stronger with each day they were together. After they married, he'd given up his apartment and he and Kate shared the third floor loft so Shamus wouldn't be alone. A second floor bedroom was being redecorated for Jared's office.

"It's enough," Shamus decided. "Some people thought old Jacob was just spinning a yarn and now we know it wasn't a yarn. I'm happy."

"So what will you two do?" Kiki asked Kate.

"I finally made Dr. Phillips a happy man. I agreed to start teaching full time at the beginning of the spring semester," she replied. "And Jared's hoping to find out more about that Wells Fargo robbery, so he can write up the find. The authorities followed our directions and traveled out there to retrieve the gold and the skeletons. One of the men turned out to be a lovely character named Pig Nose Pete and the other was Clay Stone, both very unsavory characters and well known to the law back then. When they disappeared so abruptly most people thought they went down to Mexico. There was a bounty on each of them and they had quite an extensive history of train and bank robberies.''

"Plus, we need to decide where to go on our honeymoon," Jared injected.

Kate snuggled up to him. "I've been thinking about that," she murmured.

He looked a little suspicious. "You have?"

She nodded. "Someplace quiet, out of the way. Warm sand, fun-filled days under the sun, a romantic starry sky with just us to savor it," she said huskily, tracing her fingertip around his mouth. "A place where we won't be disturbed by others. I'm talking about privacy galore, Wyatt."

He began to relax. "Sounds great. Are we talking South Pacific or Caribbean?"

Kate flashed him a dazzling smile and he doubted he would ever have enough of her. "Arizona is lovely this time of year, darling."

Jared's eyes widened. "No! There is no way I intend to go back there. I haven't even recovered yet from the idea of almost getting killed."

"He's right, Kate. We've learned enough," Shamus interjected.

Kate kept her attention trained on her husband. "One sleeping bag this time," she murmured. "And you already know you won't have to worry about snakes. Think of it, Jared. Just us in those big *lonely* mountains. Doesn't that just conjure up some real interesting ideas?''

Jared knew he would lose the war, but he'd try to win one battle, no matter how small. "You honestly think we can pull this off and find that mine according to some chicken scratches you found on the wall?"

Kate flashed him a grin identical to her grandfather's. "Trust me."

HARLEQUIN
American Romance®

COMING NEXT MONTH

#373 HEARTS AT RISK by Libby Hall

Reporting for an underground newspaper, Jennifer Wright champions counterculture causes—and fears love's dangers. Test pilot Lij Brannigan explores the limits of speed and performance in experimental jets—and struggles with his own demons. And on the day man takes his first step on the moon, the antiestablishment journalist and the fearless top gun enter an unknown world— one that mingles age-old desire and space-age conflict. Don't miss the next A CENTURY OF AMERICAN ROMANCE book!

#374 LAZARUS RISING by Anne Stuart

Though Katharine Lafferty was engaged to be married, her heart was still in mourning. When Katharine had been nineteen and a college coed, Danny McCandless had been twenty-four and a cool-headed criminal. In her innocence, Katharine never thought that Danny might be bad for her. Now, ten years later, the shock of Danny's death lingered—but it was nothing compared with the rude shock of seeing him again.

#375 DAY DREAMER by Karen Toller Whittenburg

At first Jessica Day thought she had just imagined him. But soon she realized that she could never have imagined anything half so strange and wonderful as Professor Kale Warner and his oddball tale of stolen research and cloak-and-dagger antics. And, even as Jessie was drawn into Kale's adventure, she wondered if someday she'd be left with only unbelievable daydreams of a man she could never forget.

#376 MAGIC HOUR by Leigh Anne Williams

Oscar-winning director Sandy Baker wanted no partners on or off the set. But Victoria Moore couldn't help getting involved—her first and most autobiographical novel was being brought to the screen. Delving beneath the written word, the charismatic filmmaker uncovered Victoria's private sorrows and secrets. And despite the risks to her career and heart, Victoria couldn't suppress a burning need to know this man, this stranger, who understood her like a lover.

HARLEQUIN
American Romance®

RELIVE THE MEMORIES....

From New York's immigrant experience to San Francisco's great quake of 1906. From the muddy trenches of World War I's western front to the speakeasies of the Roaring Twenties. From the lost fortunes and indomitable spirit of the Thirties to life on the home front in the Fabulous Forties...**A CENTURY OF AMERICAN ROMANCE** takes you on a nostalgic journey through the twentieth century.

Glimpse the lives and loves of American men and women from the turn of the century to the dawn of the year 2000. Revel in the romance of a time gone by. And sneak a peek at romance in an exciting future.

Watch for all the **A CENTURY OF AMERICAN ROMANCE** titles coming to you one per month in Harlequin American Romance.

Don't miss a day of **A CENTURY OF AMERICAN ROMANCE**.

A CENTURY OF
AMERICAN ROMANCE

1960s

The women...the men...the passions...the memories....

If you missed #345 AMERICAN PIE, #349 SATURDAY'S CHILD, #353 THE GOLDEN RAIN-TREE, #357 THE SENSATION, #361 ANGELS WINGS or #365 SENTIMENTAL JOURNEY and would like to order them, send your name, address, and zip or postal code, along with a check or money order for $2.95 plus 75¢ postage and handling ($1.00 in Canada) *for each book ordered*, payable to Harlequin Reader Service, to:

In the U.S.
3010 Walden Ave.
P.O. Box 1325
Buffalo, NY 14269-1325

In Canada
P.O. Box 609
Fort Erie, Ontario
L2A 5X3

Please specify book title with your order.

CA

You'll flip . . . your pages won't!
Read paperbacks *hands-free* with

Book Mate • I

The perfect "mate" for all your romance paperbacks

Traveling • Vacationing • At Work • In Bed • Studying
• Cooking • Eating

Perfect size for all standard paperbacks, this wonderful invention makes reading a pure pleasure! Ingenious design holds paperback books OPEN and FLAT so even wind can't ruffle pages — leaves your hands free to do other things. Reinforced, wipe-clean vinyl-covered holder flexes to let you turn pages without undoing the strap . . . supports paperbacks so well, they have the strength of hardcovers!

Pages turn WITHOUT opening the strap.

SEE-THROUGH STRAP

Reinforced back stays flat.

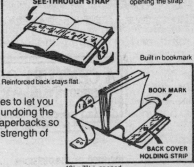

Built in bookmark

BOOK MARK

BACK COVER HOLDING STRIP

10" x 7¼", opened.
Snaps closed for easy carrying, too.

Harlequin Superromance.

THEY'RE A BREED APART

The men and women of the Canadian prairies are slow to give their friendship or their love. On the prairies, such gifts can never be recalled. Friendships between families last for generations. And love, once lit, burns hot and pure and bright for a lifetime.

In honor of this special breed of men and women, Harlequin Superromance® presents:

SAGEBRUSH AND SUNSHINE
(Available in October)

and

MAGIC AND MOONBEAMS
(Available in December)

two books by Margot Dalton, featuring the Lyndons and the Burmans, prairie families joined for generations by friendship, then nearly torn apart by love.

Look for SUNSHINE in October and MOONBEAMS in December, coming to you from Harlequin.

MAG-C1R